CLOSE TO THE HEART

ASPEN GOLD SERIES BOOK 9

DEBRA HINES

My strength and my courage is the Lord.
Isaiah 12:2

For Ron
Thank you for your love and support,
for making sure that I didn't go hungry,
and for filling in wherever you were needed.

CLOSE TO THE HEART

He raised her child as his own.

An unexpected phone call summons widower Murphy Webster back to Spencer, Colorado. He promised his dying wife their daughter would never know she was adopted, but while settling his brother's estate, he encounters a shocking revelation. His adopted daughter is the child of the woman he's loved since boyhood. Does this discovery change that pledge? Murphy's bittersweet devotion to Cora poses another excruciating question. How can he compete with a memory?

Spencer antique purveyor Cora Fleming is driven to find the baby she gave up for adoption over forty years ago. When Murphy Webster walks through her door, Cora discovers the skinny, awkward boy she'd climbed trees with has matured into a handsome man, whose arresting gray eyes spark feelings she never thought she'd experience again. Will secrets revealed fulfill love's dreams or tear love apart?

PROLOGUE

Cora Fleming smiled and accepted the flute of Prosecco Joyce Bennett handed her. "Thanks. Hopefully this will settle my nerves. I'm not used to being in the spotlight."

Joyce, Spencer Historical Society's newly-installed president, sipped from her own glass, branding the rim with her vibrant red lipstick. "You deserve to be honored for your service over the years. Now that you're retiring and your new book on Spencer's history is out, tonight's celebration here at the restored schoolhouse is the perfect occasion."

The cold, bubbly beverage tasted of crisp pears on a blistering summer afternoon. Cora stood behind the teacher's desk and surveyed the people milling around the brightly-lit room. "I have you to thank, Joyce. Without your encouragement, editing and organizational skills, my book would have wilted on the vine."

Joyce gave her a quick, affectionate hug. "As soon as I had a peek at your meticulously documented manuscript and the photographs you'd collected, I knew the book would be an asset, not only to the historical society, but as a marketing tool for Spencer's tourist trade."

"*Spencer, the Town and the People* was a labor of love. The booklets I'd written on Spencer's colorful past and legends inspired me." Cora raised her glass to Joyce in a mini-toast. "I'll leave the commercial aspects to you and the chamber."

She smiled to herself. Joyce was the P.T. Barnum of their thriving mountain town. The vivacious woman had migrated from the Chamber of Commerce to the historical society, infusing its flagging membership with her industrious enthusiasm. Once she'd determined Joyce's heart was in the right place, Cora had endorsed her for president.

Cora frowned. "I'm getting butterflies in my stomach at the prospect of standing up and making my speech tonight."

Joyce patted her shoulder, her tone breezy. "You'll be fine. Drink the rest of your wine and try to eat a little. You've got about a half-hour until the program begins. We'll show the video first. I'll follow with the presentation, you give your remarks, sign copies of your book and you're done."

"Easy for you to say." Cora sighed and shifted her cramped feet in the unfamiliar flats. She wished she'd worn her comfy sandals, but the beat-up leather footwear would've clashed with her tailored slacks and silky tunic top.

"Oh boy," Joyce whispered. "I'm being summoned. Excuse me."

Cora finished her Prosecco and eyed the buffet set up along the back wall. She toyed with the idea of cheese and crackers, heavy on the crackers, but her stomach revolted. Eating after the speech was a better plan.

Gazing around at the one-room schoolhouse's freshly painted walls and the restored windows letting in the waning sun, Cora was filled with a sense of pride.

Once the society had gotten the ball rolling, the entire community had contributed to the renovation by pitching in with monetary donations as well as old books, report cards and other classroom memorabilia. The historical society had been able to move the derelict structure from the abandoned construction site to its present location in Olde Town.

Guests hovered between the rows of desks and engaged in animated conversation. Cora spotted her reclusive friend and neighbor, Jesse Webster, hands in his pockets, examining the class photographs displayed near the front of the room. Cora's apprehension about her speech evaporated. Just the person she'd wanted to talk to.

"Jesse. What a nice surprise. Thank you for coming. I know social get-togethers like this aren't your thing."

The tall, elegant man turned at her greeting. A pleased smile animated his handsome face and pale blue eyes. "Cora, I'm always willing to make an exception for you."

"Where's Stuart?"

"He's waiting in line to buy your book." Jesse enveloped her in a friendly embrace. "Congratulations on both counts. Maybe now that you're retiring I can convince Stuart it's time to quit the gun business and start looking for our Italian villa."

"I don't understand why he didn't sell his shops at the same time you closed your law practice," Cora said.

Jesse shrugged. "I argued my case, but the stubborn man wasn't ready. Maybe…." An expectant grin crossed his features. "Maybe Thursday, after he's had a glass or two of wine, you and I can nudge Stuart a little closer to Italy. We're having Frankie Spampanado's deliver."

Her friend's lighthearted conjecture regarding his spouse's cautious nature sparked another idea. "I was going to bring a new card game for us to try this month, but I'll gladly endure dominoes again if it'll butter up Stuart a little more."

Jesse laughed outright. "Good idea. I think fate is on our side."

Cora hoped Jesse was right and providence was in their corner. Her corner to be specific. A quick glance assured her their conversation would remain private. She touched his sleeve, inhaled a fortifying breath and lowered her voice. "Jesse—-"

"Aunt Cora! Jesse!" Miranda Elliot strode towards them, still slim in dark slacks and a smocked top. Her green eyes brimmed with urgency. "I'm sorry to interrupt your conversation, but the photographer from the Herald is here and Joyce asked me to remind you the program begins in ten minutes."

Her news would have to wait. Unconsciously cupping her palm over the concealed ring beneath her blouse, Cora reluctantly switched the gears of her mind back to tonight's festivities.

"Calm down, Mandy. You'll get your baby all upset."

Miranda placed a hand on her abdomen. "I know. Don't tell Declan. He's already over-protective."

Cora planted a quick kiss on Jesse's cheek. "Let's talk later," she whispered.

He arched a white brow and retreated behind his amiable smile. "I'm happy for you, Cora. We'll see you Thursday night." He nodded at Miranda. "You're looking well, Miranda. Congratulations."

Jesse had given no indication he'd stick around after the festivities. She didn't expect him to, but she fervently hoped he would. Cora followed Miranda to the back of the building, fielding well-wishes from friends and acquaintances.

Immediately after the photo shoot, the overhead lights flickered and the program commenced. The video was a montage of photographs, chronicling her years with the historical society. The nostalgic images, paired with wistful background music, called to mind fond memories and past members she'd worked with, Grandma Binney among them. Cora's eyes misted.

John Lennon's song *Imagine* accompanied the last round of photographs in a moving tribute to the glory days of the schoolhouse. Class pictures from the educational structure's inception to the end of its years of service hovered and flashed off the screen in a series of special effects. Her grade school classmates bearing toothy smiles evoked the piercing smells of chalk dust and leaded pencils. Snapshots of dances and academic events culminated in a Polaroid photograph taken at an end-of-year picnic at Brook Park.

The three of them stood in front of the gazebo, their arms casually draped around one another, David on the left, Cora in the center, and Murphy on the right. Carefree youth suspended for eternity. She'd worn her favorite yellow spaghetti-strap dress. Both the guys sported Madras shirts and cut-offs.

Cora clasped the ring she wore around her neck on a silver chain, her attention riveted on the tall, slim boy with the dark, curly hair and laughing eyes.

The video ended to polite applause. The blinding overhead lights blinked on, dispelling the image, but her sorrowful memory remained. Cora repositioned the ring beneath her neckline and, breathing deeply, struggled for composure.

Joyce called her up front where she was presented with an engraved plaque, a gorgeous bouquet of mauve roses and a gift certificate. Gazing out at the sea of friendly faces, her nervousness vanished and she spoke straight from the heart, her handwritten remarks forgotten in her pocket.

Humbled by the applause and relieved the ceremony was over, she had enough time to gulp a glass of cold water and eat a slice of cheese sandwiched between two crackers before Joyce whisked her off to sign books.

"Congratulations, Cora." Last in line, Willa Spencer approached, clutching a newly-minted copy of *Spencer, the Town and the People* for her to inscribe. "I can't wait to show the finished product to Jakob. He sends his regrets."

"The historical society owes him a debt of gratitude for

his hand in moving this building and hiring Declan to supervise its restoration." Cora signed the title page and handed the book back to Willa with an appreciative smile. "Thank you for the cover art."

"My pleasure, Cora. The society put together a beautiful celebration. I loved the video, although I choked up a little. The music took me back to some tumultuous times."

Once Willa departed, Cora sagged back in her chair and closed her eyes. Willa's remark had hit home. The early seventies had not only rocked the country with social upheaval, but Cora's shattered personal life as well.

The small entry room where her table was set up was deserted. She stood and stretched. Joyce had brought her a piece of cake, but she was hungry for more of the cheese and crackers.

Jesse walked in from outside, a concerned smile creasing his face. "You were about to tell me something when we were interrupted."

Cora's spirits rose, her fatigue and hunger forgotten. "Jesse, thank you for staying. You don't know how much I—-"

"Joyce waylaid Stuart about some guns her husband inherited, but I don't know how much time we have." He sat on the spare chair and gently grasped her by the arm to join him .

The taxing events of the evening and the emotional impact of David's image in that last photo brought unexpected tears to her eyes. Pressing her lips firmly together, she searched her friend's compassionate features. "Jesse, I'm finally doing it. I'm searching for my baby."

He nodded. A resigned smile deepened the lines around his blue eyes. "I figured you would eventually."

"Two weeks ago, I engaged an online detective agency that specializes in locating children given up for adoption." Cora twisted her hands anxiously. "I understand she's a grown woman by now living a life of her own. I don't know if anything will come of it, but I had to try. I couldn't get her off my mind."

Jesse cradled her hands between his. After a thoughtful silence, he spoke in a low, soothing tone. "Cora, I know you've been thinking about finding your child for years. It hasn't been an easy decision."

"I'm excited and I'm terrified. I had to tell someone." Her gaze locked with his. "And you're the only one left who knows my secret."

CHAPTER ONE

Cora Fleming finished sweeping the wide front porch and leaned against the broom. The balmy wedge of bright Colorado sunshine revitalized her. She stared at the blue-and-white for sale sign that the realtor had planted in her lawn earlier this morning. The woman had assured Cora that Spencer's flourishing summer tourist season was the perfect time to list her Victorian home and shop. Customers who treasured antiques and patronized The Attic would be Cora's key potential buyers.

The realtor had left Cora an embossed company folder containing her card and a recommended to-do list, including the name of a professional stager she highly recommended.

Cora harbored misgivings about her decision. She had never planned to sell the Victorian structure that had served as her home and antique business for over forty years. What would Grandma Binney say? Her beloved grandmother had left Cora the house and the shop. But once Cora had made the decision to find the baby she'd been forced to give up for adoption and engaged the detective agency, she'd sat down at her kitchen table and had taken stock of the direction her life was taking.

Next to locating her daughter, she'd always wanted to travel to far-flung places like the South Pacific while she was still active. If she was tied to the business, she couldn't take the time off. Determined to follow through on her travel resolution, she'd applied for a passport and called Hometown Real Estate.

She'd stay in town until she'd located her child. Cora had no control over how long the process would take, but if her daughter was searching for her biological mother that would speed things up. It had been only ten days since she'd put the ball in motion, but waiting was hard and contrary to her nature.

Cora religiously checked her emails each morning before opening the shop, and after she closed. Most days, The Attic and her active participation in the community had kept her busy enough that she hadn't had time to stew about all her unanswered questions.

Now she was retired. Her long-standing commitment to the historical society was officially over, as of today when she handed over everything to Joyce.

Oh crap. Joyce would be here any minute to pick up the executive binder and files. Cora had meant to bring them down with her this morning. Setting the broom aside, she pushed through the half-open door and nearly ran over Agnes. The cat leapt out of her way and vanished into the dim interior of the shop.

Bustling through the kitchen, Cora's hip connected with the heavy maple chair angled in front of the counter. She yelped a curse and massaged the throbbing joint as she climbed the back stairs to her bedroom. "You'd think I'd have learned to put things away by now."

The doorbell rang.

Joyce. Cradling the binder and toting the portable file case, Cora cautiously descended the remaining steps to the kitchen.

"I'm coming." Giving the offending chair wide berth, Cora pasted a welcoming smile on her face and rushed into the entryway. "Sorry Joyce…."

The greeting died on her lips.

Stuart. Jesse's lean, silver-haired spouse stood in the doorway, his stricken face wearing a dazed expression. He pressed his lips tight together, but his chin quivered.

Cora's breath hitched in her throat. The file case hit the floor and tipped on its side. The binder slipped from her grasp, landing square on her sandaled feet. Ignoring the shooting pain, she pressed her hand over her pounding heart. "Stuart! What's wrong?"

"Jess…." his throat worked. "Jess is…." He raised a hand to his eyes. "He's gone, Cora. He died."

A summer afternoon, years ago, flashed in her mind. David.

She blinked the image away and gathered Stuart in a clumsy embrace. Cora recalled her recent encounter with Jesse at the schoolhouse. She'd cherished his thoughtful silence, his compassionate, understanding ear. The light in his blue eyes as he'd laughingly recruited her help in convincing Stuart to retire.

Stuart wept soundlessly, his arms squeezing her as though she were a rag doll.

Cora pressed her cheek against Stuart's shoulder. She wept for Jesse, for Stuart, and for the fickleness of life.

Finally, Stuart heaved a sigh. Releasing her, he pulled a handkerchief from the back pocket of his jeans. He wiped his face and blew his nose. "Sorry. I can't stop crying. Jess always said I was an over-emotional slice of humanity."

Cora sniffed and nodded, searching the folds of her skirt for the pocket containing her own embroidered scrap of fabric. "He always did have a way of mixing the eloquent with the mundane."

Stuart managed a shaky laugh. He folded his arms and

looked down at the floor. "I came directly from the hospital. I wanted you to know…." His voice wavered.

He grimaced and cleared his throat. "I still have to call Jess's brother on the west coast. I'm not looking forward to that."

Cora nodded in sympathy. Murphy Webster was Jesse's younger brother and David's best friend. She hadn't seen Murphy since he'd gotten married and moved to San Francisco. That had been a lifetime ago.

Stuart sighed again and squinted at the face of the grandfather clock standing sentinel at the entrance to the shop. "The bank will be open in a few minutes. Our papers are in the safe deposit box. Jess was the planner. He had me sit down and make my own will out as soon as we were married."

Plunging his hands into his pockets, Stuart's agonized gaze swept the ceiling, the walls. A muscle twitched in his jaw.

Poor Stuart. She knew how deep the pain of loss could cut. She couldn't think about Jesse right now. Thinking about losing Jesse would invariably lead to thoughts of David. A stray tear breached her dammed grief and leaked from the corner of her eye. If Stuart stayed here much longer, she'd be swept away in another unbearable tide of the past and her own sorrow. She couldn't give in to the feelings.

The clock struck the hour. Cora patted Stuart's shoulder and managed a tremulous smile. Biting her lip, she stooped and retrieved the binder. "I had better open the shop. If there's anything I can do—-"

Such a trite, helpless phrase. She hated useless platitudes, but she didn't know what else to say. She blotted her wet eyes with the crumpled hanky still fisted in her free hand. "I'll brew us a pot of strong, black tea. It's usually not too busy the first hour."

Stuart shifted toward the door. "Tea's not what I have in

mind, but you're an angel to offer. Guess I'll head over to the bank. Then give his brother the call."

Turning back to her, Stuart speared his hand through his hair. "God, I hate giving news like this over the phone." He crushed her in another hug and planted a quick peck on her cheek. "Thanks for everything."

Cora stood on the threshold, clasping the binder to her chest until Stuart crossed the street and climbed into his truck. She didn't envy him having to call Murphy. Leaning against the doorframe, she closed her eyes, trying to remember Murphy's face the last time she'd seen him.

The only image she could conjure up was inextricably linked to the distant summer afternoon that David had died. Murphy had been wearing cut-offs and a white baseball shirt, his tanned, skinny arms hanging awkwardly at his sides. Before he'd opened his mouth, the haunted expression in his gray eyes had told her everything.

Cora inhaled deeply, shoving down the dark memory. She imagined Murphy would be coming back to Spencer for Jesse's memorial service. The prospect of reuniting with her old friend after years of separation, sparked her boundless curiosity.

The rumble of a powerful engine split the silence. Stuart's new Ram truck was a gas hog, spewing diesel fumes and carbon into the once-pristine mountain air.

Shaking her head, Cora planted her hands on her hips and stared after the obscene vehicle until it rounded the corner and disappeared. She'd better wash her face and get her ducks in a row before Joyce showed up.

❦

Murphy Webster ignored the new ringtone announcing a call. He'd meant to mute his new, smarter phone before stepping aboard the *Stargazer*, but the buttons and commands were different. The gentle rocking of the boat beneath his feet reassured him. Life was good. The *Stargazer* was his and, with sails unfurled, she would take him around the world.

Palms flat, he leaned closer and squinted down at the chart spread out on the table. He fished around in his pockets and lifted the pile of papers on the nearby bench. Shaking his head, he laughed softly to himself. It didn't matter how many pair of readers he had, he could never find them when he needed to see.

The phone rang again. He blew out an exasperated breath and stared up at the low cabin ceiling. Shannan and Trinity almost always texted him. It was probably a political robo-call, or someone asking for money.

He'd run out to the car, trade out the phone for his emergency glasses in the glove box, and finally get back to plotting the first leg of his trip.

Murphy climbed out on the deck where a stiff breeze swept through his hair. The fog was rolling in, swallowing the light and warmth of the afternoon sun. He'd meant to come out in the morning, but after mowing the lawn he'd had to tie up some loose ends concerning his final legal aid case.

He was officially retired, but retirement wouldn't feel real until he cast off and sailed under the Golden Gate Bridge.

The damn thing went off again. He held the phone at arm's length and peered at the screen. Jesse.

Murphy grinned. A conversation with Jesse was a welcome interruption. His brother in Colorado rarely called. They'd trade legal war stories, he'd ask Jesse how the fishing was and Murphy would give Jesse an updated itinerary on his voyage.

Murphy pressed the phone against his ear. "This is a pleasant surprise."

"Hello, may I speak to Murphy Webster?"

It was hard to hear above the wind and the marina traffic,

but it wasn't Jesse. The guy's voice sounded odd. Murphy frowned. "Speaking."

Silence. A deep sigh. "My name's Stuart Fiske. I'm a close friend of Jess's. There's no easy way to say this."

It sounded as though the man was crying. Murphy rubbed his neck harder. His stomach knotted. "Hold on a minute."

Rushing to get below, he missed a step and slid the rest of the way into the cabin. He scrambled to his feet and shut his eyes.

Don't say it.

"Jess passed away—-early this morning." The guy choked.

No, not Jesse. Not his big brother. Murphy's throat tightened and his own voice sounded strangled. "How did it happen?"

He sank onto the cluttered bench. The amplified crackle of papers under his butt echoed in his ears.

"The doctors think it was an embolism."

Murphy nodded as though the man was sitting across the table from him.

The friend cleared his throat. "I apologize. I hate doing this over the phone. Jess left specific instructions regarding arrangements. He wanted his body donated. His organs have already been harvested. There's a sealed letter here with your name on it. He left me one too. He named you executor."

Murphy gripped the table edge and rose to his feet. Papers and charts cascaded onto the floor. He crossed the narrow cabin to the galley, tore a ragged sheet off the paper towel rack and scrubbed his face. "I'll book a flight."

Doing something, even something as commonplace as booking an airline ticket was better than dwelling on his brother's sudden death.

"I can pick you up at the airport."

"That's okay, I'll rent a car, but thanks. What number can

I reach you at?" Murphy grabbed the pen he'd been using. "Stuart, right?"

"Yes, Stuart Fiske. You can call Jess's phone. Figured I'd better look through his contacts and notify everyone."

Murphy heard the distinct rattle of ice cubes against glass. A hefty splash of scotch would hit the spot right about now. He glanced at his watch. Normally, he had his first drink at five, but to hell with that.

"Jess only had three people listed in his phone, besides me."

Stuart's voice jolted Murphy back to the pressing matters at hand. Not surprising. Jesse had become pretty much of a recluse, especially since he'd retired and sold the family law practice.

"You, a Shannan Thomas—-"

"Thompson. She's my daughter, Jesse's niece."

"Sorry. Shannan Thompson, and his neighbor, Cora Fleming. That was it. You, me, your daughter and Aunt Cora."

The ice rattled again and Stuart sighed. "I can see the bottom of my glass. Time for a refill."

Murphy could feel his composure slipping.

"What do you mean by 'Aunt' Cora?" He fumbled in the compact cupboard over the bar and snagged a squat tumbler. "The Cora Fleming I knew had no brothers or sisters to have nieces and nephews."

"Don't have a clue, but years ago when I first visited Spencer and Jess introduced me, she referred to herself as Aunt Cora. I thought it was odd at the time, but the name stuck, and it fits her now. I'm going to go get that drink. I'll wait to hear from you. Wish we could've met under better circumstances."

He hung up before Murphy could thank him. Murphy frowned and tipped the half-empty bottle of scotch, filling his glass a third full.

Aunt Cora? He gulped a fortifying swallow of the smooth liquor as he opened the tiny freezer to get ice. The whiskey burned going down, leaving a consoling trail of heat in its wake.

Murphy splashed more liquor over the ice and sipped. Aunt Cora sounded like an old lady. The Cora Rose Fleming he remembered had been a tall slender girl with deep brown eyes, long russet hair and a very passionate heart. 'Hippie heart,' he used to tease her. A very passionate heart reserved for one man only, and that man hadn't been him.

Braced against the counter, Murphy raised his glass and swallowed. The alcohol fumes stung his nostrils. Let's not go down that road.

Phone in one hand and drink in the other, he concentrated on navigating across the swaying boat over to the sitting area.

He set his glass on the low table and thumbed his travel app. The glowing screen blurred. Damn.

Blinking hard, he dropped his phone in his lap and pressed the heels of his hands over his eyes as though to stem his gut-wrenching sorrow.

Losing Jesse was like losing Davey, Nan and the baby all over again. His best friend, then his wife and his infant son.

The muted chime of a notification roused him. His daughter, Shannan.

Dinner tonight? My famous clam chowder! Need 3 small sourdough bread bowls.

Shannan and Trinity. His anchors. Murphy grinned. Wiping his damp palms on his slacks, he texted.

You bet. Usual time?

He sipped his drink and opened his travel app. Another message appeared at the top of his screen.

Mom says yes. Add ice-cream for you and me.

Murphy sent his granddaughter a thumbs up emoji, made his flight reservations and arranged for a rental car. Phones were a nuisance but they sure came in handy. He closed his eyes and smiled. The heaviness in his chest had eased. He wouldn't have to go home to his big, empty house and eat alone tonight.

His smile faded. He'd tell the girls about Jesse after dinner. Murphy cast a wistful glance around his boat's spacious living area. He'd been within spitting distance of his dream. Once again life had happened.

He rubbed the back of his neck and sighed. The delay couldn't be helped. He'd settle his brother's estate and pick up where he'd left off.

Murphy relaxed back against the cushions and savored another swallow. Spencer, Colorado. He hadn't been home in years. It would be nice to see Cora again. Had she changed as much as he had?

CHAPTER TWO

The following morning, after a light breakfast of toast and coffee, Cora switched on the lights and pulled up the shades in the large open parlor and dining room that served as The Attic. She'd had the dream again and endured another long, sleepless night, but Friday was one of her busiest days and she couldn't afford the luxury of going back to bed.

Perching on the edge of the glass display counter, the tortoiseshell cat extended her body down toward the floor as far as she could. She finally let go and landed with a thud, followed by a loud hurry-up-and-feed me yowl.

"Bossy old lady." Cora stroked Agnes' hard little head until the purring feline darted off in the direction of the kitchen, her tail ramrod straight. Even at her advanced age, Agnes was still frisky.

Cora trailed Agnes into the kitchen. She hummed as she rinsed out the empty can. The more she thought about her decision to sell, the more her gut told her it was the right thing to do.

Over the years, she'd learned often the hard way to listen to her gut. David had always laughed, arguing that it was the heart one should listen to. Cora had stubbornly maintained that the gut and the heart were connected.

The chime sounded, announcing a customer. She shut off the faucet and wiped her hands on a dishtowel. "Well, Agnes, looks like we're starting the day off with a bang."

She looked at the floor where Agnes had been eating only minutes ago. Among other aspects of the cat's temperamental personality, her tortie was perpetually curious and had gone to investigate.

A slender teenage girl with a mop of curly black hair stood inside the parlor gazing out the window at the garden. Arms folded, her head slightly tilted, she gasped, looked down and laughed. "Hi, kitty. What's this? A mouse? Do you want to play?"

Agnes meowed.

The girl crouched behind a drop-leaf table stacked with a set of Havilland china. The cat hissed. Agnes strode into Cora's view, the cat's favorite toy clamped between her whiskered jaws. Crouching at the base of the glass cabinet, she leapt up to her customary napping spot where the space heater blew warm air from the floor.

Cora scowled at the tortoiseshell, currently occupied with licking her paw and dragging it over her patrician face. "Agnes can be quite rude. She's getting cantankerous in her old age."

The girl shot Cora a fleeting glance. She ambled over to the counter. "I'm used to kitties. We have three at home. Agnes, huh?"

She wore the same ridiculous ripped-up jeans that Cora had seen on other teens around town. A faded Grateful Dead t-shirt accentuated her petite frame.

The cat interrupted her bathing ritual and gifted the girl with an enigmatic feline stare.

"So, you're Agnes, the cat. I'm Trinity, the rebellious adolescent, or so my mother says." Trinity sighed, put her hands on her knees and bent closer, her face level with the cat's.

"Careful!" Cora held her breath. Agnes could be so damn unpredictable.

Numerous clocks ticked. Outside, a large vehicle rumbled down the street, vibrating the crystal prisms on a nearby lamp.

The tortie's focus never wavered, but she closed her eyes about halfway and opened them again.

A slow blink. Cora leaked the pent-up air in her lungs as quietly as she could.

In an unhurried, fearless gesture Trinity extended her hand and stroked between the animal's ears.

"What a sweet, kitty kiss," she cooed.

Agnes closed her eyes, thrust her head beneath Trinity's multi-ringed hand and purred like a buzzsaw.

"That's definitely a first." Cora heard the amazement in her own voice. An incredible event was happening at this moment. She didn't know what it was yet, but her gut and her heart both sensed it.

As was her habit, Cora launched into her customary greeting. "Good morning, welcome to Aunt Cora's Attic where treasures lie in wait to be discovered."

The girl turned her kohl-lined eyes on Cora. A smile curved her rosy lips and brightened the hazel color of her eyes under all that makeup "What did you say your name was?"

"Trinity Thompson. My grandpa's across the street."

"Your grandpa is Murphy Webster?"

"Yeah. How did you know?"

"Well, I've known him and Jesse for years."

"Oh." The girl went back to stroking Agnes' head. "I love your cat."

"And she's certainly taken a shine to you." Curious, Cora took her place behind the counter closer to where Murphy's granddaughter stood. "So, if Murphy is your grandpa, who's your dad?"

The girl turned from Agnes, her hazel gaze unruffled. "Patrick Thompson. He's a government contractor working overseas. Mom begged Gramps to bring me with him to Colorado." Trinity rolled her eyes. "Apparently, I never listen to her because," she punctuated her dramatic statement, sketching air quotes with nimble fingers, "I'm 'hanging with the wrong crowd' and I'll 'get in trouble' while Dad's away."

Cora's lips twitched. Trinity's mocking statements echoed Cora's arguments with her mother at that age.

Agnes thrust her head under the girl's ringed fingers. Smiling, Trinity resumed stroking the cat. "We flew in from California last night. Mom's still back home in San Francisco. She'd love this place. She's always wanted to own her own antique shop."

Cora folded her arms. "Well, it's for sale."

"I know." Trinity flashed a heart-tugging grin and brandished a cell phone in a sparkly pink case. "I snapped a picture of the shop with the sign and sent it to her."

"How long will you and your grandpa be in town?"

The girl lifted a delicate shoulder. "As long as it takes, I guess. As Gramps put it, 'Jesse has a butt-load of stuff to go through.'"

Cora's eyes watered and a lump formed in her throat. She was going to miss her shy, quiet friend, his calm manner and indulgent smiles at her political rants.

Trinity's brows drew together. "Are you okay?"

Nodding, Cora swiped her fingers beneath her eyes. "I'm fine. The past week has been hard."

The teen shot her a sideways glance and ran an index finger over a nearby pile of books. "So, did you know Gramps' brother really well?"

"Yes, I did. I went to school with both your grandpa and Jesse. We attended the same one-room schoolhouse that's now a museum in Olde Town. You should have your grandpa take you to see it."

The girl nodded and sauntered back over to the windows. "Your garden's cool. Mom would like it, too."

Cora smiled and stood next to Trinity. "I like playing in the dirt."

Trinity tilted her head and crossed her arms. "Jesse was gay, wasn't he?" She slanted a shrewd glance at Cora and blew out a theatrical sigh. "Of course, when I first mentioned it to Gramps, he nearly had a stroke and flat out denied it. Until Stuart showed him the marriage license. Gramps is really conservative you know."

Cora ducked her head and chuckled. "You're correct on both counts. Your grandpa is a bit right of center."

She resisted the impulse to reach out and touch the girl's tousled curls. "Jesse and Stuart have been together for years. They were married shortly after Colorado legalized gay unions. They preferred to live separately and keep their relationship to themselves, although most of their friends and acquaintances in Spencer knew. They frequently traveled abroad as a couple."

Hands on hips, Cora squinted outside at another damn squirrel clinging upside-down to get to her bird feeder. "There are still people who tend to be narrow-minded and set in their ways, particularly the older folks. Many of them take a dim view of same-sex couples, even now."

Trinity nodded emphatically. "Yeah, it's hard for Gramps because of his religious views."

Cora plucked a loose thread from the front of her shirt and frowned. "I hope he's not giving Stuart a hard time."

Trinity shook her head. "No. Actually, Gramps has been very nice. At first, it was awkward, but I knew Gramps was warming up to Stuart when he started cracking his bad jokes. Gramps even insisted that Stuart stay with us, but he said he'd rather stay at the local B&B. He wasn't sure he'd be able to sleep at the house—-too many memories." The girl gifted her with another adorable smile. "Stuart's easy to like. Besides, he owns a string of gun shops and that's a gold star in Gramps' book."

Cora shook her head and snorted. "Your grandpa always was fond of his right to bear arms."

"So, was Gramps hot when he was younger? I've seen pictures of him, and he was pretty good looking."

"Hot?" Cora erupted in astonished laughter. Talk about changing the subject.

She gazed out the window and gnawed on her upper lip. She'd never looked beyond David. Murphy had always been David's best friend. "I guess I never thought about your grandpa that way, but now that I think about it, I remember a couple of the other girls thought Murphy was a 'babe.'" Cora darted a glance at Trinity. "That's what we called 'hot' back then."

Trinity giggled. "And you were a tree-hugging flower child, according to Gramps."

Better than a war-mongering nationalist. Cora huffed. "I still am and I'm not ashamed of it."

Though to be fair, Murphy hadn't been one of those either. According to Jesse, Murphy's number had come up in the draft, and he'd gone to Vietnam because he loved his country and he'd felt it had been the honorable thing to do.

David would have done the same, but he'd never gotten the chance. She pressed a hand to her chest. The big clock sounded a series of notes.

Half-past the hour.

Trinity peered at her phone. "Oops. Gramps is looking for me. I'd better go." She leveled her face with the cat's. "Bye Agnes. See you again soon." She flashed her heart-melting grin at Cora. "Nice to meet you, Aunt Cora. Mom's so going to love this place."

Murphy stood in the middle of Jesse's office. His brother had been a packrat, but an organized, tidy packrat. Where should he start?

The room had an abandoned, musty smell. Glass-fronted cases contained thickly bound law books arranged in alphabetical and numerical order. Labeled bank boxes were neatly stacked in threes along one wall. They looked to be old files going back to Dad's time.

The massive desk had been their dad's before Jesse had taken over the practice. Murphy ran his hand over the dark walnut finish. An unexpected wave of melancholy swamped him and pressure swelled behind his eyes. So many memories. Maybe he should keep the desk. It was like part of the family.

When he was a boy, Dad's office had been a secret, mystical room. The door had always been closed, and both he and Jesse had been forbidden to enter whether Dad was working in there or not. The fact that Henry Webster's office was off-limits made the room all the more enticing. Jesse had been content to mind the boundaries, but Murphy had been born to exceed them.

He'd been a little pain in the butt. Jesse's butt to be exact, but his big brother had always tolerated his shenanigans—-to a point.

Murphy chuckled and sank down on the worn swivel chair behind the desk. One memory in particular came to mind.

He'd been seven, maybe eight tops. Jesse would've been thirteen. Early on a Saturday morning, wearing only the white briefs he'd slept in the night before, Murphy had planted himself directly in front of the black-and-white television set.

Jesse blinked, suspending his spoon over his bowl of

cornflakes. He was already dressed, eating in the living room and resting both his big feet on the coffee table even though he wasn't supposed to.

Murphy had bigger fish to fry that morning. He rattled their father's key ring. "Mom and Dad are still asleep. C'mon. This is our big chance."

His older brother sighed and resumed eating. "Put them back, Murph. There's no secret treasure map locked in Dad's desk. All that's going to happen is that you're going to get us both in trouble."

Murphy flashed Jesse the evil eye and twisted the on/off dial. The black-and-white picture disappeared and the TV went silent. "Not if we don't get caught. C'mon. I'll give you my best shooter marble." He stole a glance at the face of the sunburst clock hanging on the wall. "We gotta hurry. C'mon, Jesse. Please, please, please?"

His brother anchored his thumb on the spoon, tilted the bowl and polished off its contents. Wiping his mouth with the back of his hand, Jesse belched and rose from the sofa. "Jesus, Mary and Joseph, Murph. Keep your crappy shooter, but for the next two weeks my wish is your command."

Murphy was so excited, he practically peed his pants. He handed the keys over to Jesse. They crept on the balls of their feet to the solid wood door that led to their father's inner sanctum. Murphy hung back, holding his breath while Jesse turned the key and grasped hold of the faceted glass knob. The door creaked loud enough to wake the dead. Jesse froze. Murphy squeezed his eyes shut and held his breath. They listened for footfalls and squeaking floorboards from upstairs. Murphy thought his head would explode.

Absolute silence.

Jesse glared at Murphy and whispered. "I swear, if we get caught, I'm gonna kill you."

Murphy's throat was so tight he couldn't even swallow.

He nodded and followed his big brother into the dim, high-ceilinged room.

Jesse went directly to the desk. After two heart-stopping attempts, he inserted the small tarnished key into the lock and slid the middle drawer open. "See. What'd I tell you?"

On top of loose papers lay a faded green ledger along with Murphy's confiscated slingshot. After accidentally missing the elm tree in the back yard and breaking the kitchen window he'd been forced to hand it over.

"So, that's where Dad put it." Murphy reached to retrieve his toy.

Jesse landed a stinging blow on his outstretched arm. He slid the drawer shut and twisted the key. "And that's where it's gonna stay."

He carefully re-positioned their father's chair and motioned for Murphy to follow him out of the room. "C'mon, doofus. You'd better get those keys back where you found them. I'll write you a list of stuff to do as payment."

Emptying the trash and handing over the fifty cents that was Murphy's two weeks' allowance had seemed a high price to pay for the disappointing results of his investigation. Knowing exactly where his prized slingshot was hidden and not being able to do anything about it only rubbed salt into the wound.

Jesse had never teased or tortured Murphy about his secret. Strong and silent, his big brother had always been good at keeping things close to the vest.

Murphy rubbed his temples. He had advocated for gay clients in San Francisco, but learning that his brother had been gay and married in the eyes of the law had shocked the hell out of him.

He struggled to wrap his mind around his brother's lifestyle. All this time, Jesse had led a double life and had chosen not to tell his own flesh and blood. Maybe if they had lived closer, and the two of them had spent more time together, Jesse would have felt more comfortable confiding in him.

A knock on the door. "Murphy? It's Stuart."

Murphy frowned. Gripping the chair, he pushed back from the desk. He'd hoped to have more time to himself to think without interruptions.

Behind him, the knob turned and the door creaked open. "Sorry, but the realtor is here."

Murphy shot a quick glance at Stuart over his shoulder. "Thanks. I lost track of time. My head is killing me. Would you mind showing her the bedrooms first? I'll take some aspirin and meet you upstairs."

"Sure." Stuart flashed Murphy a sympathetic smile and pulled the door shut.

The tightly coiled tension and grief inside him eased. Losing Jesse was rough. Nan's lingering illness and her death had been bad enough.

His gaze drifted back to the desk. He studied the tarnished keyhole. What had happened to that slingshot anyway? He pulled on the drawer. It didn't give.

He tugged at the yellowed plastic cover that draped the obsolete computer monitor. Jesse hadn't needed to keep a written ledger. Stuart had already given Murphy Jesse's letter and the will, so what had his brother kept locked away?

Murphy pulled the bulky ring from his pocket and examined the keys, one by one. They were all either too big or too narrow.

Floorboards creaked overhead. He rose and slipped the keys back into his pocket. Time to regroup and get upstairs. They'd get this appointment over with and go grab lunch. He'd ask Stuart for his recommendation.

The consultation ran longer than he'd anticipated. Murphy ushered the broker to the door, and then sent his granddaughter a text. He ambled back into the dining room, reading the message that lit up his phone.

He glanced over at Stuart. "Trinity's coming from across the street. We'll leave as soon as she gets here. What sounds good to you?"

Stuart slipped the real estate papers into a folder on the dining room table. Raking a hand through his hair, he crossed his arms and stared down at the floor. He cleared his throat. "I like the Wild Card. Food's decent. It's nothing fancy, but Ace serves a good steak. Jess and I usually ate there when I was in town."

Murphy swallowed and squeezed the back of his neck. He and Jesse had always ended up at the Wild Card too. He'd better change the subject quick.

He jangled the keys in his pocket. "Hey, Stuart. Do you know anything about the locked middle drawer in Jesse's desk?"

Stuart shook his head and frowned. "I haven't set foot inside Jess' office in years. His will and his letters to us were in the safe deposit box at the bank." The slender man's gaze shifted beyond the dining room to the flight of stairs. Grief etched his finely drawn features. He sucked in a breath and blew it out. "After Jess….after I left the hospital, I went to Cora's. She was like family to Jess and me."

Murphy nodded and clenched his jaw. His composure was slipping, but he stood his ground and listened. It was as though their shared sorrow bound them together.

Stuart sighed and rapped the tabletop sharply with his fist. "After I'd gone to the bank, I came back here to the house." He closed his eyes. "I made myself a good, stiff drink and went upstairs. I sat on Jess' bed and drank my scotch. It went down fast."

His forlorn expression squeezed Murphy's chest.

"I picked up his pillow. Jess took that ridiculous pillow with him everywhere. He couldn't sleep without it. I held his silly pillow and cried like a baby. Then I called you."

Stuart offered him a watery smile and bowed his head.

Murphy's jaw ached. He plunged his hands deep in his pockets. What could he say?

He briefly gripped Stuart's shoulder and strode toward the front door. "The Wild Card it is. I'll wait out in the car."

He squinted into the sun and gulped several deep swallows of fresh mountain air. It was a relief to escape the dark, stuffy house. He slid behind the wheel, rolled down the window and sagged against the seat. His eyes drifted closed.

The rear door opened. Trinity bounded into the back seat, her attention focused on her phone. What passed for music these days blared full volume. A disembodied rapper proclaimed his outrage over a deep primal beat, jarring Murphy's frayed nerves.

"Trinity."

His granddaughter groaned and retrieved her ear buds from her pocket. "Sorry."

Seconds later the racket cut off. Crossing her arms, she stared out the window.

Murphy rubbed his forehead. He'd told Shannan that Trinity would be bored out of her skull, but his persuasive daughter had reasoned that this would give them an opportunity to spend time together.

Stuart folded his lanky frame into the passenger side. "Sorry, didn't mean to hold everyone up."

Murphy sighed heavily and pushed the start button.

Settling Jesse's estate, dealing with his unsteady emotions and those of his brother's spouse was nerve-racking enough. Murphy wasn't sure he was up to the additional challenge of supervising his lively teenage granddaughter.

he last time Murphy had been in the Wild Card was after Dad's funeral. He trailed inside the saloon behind Trinity and Stuart. How ironic. He and Jesse had sat at the same intricately carved bar. They'd sipped good whiskey, talked a little law and shared their favorite Dad stories.

Now Jesse was gone. There would be no funeral, no grave to visit, no headstone etched with a suitable epitaph. Jesse's letter had been clear and concise. He'd wanted his body donated and his remaining ashes scattered over one of his favorite fishing lakes in Colorado. Like it or not, Murphy would respect his brother's wishes, although he was secretly glad Stuart was planning a future family gathering to celebrate Jesse's life.

Over coffee, earlier that morning, Stuart had fixed Murphy with a defiant stare. "Jess may haunt me for this, but those of us who loved him need closure."

The crossed infantry swords Murphy remembered hung beneath the familiar daguerreotype on the wall behind the bar. Murphy wandered over to the far side of the vintage mirror and smiled his relief. The pair of Colts was still there.

Ace came out from behind the bar, his seamed, brown face lighting up. "Hey, look who's here." The proprietor's keen, dark eyes settled on Trinity. "Who's the beautiful young lady?"

Before Murphy could react, his granddaughter marched over and stuck out her ringed fingers. "I'm Trinity. You must be Ace. Stuart told me all about you."

Ace laughed and pumped her hand. "That's me. Nice to meet you." He grasped Murphy's shoulder and squeezed. "Hey, sorry about Jesse. He was a good man." Turning to Stuart, Ace sighed. "It goes without saying."

Stuart raised his hand in a feeble gesture. He managed a tight smile.

Murphy buried his fists in his pockets. Apparently everyone except him had known about Jesse and Stuart. How many private conversations had Stuart and his granddaughter shared?

He scoped out the empty dance floor. *Wichita Lineman* played softly in the background. *'I know I need a small vacation....'*

Murphy cleared his throat and sought to lighten his mood. "My offer still stands for that pair of Colts."

Ace glanced in the general direction of the guns. With a low chuckle, he snapped up three menus and led them to a nearby table. "Did hell freeze over?" He grinned and handed Murphy a menu. "I can't put a price on those babies. They're part of the place."

The proprietor's good-natured ribbing was a welcome tonic. "It never hurts to ask," said Murphy.

"Lunch rush is over so I'll take care of you folks personally. What can I get you to start?"

Trinity opted for a soda. Stuart ordered a single malt. Neat.

"Sounds good to me." Murphy slipped on his readers and sighed. "Damn. I really wanted those guns."

"I'll get your drinks." Ace ambled back to the bar.

Head down, Stuart rubbed his temples.

When their drinks arrived Murphy raised his glass. "To Jesse."

"To Jesse." Trinity hoisted her soda and glanced at Stuart.

Stuart stared at Murphy. He tossed back his scotch and smacked the heavy tumbler on the table top. "To Jess."

They studied their menus in silence.

Murphy sipped his scotch. Instead of calling on Stuart to pick a restaurant, he should have asked the poor guy if he'd felt up to going out in the first place.

Trinity slapped her laminated menu down. "I'm having a meatless burger." She shrugged and grinned at Stuart, charming a genuine smile from him. "I'm a vegetarian." She stared down at her phone's glowing screen. "Stu said that the steaks here are good, Gramps."

Murphy frowned and peered at her over his glasses. Stu? Since when had Stuart become Stu?

Trinity's kohl-lined eyes widened. She leaned back and wedged her phone in the pocket of her jeans. "Sorry about the phone. Like Mom says, 'Old habits die hard.'"

She called him gramps when she was being lovable. Beneath all the makeup, Murphy caught a fleeting glimpse of the precocious toddler who had turned his heart to mush.

Impulsively, he reached to gently chuck her under her pert little chin. "I'm counting on you to help me and Stuart. We need to go through Jesse's things, particularly his files. There are some that legally we'll have to keep."

Murphy turned to the man. "If you don't mind, I thought I'd have you sort through Jesse's personal items."

Stuart nodded. He regarded his empty glass and peeked over at the bar.

Minutes later, Ace took their order and returned with a round of refills.

Trinity looked from Stuart to Murphy and sipped on her

straw. "Aunt Cora is nice. She has an awesome tortoiseshell kitty named Agnes that normally doesn't like anyone, but she came right up to me to be petted."

Stuart gaped. "Really? That animal hisses and high-tails it as soon as I walk into the shop. It didn't care much for Jess either. He used to refer to the cat as 'old miss high and mighty.'

"The only time I ever saw Cora truly angry was when I threatened to shoot the cat after it climbed up my leg. I wasn't really serious, but I thought she was going to go postal. She said if I so much as brought a BB gun into her shop, she'd call the sheriff.

"When I jokingly brought up the Second Amendment and informed her that I had a permit to carry, she ordered me to get the hell out.

"Jess and I went back over later that afternoon and apologized. We practically had to swear an oath not to ever threaten Agnes or mention guns again." Stuart closed his eyes and sipped his drink. "Cora can be one fiery woman when she's crossed."

Murphy raised his glass in a silent toast. A true statement if he'd ever heard one. He recalled their frequent heated arguments over the Vietnam War, the race riots and marijuana. "Cora always was opinionated."

He grinned at Trinity. "Does she still wear her long, hippie skirts and Birkenstocks?"

Trinity cast him a sly look. "You should go over and see for yourself. She asked about you." The light in her hazel eyes danced. "I think the two of you would make a cute couple."

Murphy managed to swallow his mouthful of scotch without choking. If she only knew. "I'm way past the 'cute couple' stage, pookie-poo. The only woman in my life now is *Stargazer*."

Trinity rolled her eyes. "You can't talk to a boat, Gramps. Besides, Aunt Cora looks lonely in that big old house all by herself with—-Trinity gestured air quotes, 'old miss high and mighty.'"

His granddaughter sucked the last dregs of her soda. "I sent Mom a picture of The Attic. Aunt Cora is selling her business and Mom has always wanted to own an antique shop."

Murphy sat back with an indulgent smile. "Your mother already has her own business."

Ace appeared carrying a tray loaded with a basket of rolls, salads and their meals.

Trinity cut her veggie-burger in half. "I know, but antiques are Mom's passion and she's getting tired of working sixty-hour weeks."

"And she used to call me a workaholic." Murphy inhaled his steak's rich, savory aroma. Wielding his knife and fork, he sliced off a generous bite. The beef was as juicy and flavorful as it smelled.

Stuart shook his head and reached for his drink. "Cora hadn't said a word to Jess or me about selling. I was so upset about Jess…." Stuart sighed. "I didn't even notice the sign until the next day, and I was shocked. Cora is practically an institution in this town and The Attic is a Spencer landmark."

"Aunt Cora is such an interesting person." Trinity dipped a French-fry in her container of catsup. "She dresses like a hippie, but she wears her hair in an awesome coronet braid."

Murphy shaved off another slice of steak. Shannan was grown and Nan had passed away before Murphy had thought about Cora again. Lonely and lost, he'd floundered for a couple of years. Several times, he'd almost called her. Then he'd remind himself that Cora's heart would always belong to Davey, and he'd moved on.

It wasn't in the cards.

Over the years, his visits to Spencer had been few and

short-lived. Murphy had never stopped in at the shop to see her. There had been too many painful memories.

Now that he'd retired and bought his boat, he focused only on sailing lessons and plotting his dream voyage.

"Gramps?" Trinity's voice disrupted his thoughts.

"What?" Murphy stuck another delicious morsel into his mouth. He loved Trinity dearly, but her everlasting curiosity threatened his peace of mind.

"Aunt Cora said she went to school with you and Jesse in a one-room schoolhouse. She said some of the girls considered you a 'babe.' What did she look like, then? Did she wear her hair long, with bangs, like Nana did in her old school pictures?"

Murphy polished off the rest of his drink and attempted a light-hearted chuckle. "Trinity Grace, I can't eat and answer all your questions at the same time."

All his granddaughter's talk about Cora, on top of his mounting legal and family obligations, unsettled him. His long-awaited plans were unraveling and slipping out of his control. Jimmy Stewart and *It's a Wonderful Life* came to mind. Murphy's dreams would keep getting postponed just as George Bailey's had. Only there wasn't a benevolent, geriatric angel to pester him about getting his wings.

Jesse's unexpected death was a dutiful distraction. Cora Rose Fleming was not. Nothing else was going to interfere with his expedition.

Once the immediate legalities were attended to, and as soon as Jesse's house was cleaned out and listed, Murphy would shake Stuart's hand, clap him on the back and wish him all the best. He and Trinity would fly home to San Francisco, where he'd hand her back to Shannan, kiss his girls good-bye and head out on the first leg of his adventure.

The scotch had worked its magic. He cast a genial smile at Stuart. "This steak is outstanding. You were spot on, my man."

Out of the corner of his eye, Murphy saw Trinity open her mouth as though to pursue the subject of Cora, but Stuart subtly lifted his hand in a cautionary gesture and shook his head.

Trinity pushed her plate aside. She aimed an irate scowl at Murphy before turning her attention to her ringed fingers.

The corners of Stuart's mouth twitched. He casually snagged a roll from the basket and pointed at Trinity's plate. "I'll take those fries if you're done eating."

"Sure," she said, her tone flat, her face expressionless. She nudged her plate in Stuart's direction.

Murphy mixed another dollop of horseradish into the sour cream blanketing his potato. He appreciated Stuart's diplomacy, especially where Trinity was concerned. He liked Stuart. The man was friendly and he knew his guns, but thinking of him as Jesse's partner would take time and some getting used to.

❦

Trinity itched to check her phone, which had vibrated with several notifications during their meal. Her grandfather had deliberately refused to talk about Aunt Cora anymore, which sucked. She would've pushed him if Stuart hadn't given her the look and kicked her under the table.

Her grandfather's mind was obviously somewhere else, and that somewhere else was most likely his precious boat. Lately, that's all he thought about. She might as well be invisible.

She could hardly wait to leave the Wild Card and get back to Jesse's house. At least she could hang out upstairs and listen to her playlist. Or better yet, go back to Aunt Cora's to pet Agnes.

Instead, Grandpa and Stu decided to stop at some gun

shop. Trinity waited in the car and traded text messages with Merida, one of her older friends Mom disapproved of.

As soon as they pulled into Jesse's drive and the car stopped, Trinity was out the door and halfway across the street to Aunt Cora's. Grandpa and Stu were still BS-ing about guns, and they apparently didn't know or care what she was doing.

Trinity smiled to herself. Sometimes being invisible had its advantages. Maybe Grandpa wouldn't talk, but this was the perfect opportunity to chat more with Aunt Cora.

She'd just met the older woman, but she'd immediately tuned in to the lady and her cat. Maybe because Nana was gone and she missed her own kitties back home.

Trinity jogged up the uneven walk and entered the house. The bell chimed over the door and faded into silence. She stood uncertainly in the deserted hall. "Aunt Cora?"

Agnes padded up to her and meowed.

"Hi, kitty." Trinity bent and ran her palm along the tortie's arching back before strolling into the shop. Her phone vibrated with another notification.

"I figured it was you as soon as Agnes perked up and jumped off my lap." Aunt Cora smiled and rose from an antique rocker behind the counter. "Today was busy. Three busloads of people came through the shop. Everyone was buying and I sold a collection of Madame Alexander dolls."

"Cool." Trinity peered at her phone and laughed. "Holy moly, Aunt Cora! My mom just sent me a text. She loves the picture of your shop that I sent her. She's thinking about coming out to take a look for herself."

Snatching up the cat hovering at her feet, Trinity buried her face against the feline's soft fur. Agnes stiffened and gave a low, protesting growl. Razor-sharp claws pricked Trinity's skin through her thin shirt.

"Y-ouch." She released the furious cat, which thudded to the floor and vanished behind the counter.

"Sorry." Trinity furiously rubbed her stinging skin and glanced at Cora. "I'm super excited. Once she actually sees The Attic, I'm positive she'll make you an offer. Spencer isn't that far from Denver, and there are small municipal airports that are even closer for my dad. We can move here and I can help Mom in the shop."

She stopped and stared into the woman's baffled brown eyes. What about you, Aunt Cora? Why are you selling everything? Where are you moving to?"

"Good grief, that's a lot of questions." Cora walked out from behind the counter. "I think it's time for a pot of tea and my famous lemon cookies. Give me a few minutes to close up."

Trinity sighed. She was being a Nosy Nelly and her mouth had gotten away from her again. Dad's pointed scowl came to mind. He'd been gone so much lately his scowl was all she seemed to remember. That and the constant arguments he and Mom had. Sometimes they'd yell so loud Trinity could hear them above the music playing through her earbuds.

Trinity followed Aunt Cora into the kitchen. She examined the old-fashioned fixtures, comparing them to the modern appliances and granite-topped counters at home.

Mom would definitely gut this room. Her Zen philosophy would kick in. The stacks of mail and catalogs would be gone, the updated countertops bare and pristine.

"Wow." Trinity paused in front of the retro white-enameled fridge with its rounded edges. She inspected the cards and photos hanging from a 'mishmash of magnets,' as Nana would've called it. "Are these your family?"

Aunt Cora struck a match and lit a blue circle of flame under the kettle. She filled a blue teapot with hot tap water. "Those are the people I consider my family. Both of my parents are gone, along with my Grandma Binney, who owned this place before me."

Trinity turned back to study the assorted pictures. Who were all these people? It would take forever to answer all the questions swirling around in her head.

"Since you're over there would you please get the milk out of the refrigerator for me?"

"Sure." Trinity grabbed the carton out of the refrigerator and set it on the table. "Is there anything else I can do?"

While Aunt Cora brewed the tea, Trinity set the table.

She crossed her arms and gnawed on her nails. The shop was basically clean and organized, except maybe Agnes' bed on the counter, but this kitchen was a total deal-breaker. She glanced up at the ceiling. The upstairs rooms were probably equally chaotic. Trinity could offer to help the woman stage her living quarters. She'd talk to Gramps and Stu first before mentioning it to Aunt Cora.

Trinity sat at the table across from the older woman. "Your kitchen is like a book, filled with lots of stories."

Aunt Cora reached for the tin and popped off the lid. She smiled and gazed around the room. "I suppose it is. Here, try the cookies."

They smelled really lemony. Trinity chose a pale, yellow frosted cookie and took a tentative nibble. It tasted buttery, sweet and tart all at the same time. She took another bite. "Yum, these are the bomb."

Aunt Cora cradled her mug in both hands, a faraway look in her eyes. "Mandy and her cousin Nikki loved my lemon cookies. They'd come here after school and head straight for the kitchen."

Trinity straightened and scooted her chair closer. "Who are Mandy and Nikki?"

Agnes appeared out of nowhere and launched herself into Aunt Cora's lap. The cat sniffed and circled once before settling down and curling into a ball. The older woman smiled and caressed her cat's mottled head until the kitty's contented purr buzzed louder than the refrigerator. "Mandy and Nikki were about your age when they first came into my shop looking for Halloween costumes. Mandy still lives here in Spencer. She and her husband, Declan, are expecting a baby this fall."

Trinity finished her cookie along with a cup of warm, milky tea. She wiped her sugary lips with her napkin. "I'm stuffed. I ate a huge lunch at the Wild Card."

She wished she could stay. She wanted to hear the stories behind all the pictures on the refrigerator, but she had probably better get back to the house in case Gramps and Stu actually noticed she was gone.

Trinity picked up the milk carton and returned it to the fridge. "Gramps isn't big on sweet stuff, but I'll bet Stu would like these."

Cora nodded and her mouth tilted in a grin. "Oh, he does. Jesse did too. I used to take over a fresh batch every Christmas."

She laughed softly. "After the first year, the two of them made me promise to continue the tradition, but only at Christmas, for the sake of Stuart's waistline and Jesse's blood sugar."

"Go ahead and take the cookies with you. You can share the rest with Stuart. It's not Christmas, but he can use some cheering up." Grabbing the tin, Trinity impulsively planted a quick kiss on Aunt Cora's warm, soft cheek, catching a whiff of vanilla and something flowery. "Thanks."

Trinity paused thoughtfully on the porch steps and gazed across the street. Jesse's gray Victorian house was a lot like Aunt Cora's.

Trinity imagined what it had been like when Aunt Cora, Jesse and Gramps were kids. It was hard to picture Gramps as a kid, except for the few times he'd taken her and Mom out on the bay in his boat. He'd been happier when Nana was alive.

Trinity missed his deep, booming laugh and the way his

eyes twinkled, how all of a sudden he'd hug Mom and plant kisses on her face, making her loosen up and laugh back.

Back then it had seemed like both Mom and Gramps gave themselves permission to be happy and enjoy life instead of being responsible all the time.

Trinity sighed and chewed on her lower lip. She wished for more days like those.

The front door on Jesse's house opened and Gramps appeared on the front porch. Trinity waved the tin and trotted down across the street. She couldn't wait for him to try one of Aunt Cora's cookies and tell him that Mom was interested in taking a closer look at The Attic.

CHAPTER FOUR

*M*urphy grasped Cora's tin off the dining room table. He, Trinity and Stuart had devoured her lemon cookies in the space of a day. Glancing in the hall mirror one last time, he smoothed the cowlick on the back of his head and left the house.

Lingering on the walk leading to the street, he jingled the keys in the pocket of his khakis.

Cora's house dominated the large lot. If memory served him right, behind the Victorian structure had been Grandma Binney's flower garden and a good-sized apple tree.

When they were growing up, Grandma Binney had owned the house and the shop. Murphy shook his head and grinned to himself remembering the summer he, Jesse and Cora had persuaded Grandma to let them build a tree house. Back then, Cora's long thick braids had annoyed her to no end, but they'd been irresistible to a ten-year-old boy. He'd loved tugging on them to get a rise out of her.

Picturing Cora Fleming climbing the apple tree as an agile twelve- year-old wearing cut-offs and a sleeveless blouse helped ease his apprehension about meeting up with her again. His heart thudded uncomfortably against his ribs, but he mobilized his legs and put one foot in front of the other.

The front door was painted the same bright daffodil yellow, as it always had been, but the faded red sign had been replaced with an oval, electric one.

Murphy inhaled a fortifying breath and entered the brightly-lit foyer. A bell chimed, sucking him unwillingly into the murky past. The last time he'd been in here had been the day Davey had drowned. Frowning, he rubbed his irritable stomach.

"Good morning. Welcome to Aunt Cora's Attic, where treasures lie in wait to be discovered." The tall woman raised her hand to her throat.

Murphy stood, wordlessly trapped in the eerie recollection of that long-ago afternoon. Finally, he thrust out the colorful tin. "Thank you for the cookies."

Five seconds stretched to ten. Cora stepped closer and took the container, the same haunted memory of that long ago afternoon reflected in the soulful depths of her beautiful brown eyes. "You're welcome."

Setting the tin on a narrow console table, she gave the barest shake of her head and embraced him, enveloping Murphy in a warm, fragrant cloak of lavender-scented vanilla.

"I'm so sorry about Jesse," she said.

Murphy closed his eyes against the rising tide of grief that flooded him at the recollection of all the people he'd loved and lost. Jesse, Nan, the tiny white casket containing their infant son, and Davey.

Davey. Always larger than life.

His charming best friend was frozen forever in Murphy's mind. With his boyish good looks and the Spencer name and fortune, the one thing David Spencer had possessed that Murphy envied most was Cora Fleming's heart.

Murphy tightened his arms around her slender form, and

God help him, nestled his face in the sweet space between her neck and shoulder.

He heard the sharp intake of her breath. She clenched her fists between his shoulder blades, tugging at his shirt. How many times as an adolescent kid had he'd imagined holding Cora like this? Murphy sighed, inched her closer, and sank deeper into the paradise of her nearness.

Immediately, Cora withdrew. Eyes downcast, she retrieved the cookie tin, hugged it to her chest and strode briskly into the shop. "I'll put this over on the counter for now."

Rubbing the spot on his cheek that had come into contact with her smooth skin, Murphy followed her over the threshold. A blur of movement he belatedly registered as a cat brushed past his leg.

Cora's regal posture was discernable in spite of her oversized baggy sweater. Smoothing both hands over the braided coronet of her hair and down her skirt, she finally turned to face him, cheeks flushed, her wide eyes bewildered.

Crossing her arms, she gave a breathless laugh. "This is a surprise. Obviously, I knew you were in town, but you're the last person I expected to see."

Murphy longed for the easy stream of conversation and witty banter they had once shared.

He rubbed his mid-section. "I ate too many of your lemon cookies, but they were worth it. Stuart and I almost came to blows over the last couple."

The corners of her mouth lifted. "Stuart is crazy about those cookies."

The tightly wound tension in his shoulders eased. Murphy rubbed the back of his neck and wandered over to the windows overlooking the garden. The apple tree was still standing sentinel, though a bit more gnarled. He squinted and wondered if a remnant of their tree house remained hidden amid the lush proliferation of leaves. "Stuart's been very helpful. He's nothing like I imagined."

Cora joined him. "Stuart and Jesse enjoyed many happy years together. Like most couples, they were different, yet they suited one another."

"How did they meet?" Murphy was curious about the part of his brother's life he'd kept private.

Cora stared beyond the window glass. "At a gun show of all things. Jesse did like to hunt and freeze his own venison." She flashed Murphy a reproachful glance. "Unlike you and your NRA buddies, Jesse didn't kill deer only for sport."

Murphy opened his mouth to protest, but Cora lightly smacked his arm and grinned. "Just kidding. Got you, didn't I?"

Seriously? Knowing Cora, and after Stuart's recent anecdote about shooting her cat, Murphy suspected she'd meant what she'd said. He sought a clever retort and failed.

She grasped him by the arm, the pressure of her warm, slender fingers a pleasant sensation. "Let's sit outside. It's such a beautiful day. Sundays don't usually get busy for another hour and if I keep the back door open I can hear the chime."

He allowed her to tow him between the pocket doors, through the dining room and into the kitchen, which seemed unchanged in its yellow-walled busyness and clutter.

Once they cleared the porch and descended the steps, Cora released him and bustled ahead to the wrought-iron table and chairs. She swept off a seat with her hand. "Now you can sit without getting your pants dirty."

The sun gleamed on her bent head, highlighting the numerous silver strands amid her braided hair. Sighing, she raised the hem of her baggy sweater, dusting leaves and twigs off the top of the table.

Murphy sat and crossed one ankle over his flexed knee. "Cora, will you please stop fussing and sit so we can talk?"

She frowned and settled on the chair across from him.

"That's better." Lounging back in his seat, he squinted into the sun.

She narrowed her gaze and leaned forward, resting her arms on the table. "You should be wearing sunglasses."

The neckline of her baggy shirt gaped. Murphy averted his gaze, but not before he glimpsed the glittering ring resting on the swell of her breast.

Davey's ring. Cora still wore it next to her heart.

Incredible. Murphy shook his head, looking around the yard, looking anywhere but the hollow of her breasts and the damn ring. "I don't see you wearing sunglasses," he quirked a smile. "You're as bossy as you ever were."

She blinked, straightened her shoulders, and stared back at him. "Did you come over here to goad me into an argument, or do you want to hear more about how your brother met Stuart?"

On impulse, Murphy reached out and clasped her wrist. "I came over here to give you back your cookie tin and to see you."

Her eyes fluttered shut. Gently withdrawing her hand, she sank back on the chair, absently toying with the chain around her neck. "It's good to see you, Murphy. So many years have gone by since that day. All those memories hit me at once. Trinity—-"

Murphy recalled his inquisitive granddaughter's abundant enthusiasm after her visit to Cora's yesterday. Trinity had probably talked the poor woman's ear off and peppered her with questions. He sighed. "Is she being a nuisance? Starting tomorrow, she's going to be too busy to bother you. I'm having her help me go through Jesse's office. He'd kept files going back fifty, sixty years."

Cora beamed, affording him a glimpse of the young woman he remembered. "Trinity is no bother. She's a precious breath of fresh air. She told me her mother is looking for an antique shop like mine."

Murphy swept his gaze over the back of the house. "Shannan's always loved vintage furniture and knick-knacks. Pat's away most of the time, and I think she's searching for something to fill her days. She's not one to rest on her laurels." He smiled across the table at Cora. "I'm afraid she reminds me of you. Busy, busy, busy."

Regret stole across Cora's features. "She should be careful not to be so busy that life passes her by. She should cherish her family—-you, her husband, and especially that darling daughter of hers."

Smoothing the palm of his hand over his trouser leg, Murphy focused on the ornate iron tabletop. "Nan's been gone almost five years and I wish I had spent more time with Jesse."

Reaching out, Cora squeezed his arm. "I'm so sorry, Murphy. I'm glad I had a chance to talk to Jesse last week. We were supposed to get together tonight for our monthly dinner."

His brother's death and returning to Spencer had stirred up painful enough memories. Seeing Cora again, holding her in his arms, only hammered home the stunning revelation that his feelings for her had retained their fierce intensity.

A warm current of air stirred the leaves on the apple tree. White cumulus clouds drifted across the blue sky, reminding him of lazy, carefree summers as a kid. Those had been happier times when climbing trees and running down the ice cream truck were the only passions occupying his mind.

Time to lighten up the conversation. He scratched his jaw and shot Cora a wry grin. "Shannan's going to be forty-seven on her next birthday, and she's not happy about it one bit. But Trinity's our little ray of sunshine."

Cora graced him with another of her radiant smiles.

"That's a perfect description. I felt that way the minute I saw her. She's even bewitched my ornery cat."

Murphy chuckled. "That girl and her cats." Slouching on his chair, he extended his legs. "Trinity was a surprise. Shannan and Pat had given up on having children and poof, Shannan got pregnant. Given her previous miscarriages and history of high blood pressure, the doctor put her on bed-rest, which nearly drove Shannan off the deep end. However, as soon as she looked into that baby girl's face, Shannan declared that all the precautions had been worth it."

"Your granddaughter is as sweet as she is beautiful." Cora's soft response matched the feeling in Murphy's heart.

"That she is. Oh, don't get me wrong, Trinity has her stubborn side. She and her mother have been butting heads lately. Trinity's extremely bright for her age. Shannan's worried about her involvement with an older, more sophisticated crowd. That's part of the reason I brought her out here with me."

Cora nodded, a frown creasing her brow. "Trinity mentioned her mother's concern about her associating with the wrong people. The drug culture terrifies me. The limited experience I had convinced me of that."

Murphy studied the woman sitting across from him. In her youth, Cora Rose Fleming had been an extreme political activist. Regretfully, some of her actions overshadowed her good intentions. His granddaughter's passionate nature reminded him of Cora's.

"Trinity has assured us she's not about to screw up her life with drugs, but she's participated in several demonstrations. These people she refers to as friends belong to a radical worldwide environmental organization. Although this group has raised environmental issues to public knowledge, some of their direct actions have sparked fines and suspended sentences for several of their activists. Trinity was damn near arrested."

Cora's brown eyes widened. Bright spots of color stained her cheeks. She compressed her lips until they whitened. When she spoke, her low voice shook. "What the hell, Murphy? Haven't you learned anything in the last decades?"

If he hadn't, apparently she hadn't either. A flippant response rose to mind, but given Cora's fiery reaction, Murphy kept his mouth shut.

Relying on his career in the courtroom, he dispassionately told himself this was not so much about Trinity as it was about the legal and moral principles he'd believed in and subscribed to his whole life.

Sublimating his emotions for the sake of argument, he folded his arms over his chest. "Laws are the foundation of society, Cora. Without law and order there is chaos. You saw what happened in the seventies."

Cora shot to her feet. "Thank God for civil disobedience and free speech. Thank God for Susan B. Anthony and woman's suffrage, Martin Luther King and the civil rights marches. You mean to tell me you believe your sacred laws of denying women their right to vote, and school segregation were morally correct before?" She gave a harsh laugh. "Why am I not surprised? You're a privileged white man with a straight white man's entitled attitude."

Murphy curbed his heated response. Coming here had been a mistake. He should've known. No matter how convincing his argument, Cora wasn't going to change her mind. Their fundamental disagreements would always stand as a wall between them.

❦

Cora clenched the table with trembling fingers. Adrenaline rocketed through her body.

To his credit, Murphy actually looked taken aback.

Astonishment flickered in the depths of his gray eyes. "Now you sound like Trinity."

Murphy had aged well. His gaunt, narrow face had filled out and grown handsome. She tried not to think of how she must look without makeup, without even so much as a touch of lipstick.

He tipped his face up to the sky and laughed. "Oh my, Cora. Just like old times. We can't discuss anything without turning the subject into a debate."

She hugged herself and struggled to contain her boiling emotions. "A debate, my ass."

Cora turned her back to him so he wouldn't see the wounded tears that stung her eyes. How had their conversation strayed from Jesse and Stuart to the social revolution of the seventies and her part in it?

To her horror, her voice came out breathless and choked. "It's never been a debate with you, Murphy Webster. It's always been a battle."

A magpie glided down from the apple tree and landed on the weathered birdbath.

Murphy sighed and came to stand behind her. He cupped her shoulders with his warm hands. "I always seem to rub you the wrong way. I'm sorry, Cora Rose. I'll leave."

He smelled good, like lime and spice. She swallowed and closed her eyes. She listened to the whisper of his feet retreating through the grass and up the steps of the back porch. The screen door's dry hinges emitted a plaintive squeak followed by an earsplitting crash as the door banged shut.

Cora flinched, clamping her lower lip between her teeth. A desolate wave of loneliness swamped her.

The ring lying against her breast was cold comfort this morning. David would always hold a cherished, tender piece of her heart, but his memory was being replaced by the cry of her baby, whose first vibrant wail still echoed in her ears.

Cora remained outside in the yard. She roamed the sun-washed garden, seeking solace in examining her hardy roses and pinching off dead blooms.

Straightening from her stooped position, Cora arched her back and studied the gnarled apple tree. She envied the family Murphy possessed with such confident, loving assurance.

What if she couldn't locate her long-lost daughter? The idea was unbearable. An equally frightening prospect occurred to her.

What if she did? What if her daughter rejected her?

Her life had rounded a corner and she was navigating an unfamiliar course.

Add to that uncertainty her thrilling response when Murphy had appeared on her threshold. Her consoling hug had instantly shifted from the forged link of their past to the pleasurable comfort of connection, of one lonely soul drawing physical solace from another.

Cora touched her fingertips low on her neck recalling the surprising strength of Murphy's answering embrace, the breathtaking sensation of his skin against hers.

His lime and spice scent and the reassuring heat of his solid grip on her shoulders lingered in her memory.

The faint sound of the door chime came from inside the house. Cora lifted her chin and wiped her hands down her long skirt.

At this crucial hour of her life, an autumn romance already weighed down by a lifetime of long-buried feelings and heartbreak was the last complication she needed. The time for that kind of relationship was long past.

CHAPTER FIVE

*H*ands fisted in his pockets, Murphy stepped off the curb and crossed the deserted street. He felt as though he'd been hit by a bus. He knew now why he'd avoided visiting Cora the few times he'd been in town. He'd been right to avoid her.

Nothing had changed. Davey might be dead and buried all these years, but he lived on inside the walls of the house across the street. The ring that Cora still wore around her neck was testament to that fact.

Murphy's visceral response to Cora's embrace was disturbing. She'd put her arms around him and immediately resurrected all those old feelings he'd buried.

He swallowed the hopeless lump rising in his throat and stepped inside Jesse's house. The house he and his brother had grown up in was still packed tight with more gut-wrenching memories.

A generous splash of scotch from the new bottle he'd bought to replace the one he and Stuart had depleted sounded tempting, but it wasn't even noon yet, and he had Trinity to consider.

She leaned against the dining room wall and glanced up

from the glowing screen of her phone, her bright eyes expectant. "How'd it go?"

His heart swelled with tender love for his granddaughter. He'd bought into her romantic notions, and deep-down he'd wished she'd been right. He hated to disappoint her.

Murphy forced a smile and lifted her off her feet. He hadn't hugged her like this in a very long time. She was a lot heavier than she used to be. He gently released her and tousled her soft curly hair.

"Geez, Gramps. I'm not a little kid anymore." Trinity grinned in spite of her exasperated tone. She slipped her phone into the back pocket of her jeans. "I knew it. After mom buys the shop, we can move here and you and Aunt Cora can sail around the world on your boat."

Not even in your wildest dreams, sweetheart.

The thought of rattling around in this gloomy house all day, sorting through his dead brother's possessions was unbearable. What time had Stuart told him he'd be back from Loveland?

Switching on the overhead light, Murphy scoured the objects occupying half of the dining room table. "Trinity, have you seen my phone?"

Rifling through papers, he flipped open the realtor's portfolio. "I swear I left it on top of my briefcase like I always do," he muttered to himself.

Between Jesse's sudden death, living out of a suitcase, and this morning's altercation with Cora, he was losing his mind.

Trinity jogged back into the room and handed him his phone. "Sorry, Gramps. I plugged it into my charger. Stu called while you were gone, and your phone was dead. He wants you to call him back."

Murphy tapped the lit screen, putting the phone on speaker. "Stuart?"

"Hey, Murph. I've been thinking about Jesse's service. I've got some dates to run by you."

The hard lump of grief in his throat returned with a vengeance. Murphy dipped his head and swallowed. Unable to speak, he nodded and swallowed again.

"Murphy? You there?"

Trinity slipped her arm through Murphy's. Squeezing his free hand, she rested her head against his shoulder. She said, "Hey, Stu. Is it okay if you talk to Gramps about that tomorrow? I begged him to take me around Spencer and show me the sights. We're going to spend the day together like we used to, 'before I grew up and got sassy,' which is a direct quote."

She was right. His sassy granddaughter had grown up, mastering the art of adult subterfuge. A sad smile tugged at his lips. Murphy closed his eyes and gripped her hand more tightly.

"Well, sure thing, honey. I think that's great." Stuart's voice squawked from the speaker. "Murph, I just want you to know I'm finally getting on top of this. Emotionally, I mean. I've informed my store managers that I'll be taking time off, and it's all arranged. I'll be available twenty-four-seven."

"That's awesome, Stu. Thanks," Trinity interjected. She slipped the phone from Murphy's unresisting grasp and flashed him a conspiratorial smile. "We're planning to start first thing tomorrow at nine. I negotiated the time with Gramps, and he actually agreed."

Murphy raised his brows. Give that girl an inch and she took a mile.

"You're sure about that?" Stuart's amused tone contained a note of caution.

Clearing his throat, Murphy gently pinched his sweet granddaughter's soft cheek. "Trinity argued her case brilliantly. We'll see you in the morning."

"Sounds good, Murph. 'Bye."

Trinity tapped the screen and handed the phone back to Murphy. Flinging her arms around his neck, she hugged him and planted a quick sugary-smelling kiss on his cheek. "Let's go."

He rubbed the tacky spot on his skin. "What are you wearing?"

Trinity paused and turned in the open doorway. She laughed and pursed her lips. "It's fruity passion lip gloss." She wiggled her ringed fingers. "C'mon. Like you're always saying, 'Time's a wasting.'"

Murphy locked the door and followed her out to the car. He was looking forward to spending the day with her. Trinity's cheerful mood had lifted his spirits. He hoped he could keep up. Come five o'clock, he was going to need that scotch.

He backed out of the driveway onto the street and glanced to his right. A group of women were heading up the walk to Cora's shop.

This morning had been a disaster. His encounter had only served to point out that he and Cora Fleming were like oil and water. Regardless of Trinity's romantic, match-making notions he needed to constantly remind himself of that.

In less than a months' time, if there were no snags regarding Jesse's estate, he'd be aboard the *Stargazer*, sails full out, tasting the cool, salty breeze of the sea on his lips.

❧

Olde Towne was packed with cars, buses and tourists. Murphy managed to squeeze the Prius into a narrow slot behind a bank of shops. He cracked the door, careful to avoid hitting the mini-van parked inches away. "This little car has its advantages."

"That's what I've been trying to tell you, Gramps. If there were more hybrids out on the road and less trucks, we'd be leaving a smaller carbon footprint on the earth."

Trinity climbed out of the car on her side and joined him under the intense Colorado sun. She linked her slim arm through his. "Stu says he agrees with me, but insists he still needs his truck. I think it's because he has to maintain his white American male image."

Murphy chose to ignore Trinity's sarcastic remark. He'd fulfilled his quota of arguments today. He wanted to spend a nice apolitical afternoon with his granddaughter. He bumped against her, playfully knocking her off balance. "Let's walk around. According to Spencer's website there's some of my history down here."

"Sure." Trinity craned her neck to look in all directions. She bumped him back and hugged his arm. "I'm glad Mom made me come with you."

Murphy laughed and planted a light kiss on the top of her head. "Me too, pookie."

It had been years since Murphy had been down in this area. He'd forgotten that Sunday in the summer was the worst possible time to explore Spencer. The sidewalks were a minefield, packed with couples and families with children in tow.

Trinity dragged him along allowing no time to pause to read signs or peer through the windows into the shops and businesses that lined Brook Park Road. Quick glances at additional buildings informed him that Olde Town had undergone a massive transformation since he'd last been here.

They crossed Cherry Grove Drive and walked down East Brook Park Road. The one-room schoolhouse sat surrounded by a picket fence. Poignant memories washed over him again. Sunlight bounced off a fresh coat of white paint. The bell Mrs. Winston had rung every morning to summon them inside had been sandblasted clean of rust and now hung in its customary place in the tower.

"Wow." Trinity jogged up the steps ahead of him and disappeared into the building.

Murphy trudged up the risers in her wake, reluctance

pooling in his stomach. Summer cooled and morphed into a crisp fall morning. High-pitched voices of children split the air.

Rapid images flitted through his mind: Jesse, sitting by himself in the far corner of the schoolyard under the tall, blue spruce, his nose in a book.

Davey, thumb poised behind his shooter, golden eyes intent, taking aim at the smaller scattered marbles within the dirt circle.

Kneeling immediately behind him, gingham dress tucked under her knees, Cora Fleming with her worshipful brown gaze focused on Davey's bent head.

For crying out loud, Murphy. Get over her.

He noted the gleaming brass knob on the open door. The old one had been tarnished from hundreds of children's fingerprints.

The restored interior evoked the past, though the paint was fresh and the wall was free of scuff marks. The narrow entry was lined with a row of hooks where they'd hung their coats and placed their boots beneath. A glass case against the opposite wall contained an exhibit of frayed books and report cards with barely legible inscriptions.

Murphy angled past a family blocking the entrance to reach the larger room. Trinity stood up front absorbed in the objects on the teacher's desk.

Sun streamed through the narrow windows on both sides, calling to mind the warm, earthy smell drifting in through the open windows on spring days.

"Gramps, come here." Trinity waved and moved to the bank of photographs in the corner up front.

Murphy dutifully complied.

Trinity pointed to a faded black-and-white photo collection. "Look. They have old class pictures. I found you, Nana, Jesse and Aunt Cora."

Murphy fished in his shirt pocket. He'd left his glasses at

the house. He peered closer. Sure enough, there was his toothy smile and his perpetual cowlick sticking straight up.

Jesse stood in the middle of the back row, his expression agreeable, as though complying with another requirement of his academic career.

Murphy spotted Cora, rigid and solemn on the far end. Because of her height she'd always been stuck in with the older boys and she'd hated it.

He stepped closer. Where was Davey? The damn print beneath the photo was too tiny to read. He squinted, scanning the students' faces again. Davey's older brother, Jakob was there, mugging a roguish grin for the camera.

Murphy straightened. "Trinity, what's it say below the names?"

"The following students were not present. Susan Jensen, Carl Loomis and David Spencer."

Trinity remained focused on the picture. "Aunt Cora was the tallest girl. She should smile more. It makes her look younger and prettier. Don't you think?"

She tugged at his shirt sleeve and slanted him a teasing glance.

Murphy rocked back on his heels and folded his arms. Nope, he wouldn't take the bait.

Above the class photo were vintage fifties portraits of Mrs. Winston and the school's administrator.

Trinity sighed in surrender and wandered over to the nearest row of desks.

He stuck his hands in his pockets. Mrs. Winston had been strict, but fair. The only time she'd ever lost it was the time he and Jakob had put a rubber snake on the chalkboard tray. Murphy studied the scarred wooden floor with a smile.

He and Jakob had been a volatile combination. They couldn't seem to keep out of trouble and often had to be separated.

"Gramps." Trinity tugged on his arm, her ringed fingers

cool against his skin. His granddaughter's hazel eyes shone with excitement. "I discovered something else."

Murphy blinked and followed her down an orderly row of desks that had been bolted to the floor.

"Look at this." Trinity rubbed her finger over a corner of one desk near the carved groove at the top for pencils and pens.

Again, he fished fruitlessly in his empty shirt pocket before squinting down at the dark surface. "Help me out here."

Trinity trained her phone's flashlight on the wood. "It's hard to see, but there are carved initials. D.S. and C. F. C F has to be Cora Fleming, but who is D S?"

Murphy remembered Cora etching the initials into her desk with the point of her metal compass. A tiny bit every day. She'd eventually confessed her transgression to Mrs. Winston. Davey had frowned. Cora's enormous brown eyes had filled with tears, and Murphy had harbored the futile wish that she'd get so mad at Davey, she'd turn to him.

Murphy folded his arms and forced a teasing note in his voice. "How do you know it's Cora Fleming? There was also a Carolyn Fitzgerald back then, miss smarty-pants. Come on, it's getting stuffy in here and I'm hungry. Let's find some place to eat."

Trinity didn't need to know that Carolyn had been seven years old. He wasn't up to telling his incorrigible grand-daughter about Davey. Not yet. The romance and the drama would be too appealing.

Outside in the heat, vehicles carrying tourists clogged the street. A young woman occupied with her phone bumped into Murphy and excused herself. Nodding, he leaned close to his granddaughter and lowered his voice. "I would pick a Sunday to sightsee."

Trinity's light-hearted laugh boosted his mood. "Mom

would say the tourist traffic was good for business." She glanced across the street. "Look, Olde Town Soda Shoppe."

"It's going to be mobbed."

Trinity ignored his forecast. Clutching his hand, she dragged him into the stream of humanity blocking traffic.

She insisted on checking inside to see how long the wait would be. Murphy wandered under the awning and leaned against the building. He closed his eyes, wishing he was aboard his boat sipping a scotch over ice.

"You were right. It's complete chaos in there." Trinity's breathless voice rang in his ear. She paused and peered closer. "Gramps, you look beat. Mom told me to make sure you drank plenty of water." She cleared her throat and the corners of her mouth turned up. "Instead of scotch."

Murphy tamped down his irritation. "Your mother can be so annoying, to quote someone I know. Doesn't she realize that scotch is the new water?" He chuckled at his own joke and playfully pinched her pert nose.

Trinity rolled her eyes and led the way along the sidewalk past the pungent, enticing aroma of Wild Bill's Smokehouse. "Is there any place that isn't crowded?"

Rubbing the back of his neck, Murphy exhaled a weary sigh. When the traffic signal on the corner turned green, he stepped off the curb and took the lead. "Let's get off the main drag and find a place that's quiet so I can think."

It was a hike, but they finally arrived at the lot where he'd parked the car, and with the aid of Trinity's phone, they drove the short distance to Pearl's Café. Trinity raised her device with an impish grin "See, aren't you glad I had my phone with me?"

Murphy swung the door open for her. Yes, but he wasn't about to tell her that. She'd take his agreement as tacit permission and there'd be no stopping her. "Your great-grandpa used to bring Jesse and me here for burgers and fries."

Trinity laughed and slipped her phone in the back pocket of her shorts. "Never mind. I know you are." She glanced around the restaurant and inhaled deeply. "It smells so good in here I could almost eat a burger. Almost."

A pretty young woman dressed in jeans and wearing a red bibbed apron looked up as they entered the building. She snagged two brown-bordered menus and strode in their direction. "Hi there, my name's Piper. Welcome to Pearl's. Right this way, please."

Piper sat them in a booth along the wall. "What can I get the two of you to drink?"

Trinity looked up from her menu. "A gigantic glass of ice water please."

"Water sounds good." Murphy waited until the server left. "I figured I'd better drink the water first or you'll be lecturing me my whole meal and I wouldn't be able to enjoy my chocolate malt."

❧

Trinity lifted the dripping straw out of her glass and sucked the thick, creamy mixture off the end. She stifled a soft belch and glanced down at the remains of her grilled cheese. "That's the best malt ever, but there's no way I can eat any more."

Gramps wiped his mouth with his napkin and surveyed his own plate. His gray eyes twinkled. "I'd say we did pretty good considering we each had our own giant malt."

She couldn't repress her giggle. Wagging her finger at him, she collapsed against the back of the booth. "Yeah, between the cholesterol and the salt, Mom would be having a meltdown of epic proportions."

Gramps' chuckle erupted into a loud laugh.

Both of them covered their mouths and craned their

necks to look out at the u-shaped counter. Gramps acting like a big kid was a little weird, but nice.

With the exception of a little girl sitting between her mom and dad, the other patrons were busy enjoying their meals. Mom would've been embarrassed. She'd be giving both her and Gramps her look of death and telling them to knock it off.

As much fun as she was having, Trinity couldn't help feeling a little bummed. She'd texted the pictures of Aunt Cora's shop to Mom, who'd called her back that night. Mom was definitely interested, but wouldn't be able to take off for another week.

Trinity watched her grandfather study the check the waitress had left on the table between them earlier. She recalled the faded class picture. Gramps with his hair sticking up and trouble written all over his face, compared to calm, serious looking Jesse. He definitely had been the naughtier of the brothers. Nana had frequently called Gramps a pistol, and Trinity now knew why. Aunt Cora was the most intriguing, with her long braids and mysterious brown eyes.

Gramps had stared for ages at the yellowed photo. He'd gotten extremely quiet after she'd read the names of the kids who weren't in the picture. What was he thinking? What was he remembering?

When she'd pointed out Aunt Cora's initials carved in the desk, he'd given her a lame explanation about how they were somebody else's and changed the subject. Gramps was an expert in avoidance when he didn't want to talk about something.

Trinity had chosen not to push him. They'd been having fun and she didn't want to ruin it. Especially after this morning.

Gramps withdrew his wallet from his back pocket. He pulled out a five dollar bill. "That should cover the tip." He grinned at her. "Good service, good food and you can't beat the price."

He drained the water left in his glass and winked at her. "So, pookie, are you ready to work tomorrow? I thought you and I would start on Jesse's office in the morning. Everything older than seven years in those boxes can be destroyed." He raised his brows. "You've got at least a week's worth of paper shredding."

Trinity gave an inward sigh and followed him up front. Her heart sank. She hated for this day to end. She'd rather be helping Aunt Cora clean and stage her living quarters than sorting through hundreds of boring files tomorrow, but she hadn't asked the older lady yet, and she'd promised Mom she'd help Gramps and cause no trouble.

Outside, he slipped his arm around her and kissed the top of her head.

She giggled and hugged his arm. "Thanks."

He slipped on his sunglasses and glanced down at her. "For what?"

She gazed up into his eyes, concealed behind the dark lenses. "For taking me out and spending the day with me. Like when I was little. We haven't gone to Golden Gate Park, the beach or the zoo since Nana died. Mom's always busy, and Dad's gone most of the time."

Gramps cleared his throat. He smiled big and patted her hand.

They paused at the corner for traffic. He patted her hand again and said in a husky voice, "Let's go take a look at the park. I want to see if the gazebo's still there."

CHAPTER SIX

*S*ince the shop was closed on Mondays, Cora usually reserved this day to straighten the store and catch up on her bookwork. This particular Monday, she was at loose ends. Still clad in her chenille bathrobe, she sat at the kitchen table toying with her braid, her mug of coffee cold and forgotten. The only habitual tasks she'd completed thus far were to brush her teeth, check her email, and feed Agnes.

Cora sighed and stared at the untouched bowl of cat food. Where was that cat anyway? She missed having her tortie underfoot.

She really should get up and look for her cantankerous old feline. It wasn't like Agnes to skip her morning meal. She wasn't getting any younger and nine lives aside, her days were probably numbered.

Cora slumped over the table and buried her head in her folded arms. Tears misted her eyes. She still hadn't received an update from the detective agency, and now that Jesse was gone, Cora had no confidant with which to share her search for her child.

Yet, she had a lot to be thankful for. Grandma Binney had

left her the house and the shop. She made a comfortable living and she had friends. Enough with the pity party.

Cora counted the muted chimes of the clock in the hall. Half the morning was already gone. She usually had a load in the washer and the bank deposit ready by now.

Groaning, she stretched her arms over her head. She had better get her butt up off the chair and get dressed. Murphy might come barging in, and she certainly wouldn't want him to see her like this.

Fat chance. She snorted and got up from the table, mug in hand. After yesterday, he'd avoid her like the plague. Murphy she could live without, but his charming granddaughter was a different story. Trinity radiated youthful energy and optimism, infusing Cora with hope for the future. A spiritual connection existed between them, one she'd recognized as soon as she'd laid eyes on the girl.

The bitter smell of scorched coffee hung in the air. Cora wrinkled her nose and emptied the pot down the drain. She filled the sink with hot soapy water. Staring at the rising cloud of bubbles, she toyed with the chain around her neck.

David.

She closed her eyes. Those stolen early mornings he'd risen from her bed to pull on his cut-offs before going back to his house. He'd plant soft kisses on her lips and comb his fingers through her hair. The even-timbre of his voice resonated clearly in her memory. "Don't look so worried, my sweet. I'll be back after work."

Cora had sworn she'd never forget, but her gauzy memories were fading. It was harder and harder to remember how he'd looked, smelled, tasted. She pressed her palms to her temples.

She'd clung to David's memory for the last forty years and she didn't want to let go, but something instinctive inside her said it was time to move on.

Turning from the sink, she wiped her damp hands on her robe and wandered into the shop.

Agnes was curled up in her bed on the counter. Cora gently stroked her tortie's warm fur. A relieved smile lifted the corners of her mouth. Stop worrying. Agnes will eat when she's hungry.

Cora paused on the back stairs leading up to her bedroom. When was the last time she'd taken Agnes to the vet? She'd check on that as soon as she'd dressed.

Once she'd washed her face, gotten dressed and fixed her hair, the day looked brighter. Cora started a load of wash, opened the window over the sink, and tidied up the kitchen.

She picked up the empty tin Murphy had returned yesterday and gnawed on her lower lip. Perhaps if there was time, she'd bake a fresh batch of cookies. Trinity loved them and Stuart could use a little cheering up. What about Murphy? Her pulse picked up at the prospect of seeing him again.

The remainder of the morning passed quickly. Her routine tasks accomplished, Cora went out into the backyard to soak up some vitamin D while the cookies cooled. The apple tree was loaded. In another month, she'd have plenty of crisp fruit for the Farmer's Market.

Cora folded her arms. In another month she might have found her baby daughter. In another month she might have sold the shop and be looking for a new place to live. In another month, anything could happen.

Jesse's house would likely be sold. Stuart had told her he wasn't interested in buying out his share and keeping the place. He was thinking of selling his gun shops and moving to Italy. Cora smiled sadly, recalling her last conversation at the schoolhouse with Jesse.

Murphy would be gone. Out of her life as quickly as he'd swept back into it.

Her heart sank, recalling his warm hands on her shoulders and his heady scent of spice and lime. She'd overreacted yesterday as she always did when her emotions were stirred up.

The cookies should be ready to frost by now. She'd take them over and apologize to Murphy before she changed her mind. Life was too short to build walls and hang onto hard feelings.

Cora couldn't help but remember yesterday. When she'd embraced Murphy, he'd responded in kind. Two lonely souls clinging to one another in mutual need.

She shook her head. She was already heavily invested in the hope of finding her daughter. A relationship of that kind with Murphy would only complicate her life and his. Better to part as good friends, bound by shared memories and nothing more.

If Trinity's mother were to buy the shop, that would be the perfect solution. Cora smiled to herself. She loved the idea of Trinity growing up here and The Attic being cared for by someone who loved antiques and would perpetuate Grandma Binney's legacy. And hers.

Cora carefully layered a dozen cookies in the tin. Halfway out the door she stopped, turned around and went back into the kitchen.

Setting the tin on the table, Cora located her purse in its customary place on the counter. Digging deep, she retrieved the one tube of lipstick she possessed. It wouldn't do to go over there looking like a ghost.

Switching on the light in the downstairs bathroom, she leaned against the sink and carefully applied the vivid rosy color. She smoothed the wayward strands of hair that had escaped from her braided coronet and critically examined her habitual long skirt and baggy top.

Stop fussing, she told herself. She was delivering a tin of cookies and apologizing to Murphy for goodness sake.

Stuart's pickup was in the driveway, but Murphy's rental

was not. Her stomach dropped. They might've gone somewhere for lunch. She squared her shoulders, crossed the
street and marched up the walk. Fine. If no one was home,
she'd leave the cookies on the porch.

Cora rapped on the weathered oak door. Her racing heart
ticked off the seconds. She stooped to set the tin on the
porch and the lock clicked.

"Aunt Cora!" Trinity sounded surprised and happy. "Ooh,
more cookies. Come on in. Gramps went to the deli to grab
some sandwiches." Her hazel eyes widened. "Nice color. That
lipstick looks hot on you."

❖

Murphy parked the car at the curb instead of the driveway.
He didn't want to have to move the vehicle later when Stuart
left. He sat behind the wheel, his gaze gravitating to the
Victorian structure across the street. In spite of dealing with
Jesse's estate, cleaning out the house and putting it on the
market, Murphy couldn't put Cora out of his mind.

The woman had even managed to distract him from his
voyage. His matchmaking granddaughter was partly to
blame with her pie-in-the-sky fantasy that he and Cora
belonged together.

He recalled his heated argument with Cora yesterday in
her backyard. He'd handled their conversation all wrong. He
should have changed the subject or kept his mouth shut. It
had been too many years since they'd sparred, and he was
rusty.

His incurable attraction to Cora Rose, on the other hand,
was anything but rusty. As soon as she'd hugged him, he'd
returned her embrace with passion. Close contact with her
willowy figure and intoxicating fragrance had elicited an
aching pleasure.

Murphy's mind flashed on the ring glittering against

Cora's breast. He shook his head with a melancholy smile and climbed out of the car. Get real. Cora and Spencer, Colorado, were nothing but temporary roadblocks. Once he was finished wrapping up Jesse's affairs, Murphy had his boat to outfit and a crew to hire before embarking on the first leg of his cruise.

He retrieved a large grocery bag and six-pack of beer out of the passenger side. Even if Shannan were to buy Cora's shop and move to Spencer, another of Trinity's daydreams, that wouldn't change the facts. Davey had always been firmly entrenched in Cora's heart and always would be. In another month at most, Murphy would be out to sea on the *Stargazer*, destination Kahului Harbor, Maui.

He walked up the driveway, skirting Stuart's truck. They'd take an hour for lunch and work until four. Six hours the first day was a good start. He and Stuart would evaluate their progress and establish a schedule from there.

Murphy depressed the brass handle and opened the front door. He paused in the entryway, waiting for his eyes to adjust.

Cora stood in front of him, wide-eyed, her hands clasped in front of her.

Murphy's heart picked up its tempo. He needed to stop grinning like an idiot and say something. He lifted the six-pack. "The guy at the liquor store recommended this local craft brew."

Cora folded her arms and stared down at the floor. "I'm afraid I know nothing about beer." Frowning, she raised her head and lifted her chin. "Murphy, I want to apologize for the way I acted yesterday."

The contrite tone in her voice, the vulnerable set of her mouth was exceedingly rare. A tender wave of emotion washed over him. His earlier intentions fell by the wayside. Murphy tipped his head and smiled. "No apology necessary."

He noted something else and stepped closer to get a

better look. Cora was wearing lipstick. She hadn't worn any yesterday, and the Cora he remembered had rarely worn any makeup.

Trinity trotted out from the kitchen and pried the grocery bag from Murphy's grasp. She examined its contents. "Let's eat. I'm starving."

Murphy sighed. "Good grief, Trinity Grace. Show some manners."

"Okay." Trinity thrust the bag back at him but addressed Cora. "Sorry."

Cora appeared not offended in the least. Her expression was one of unadulterated love. Murphy was reminded of Nan, clapping her hands and encouraging Trinity as she had taken her first tentative steps.

Cora's smile faded. She turned toward the door. "I'd better get back to the house. I'm in the middle of a dozen tasks and—-"

Before Murphy could open his mouth, Trinity seized Cora's arm. "Oh, please have lunch with us first."

His granddaughter turned pleading hazel eyes on him. "Please Gramps? I've worked hard all morning, and I'll work extra hard again after we eat."

Murphy knew he was being played, but he couldn't help himself. As distracting as Cora was, he wanted her to stay for lunch too. She'd apologized and baked them more cookies.

He handed the bag back to Trinity and kissed the top of her head. "All right, pookie, you can take it down a notch."

Murphy flashed Cora a persuasive grin. "Please stay. I can't eat the whole pastrami on rye all by myself."

Her honeyed laughter charmed him to his toes. "Well, I suppose I have to eat lunch, and I haven't had pastrami on rye in forever."

"Good." Caught up in the levity of the moment, Murphy impulsively slipped his arm around her shoulders and tugged her close.

The affectionate hug he'd just given Trinity was nothing like this. He inhaled a whiff of Cora's lavender scent and was rocked by the fierce longing to nestle his face in the crook of her neck as he had yesterday.

This wasn't yesterday. His eagle-eyed granddaughter looked on, ready to pounce on his slightest display of affection.

Mustering all the willpower he possessed, Murphy released Cora and strode over to the base of the stairs. He flashed the girls what he hoped was a credible wink and raised his voice. "Stuart, lunch is here."

"I'm coming." Stuart called. "Go ahead and start without me."

Murphy laughed, motioning Cora and Trinity ahead of him into the kitchen. "We're planning to, but you'd better hurry before I give Cora half your sandwich."

He took the vinyl-backed chair on Cora's right. "What do you want to drink? Trinity, what else do we have besides water?"

"Root beer and milk," Trinity replied, setting plates on the table.

His granddaughter's numerous rings glinted on her nimble fingers, reminding him again of Davey's ring and abruptly bringing him back down to earth. Murphy uncapped his beer and took a hearty swig. Giving in to Trinity and inviting Cora to stay for lunch had not been wise.

"Water's fine, thanks," Cora said, folding her hands in her lap. She shone her warm brown eyes on him, curving her pink lips into a charming smile. Had she put on the lipstick for him?

The woman was too distracting. He couldn't let today get away from them. It was important to establish a baseline for working through the house.

Stuart strolled into the kitchen "I'll take a beer if you're sharing." Murphy handed him a bottle. "Of course. You bought last time. Take a seat."

Trinity set a glass of water in front of Cora and popped the tab on her root beer. "Cheers. Hey, Stu, I saw two bikes out in the garage. Did you and Jesse ride?"

Stu nodded. "Mostly in the summer. We'd cycle around town and down to Brook Park for the band concerts."

"Would you mind if I rode one?" She slanted Murphy an earnest glance. "Not during working hours, of course."

"I don't mind if your grandpa doesn't," Stuart replied. "The tires are probably low. I'll check them before I leave tonight."

All three of them stared at Murphy as though waiting for his verdict. His sweet, unrelenting granddaughter was in her element. She was amazing. She'd wrapped both Stuart and Cora around her little finger. Murphy helped himself to another spoonful of potato salad. "It's fine with me." He pointed his fork in his granddaughter's direction. "As long as it's on your own time."

"Thanks Gramps." Trinity's beaming smile radiated from Murphy to Stuart and landed on Cora. "I love the lipstick you're wearing. What color is it?

Cora dropped her gaze to her plate, her voice barely audible. "I don't remember. Something—-something pink."

She had worn the lipstick for him. Pleasure flooded Murphy's chest. Cora's cheeks were turning something—-something pink too. He took a swig of his beer to celebrate.

Cora cleared her throat, smiled, and sat back in her chair.

She sipped her water. "Food tastes so much better when shared with friends," she said in a grateful tone. "It feels like ages since I've eaten a meal with anyone, except Agnes."

Reaching across the table, she squeezed Murphy's hand. "Thank you."

The neckline of her blouse dipped, revealing the delicate silver chain around her neck, reminding him of his earlier resolution. What time was it? They needed to get back to work.

"Gramps sharing his sandwich with you is sooo big. You have no idea." Trinity's unwavering gaze flickered from Murphy to Cora.

His face hot, Murphy abruptly stood, catching his chair before it toppled over. Throughout the meal, his imaginative granddaughter had watched him and Cora like a hawk, spinning an elaborate romantic fantasy that stood a snowball's chance in hell of coming true.

He dumped the remaining beer in his bottle down the sink, checked his watch and shot Trinity a pointed look. "Let's give it another fifteen minutes, and then we'll get back to work. Stuart and I want to see how far we can get today."

"But Gramps, the shredder's broken and—-"

"I'm ordering one online. You can still go through the files."

He rubbed the back of his neck. Cora or no Cora, he would settle Jesse's estate in a reasonable time frame and go on his voyage. That's the way this scenario would play out and Trinity needed to learn that valuable lesson.

"I'll go see if the damned Internet is working." He flashed Cora a polite smile. "Excuse me."

❧

Gramps could be such a downer. Trinity trudged back into Jesse's office. She shut the door and stuck in her earbuds. An acrid odor lingered in the room, compliments of the over-taxed office shredder. Stacks of manila folders littered the floor.

Boring. After doing nothing but checking dates, removing staples and shredding paper, the thought of spending the whole afternoon repeating the process was unbearable. Some of the ancient cases had been interesting, but Gramps ended that as soon as he'd caught her reading them. A lecture on client privacy had followed.

Seriously? She'd argued that all the clients had probably been dead at least twenty years. Peering over his reading glasses, Gramps had folded his arms and launched into another rant about the limited time they had to purge Jesse's files, clean out the house and get it ready to sell.

Afterward, Gramps had stared out the window, rubbing the back of his neck and not saying anything for a long time. Trinity had remained silent, sensing that a rebuttal would not be in her best interest.

What had he been thinking about? Trinity plucked out her earbuds and went over to the window. Directly across the street was Aunt Cora's.

There was definitely an attraction between Aunt Cora and Gramps. The more Trinity saw the two of them together, the more convinced she became that they should be a couple.

Aunt Cora's lipstick had sparked an idea while they'd been eating lunch. Trinity hadn't had a chance to offer to help her stage her living quarters, but giving the woman a total makeover sounded way more exciting.

Next to her smile, Aunt Cora's best feature was her large brown eyes. With a light matte shadow, brown liner along the top of her lashes and black mascara, her eyes would pop. The bigger question was how resistant would Aunt C be to cutting her hair?

Aunt C? Catchy. Better than Aunt Cora.

She grinned and swiped her phone to check out hairstyles. An angled bob would make Aunt C look younger. Trinity suspected she'd get more pushback about the haircut than the makeup.

The door creaked open. Trinity jumped and slid her phone into her back pocket. She was so busted.

Gramps frowned down at the floor and carefully picked his way across the room.

She plowed forward in his direction. "Sorry, Gramps, I got distracted. I promise—-"

Before she could get the rest of the words out, he pulled her into a bear hug like he used to when she was little.

Kissing the top of her head, he released her. "No. I'm sorry, pookie. We were enjoying a nice lunch and I practically shoved our guest out the door. I shouldn't have ordered you around like that."

She loved this side of Gramps. Trinity remembered Sunday, laughing and drinking chocolate malts at Pearl's. He'd softened since they'd come to Spencer.

It never paid to be timid. With Aunt C's makeover plan at the forefront of her mind, Trinity shot him her best smile and planted a kiss on his cheek before wading back over to the desk. Opening the top file on the nearest stack, she rigorously applied the staple puller to the thick u-shaped fastener binding the sheaf of papers.

"Maybe you should go over and apologize to Cora," she slyly suggested, purposefully leaving the aunt part off.

Gramps jingled the keys in his pocket. "Maybe I should."

His voice sounded thoughtful. Trinity glanced up. He was staring out the window again. She noticed little things about him she'd never seen before, like the cowlick that stuck up in his perfectly-styled hair. How well he carried himself. Gramps wasn't bad looking for an older guy.

"You should smile more, too. It makes you look like a babe." She deliberately used Aunt C's term for hot.

Gramps turned from the window. He folded his arms and narrowed his gaze. "Just what are you getting at, Trinity Grace?"

He didn't sound mad, so she doubled down. "I think you should ask Cora out to dinner—-as an apology," she added, exhaling a gust of pent-up breath.

Gramps raised his brows and laughed. "Oh, you do, do you? Any other suggestions?"

Suppressing a victorious grin as best she could, she eyed her grandfather from head to toe. "You're in Spencer, Gramps, not San Francisco. You need to dress less tailored, more casual. Lose the khakis and logo shirts. Get some jeans and a pair of boots."

His eyes twinkled, and he stroked his chin. "Well now," he drawled. "I better get myself a hat to go with them there boots. I can't be a proper cowboy without a hat."

Trinity put her hands on her hips and sighed. "I'm serious, Gramps. Not so much about the cowboy look, although the hat is kind of a cool idea."

Gramps stared down at his feet. "I suppose my tasseled loafers are a bit over the top."

He lifted a hand to the back of his neck. "That reminds me. I need a couple pairs of new deck shoes for my voyage. I'd better add them to my list before I forget."

The light in the room faded. Thunder rumbled in the distance. The narrow window of opportunity had closed. His stupid voyage eclipsed everything else in his life. Trinity pulled her phone out of her pocket and leaned against the desk, swiping through hairstyle after hairstyle, daring him to notice and say something.

Gramps turned from the window and flashed Trinity his get-down-to-business smile. He picked up the burned-out shredder. "I'll throw this out."

He scanned the dwindling wall of unopened boxes. "You haven't found any keys, have you? Let me know if you find anything other than paper clips and rubber bands." Hoisting the shredder higher, he backed out of the office. "We'll stop at six."

Folding her arms, Trinity glared at the vacant doorway. She couldn't resist adding, "Don't forget to add deck shoes to your list."

"I'd already forgotten. Thank you, pookie."

Her sarcastic comment had gone right over his head.

Trinity groaned and pressed the palms of her hands against her temples. She wanted to slam the door and scream the ultimate cuss word at the top of her lungs. No way in hell would he be able to ignore her then.

Wait five minutes. If after that time you're still so inclined, by all means go for it. But be prepared to suffer the consequences.

Mom's often unwanted advice. Trinity stalked over to the window, kicking crap out of her way.

Five minutes.

A bolt of lightning forked across the slate-colored sky. Deafening thunder followed close on its heels. Fat raindrops smacked against the window.

Five minutes. Trinity swallowed and her vision blurred. She wished Mom was already here. Then again, it was probably better she wasn't. Not yet. Even more important than Gramps and Aunt C hooking up was Mom falling in love with the shop and buying it. It was critical for her to see the shop and the house in the best light possible.

What if someone else made an offer before Mom could fly out here to check out The Attic?

Trinity refused to entertain that idea. Aunt C wanted them to have the shop. She could tell by Aunt C's hopeful expression upon learning Mom was seriously interested.

Realizing she was biting her nails, Trinity frowned and wiped her hand on her shirt. But as her mother was fond of reminding her, there were no guarantees in this life.

CHAPTER SEVEN

*A*fter Murphy had rudely ended lunch, Cora returned home and trudged up the stairs to her bedroom. She needed to catch up on her sleep.

Murphy's high-handed treatment of Trinity and Stuart had pissed her off. Screw his smoky gray eyes and the sexy way he smiled without saying a word.

Cora burrowed under the quilt and closed her eyes. A warm, delicious heaviness invaded her body. Actually, Murphy had done her an enormous favor. He'd shattered her silly, romantic illusion. She should thank him. Her mind drifted into oblivion.

Half an hour later, a thunderous boom shook the house, yanking her out of a sound sleep. Cora bolted upright and blinked to get her bearings. Rain drummed on the roof above.

Lightning briefly illuminated the dark room. Milliseconds later, another sharp crack of thunder rattled the glass in the window. She rolled off the mattress and walked over to peer outside.

The limbs of the old apple tree thrashed in the wind. Cora flinched against a blinding flash and at another earsplitting clap backed away from the outside wall. She checked the floor around her feet.

Where was Agnes?

The cat hated thunderstorms. Instead of hiding in a safe place until the weather had passed, her tortie would always seek her out, curling around her legs and meowing until Cora picked her up.

Cora hated thunderstorms too. Not because they scared her so much but because they were a piercing reminder of a summer afternoon, years ago. That stormy afternoon David had gone out on the lake to rescue two boys in a canoe. In the attempt, he had died.

"Agnes? Kitty, kitty?" Cora rushed from the room. Clinging to the railing, she rapidly descended the front stairs and hurried into the shop.

Eerie light flickered around the drawn shades. Hugging herself, Cora approached the cat's bed atop the glass counter. A simultaneous flash and deafening peal of thunder detonated overhead. An involuntary cry escaped her.

Agnes appeared to be sleeping, curled up in her customary position, which was uncharacteristic. Cora reached out with trembling fingers and stroked her kitty's warm, yielding fur. Relieved tears seeped from the corners of her eyes.

The cat's eyes opened to mere slits, but otherwise she didn't stir.

Cora frowned and gently caressed between the tortie's ears. "What's the matter, old girl? You never nap during a storm, and your breakfast is still in your bowl."

The cat barely lifted her head and mewed.

Thunder rumbled, softer now. The storm was moving on. Cora wrung her hands, pondering Agnes' unusual behavior over the past week. Dread stirred in her stomach.

She clamped down on her lower lip and scooped Agnes

up in her arms. The tortie yowled and hissed. Her needle-sharp claws plowed the back of Cora's hand.

"Ouch!" Cora recoiled and tightened her hold.

She marched her squirming cat into the kitchen and swaddled Agnes in the terrycloth towel hanging next to the sink.

The cat glared at her, growling deep in her throat.

"Agnes. Stop. You're hurting me. Something's wrong, and we need to find out what's going on. If you don't stop, I'm going to take you to see Dr. Jack."

The tortie hated being bundled into the cardboard carrier and taken to the vet's office. Agnes' claws penetrated through the terrycloth and Cora's shirt.

With her own howl, borne of sudden piercing pain, Cora released Agnes, who twisted and landed with a thud on the linoleum. The cat fled from the kitchen and disappeared into the dining room.

Cora massaged the throbbing area over her left breast. She'd call and talk to the vet. He knew Agnes, and Cora trusted him.

Grimacing, she examined the bleeding scratches on the backs of her hands. Getting her cat into the carrier would be a piece of cake compared with everything else going on in her life lately.

❧

While the storm raged outside, Murphy called the painters and arranged for them to start on Friday. Three days wasn't much time. If necessary, he'd have the crew start on the rooms used the least and leave the office and the bedrooms for last.

Murphy climbed the stairs. He needed to get back out to the garage, but first he owed Stuart an apology. He'd been rude to Stu and Cora as well as Trinity.

The second floor was dark, except for the soft radiance coming from Jesse's room. Stuart sat on Jesse's bed, his silver head bent over an album. He looked up. His face glowed with the happiness of past memories. He gestured for Murphy to join him. "Please."

Murphy's first inclination was to remind the man about their deadline again, but wasn't that what he was apologizing for? Stuart's trusting expression was an open invitation. To hell with his deadline. Murphy sat next to Stuart on the firm mattress. Leaning forward, he folded his hands and cleared his throat. "Stuart, I'm sorry for ruining lunch. Cora was over and all of us, me included, were having a good time." He shrugged and gave the man a rueful smile. "No excuses. I acted like a pompous ass and I'm sorry."

Stuart arched a brow but humor danced in his black eyes. He cupped his hand to his ear. "You acted like what?"

Murphy's mouth dropped open. He narrowed his eyes at the man, swallowed his pride, and burst out in a hearty laugh. "I deserved that."

Stuart gave him a sympathetic smile and clapped him on the shoulder. "You've had a lot on your plate lately, Murph."

Murphy bowed his head and blew out a long breath. Having Stuart acknowledge his pain was powerful. Nan had acknowledged his pain once she'd recovered from losing their baby boy. He rubbed his arm and glanced over at the man his brother had loved. "Thank you."

"You're welcome." Stuart shifted his knees beneath the brown leather book and flipped the pages back to the beginning. "Jess wasn't as keen on a wedding album as I was, but he told me time and time again he was glad I'd talked him into one. He said looking at pictures of us celebrating our love together helped him through the lonely times. The times when I was away on business, or those extended periods of time when we lived apart."

Murphy clasped his hands more tightly. He'd always

thought Jesse preferred solitude. Throughout the years hadn't he frequently used Jesse's proclivity for privacy as a convenient excuse when he'd been too busy to interrupt his life and call his brother?

His excuses had come back to bite him when he'd stupidly knocked his phone off the deck railing into the murky waters of the marina and missed Jesse's voicemail. Three days later, after he'd gotten his new smarter phone, Stuart had called, and it had been too damn late.

He'd been unable to retrieve Jesse's last words to him. Murphy pinched the bridge of his nose and smiled weakly at Stuart. His voice came out thick. "I'm glad Jesse had the album." He honestly meant what he said next. "I'm glad Jesse had you."

Stuart's eyes shone with relief. Reaching over, his hand hovered above Murphy's leg. Instead, he gripped Murphy's shoulder. "Thanks. That means a lot coming from you." He cleared his throat. "I mean because I respect and value your opinion. You're all the family Jess had. I'd always wanted to meet you, but…."

Murphy clenched his jaw. He could fill in the blanks.

Stuart sighed and traced his finger over the glossy sleeve covering the first photograph. "Jess was too—-"

He shrugged and cast Murphy a compassionate look. "Jess wasn't sure how you'd react."

Murphy rubbed the back of his neck. "Yeah, I can imagine. I've made a few joking asinine remarks over the years about gay pride marches in San Francisco." His face heated. "No offense."

"No offense taken, man." Stuart tapped the photographs. "I'd like to show these to you. Would that be okay?"

Murphy studied the book containing a big piece of his brother's life he'd missed out on. The garage could wait. "Sure."

Stuart's expression was tender as he took Murphy

through each of the color photographs and shared his memories of their wedding with him.

The photographer's lens had captured the joy of the celebration. Jesse's face mirrored his happiness. In almost every picture he smiled or laughed.

Murphy tapped the glossy face of a group photo. "This looks like a nice place. Who are these guys?"

Stuart indicated the portly middle-aged man with a neatly trimmed goatee. "Simon generously offered the use of his beautiful log home in the Santa Christa range, south of Denver in Monument. The tall dude in the middle is Ben. He's the judge who married us."

In the next photograph, Jesse and Stuart were cutting a two-tiered tuxedo wedding cake. The banner hanging on the wall behind them read, We're legal!

While practicing general law, Murphy had paid scant attention to which states, other than California, had legalized gay marriage. Due to his upbringing and his faith, he'd been opposed to legalizing marriage between same-sex couples, although he did support their right to the civil advantages offered to married persons.

What if he'd known his brother had been gay? An unresolved question now that Jesse was dead. Still, his brother's spouse sat next to him, mourning Jesse as Murphy had mourned Nan. He still grieved for her on holidays, special occasions and at unexpected times.

Murphy briefly squeezed Stuart's shoulder. "How long were you two married?"

Stuart's dark eyes registered surprise. He gazed down at his left hand and twisted the wedding band on his finger. "It would've been six years this November. We'd planned to celebrate in Italy and stay over Christmas."

Murphy groaned inwardly in the heavy silence. He flipped to the last page and briefly closed his eyes.

Jesse and Stuart sharing the traditional ceremonial kiss.

As awkward as it was to see two men kissing, especially when one was his own brother, Murphy stared down at the demonstrative couple, striving his best to grasp another's sexual orientation and understand.

Gradually, Murphy gazed at the image with new eyes. He'd never seen his brother look like that. Jesse's tender expression shone with love, reminding Murphy of his own devotion for Nan.

Stuart splayed his hand over the laminated image. His voice came out in a husky whisper. "That's my favorite."

Thinking of Nan and now Jesse, the thick knot of grief in Murphy's throat returned. Murphy nodded, not trusting his voice.

"You skipped this one," said Stuart, paging back.

Murphy studied the picture of Stuart frowning in concentration as he adjusted Jesse's tie. Murphy laughed softly. "Jesse always hated ties. He never could quite get the hang of the knot. He'd always have me tie his."

"Jess always said that was the one thing his little brother was better at." Stuart smiled and gazed down at the picture. "Jess told me lots of stories. He said you were a giant pain in the ass when you were a kid, but you were a good man, a man of your word."

Sharing the wedding album and Stuart's consoling disclosure comforted and reassured Murphy. After all, they'd both loved Jesse. In different ways, perhaps, but love nevertheless.

Murphy rested his fingertips on his brother's image beneath the page's smooth plastic sleeve. "I can't help but wish I'd known about the two of you, but I understand why. The one thing I honestly regret, Stuart, is taking my relationship with Jesse for granted. I wish we'd spent more time together. I know we lived across the country from each other, but I could have picked up my phone and called. Hell, I could have used a couple of weeks of accrued vacation to come out and visit."

Stuart sighed. "Maybe we should have told you. We didn't know there wouldn't be time. Hindsight and all that. Jess had come up with a plan to ask you to fly out for a few days in the fall and the three of us would do some hunting. Jess figured once you and I got better acquainted, he'd sit down with you privately over a couple of beers and tell you everything. He wanted you to see how happy the two of us were together. He said you'd probably be pissed at first, but eventually you'd come around."

Murphy smiled sadly and nodded. Jesse's plan had been a good one. After getting to know Stuart and seeing their wedding pictures, he was coming around.

"I talked him out of it." Misery etched Stuart's features. "I called you a hard ass because I didn't want anyone to hurt Jess, least of all his own brother."

Murphy shook his head, his heart full of remorse. "I am a hard ass. You were right to protect him. I would've been just as shocked as I'd been when you'd told me, but after working with you," Murphy grinned, "and talking guns with you, I'd like to think Jesse had been right." Murphy tapped the wedding album. "That says it all, man."

It was Stuart's turn to bow his head and blow out a long breath.

The day's emotional turmoil had taken its toll. Murphy looked at his watch. "It's been a long afternoon. We have two more hours to work, but I'm drained. I don't know about you, but I could use a drink. Let's call it a day and have a scotch."

"Sounds good to me." Stuart laid the album on the bed. He gripped Murphy's shoulder and the corners of his mouth lifted in a perceptive smile. "I think Jess was right."

CHAPTER EIGHT

*C*ora hefted the carrier containing her pissed-off cat and entered All Creatures Veterinary Clinic. Emily Davis, the office manager, had been able to fit in Agnes the next day after Cora had called.

The waiting room was brightly lit with overhead florescent lighting. The other chairs were empty except for a petite woman with a carrier resting at her feet.

Cora checked in at the front desk. She took a seat and set the carrier down on the tiled floor. Agnes growled low in her throat.

The woman smiled and shook her head. "Cats sure let you know when they don't like something. My kitty pants and sheds terrible. She'll leave a carpet of fur in her crate and all over the examining table."

Cora returned the smile and nodded. She didn't know this woman, although she knew most people in Spencer, barring the tourists and seasonal people who rented on the other side of Twin Owl Lake.

The woman's eyes widened. "I know you. You're Aunt Cora. My friends and I love your shop. We were there on

Saturday. I found the cutest little figurine for my nostalgia shadowboxes."

Cora had been so busy Saturday that she couldn't recall seeing the woman, but she smiled to convey her appreciation. "Thank you. I'm glad you found what you were looking for."

The door to the examining rooms opened and a young woman dressed in colorful scrubs glanced at the chart she held and looked up with a smile. "Miss Kitty?"

"That's us." The woman stood and lifted her carrier. She cast a backward glance at Cora. "I'm sure I'll see you again soon. Hope your kitty is all right."

The door closed and Cora uttered a relieved sigh. She addressed the cat in the carrier at her feet in low tones. "Miss Kitty? What an undignified name that is. Agnes sounds so much better, don't you think?"

She didn't expect a response, but Cora bent down to peer at her cat with concern.

Agnes' ferocious glare assured her she was fine and still notably pissed. She pitched her low growl again.

"I know. I know. You hate this place, but I'm worried about you. You're not eating, and I want to find out what's wrong. Besides, Dr. Jack is one of your few favorite people."

Dr. Jack and now Trinity. Trinity had run out of Jesse's house and across the street as Cora had backed out of her driveway. The girl had immediately wanted to know where Cora was taking Agnes.

"Agnes?"

Cora looked up. A man leading a snorting bulldog on a short leash was heading over to the front desk to settle his bill.

The young girl smiled, holding the door to the examining rooms open.

Cora picked up the carrier. Agnes shifted inside. Her low

growl intensified into a plaintive yowl, followed by a loud hiss.

"Is that my favorite tortoiseshell patient?" The vet's deep voice greeted them from the second examining room.

He poked his head around the doorjamb, his sapphire eyes warm and open. "Aunt Cora, I haven't seen you since the Halloween Ball. Come on in."

"Hello, Jack."

"Let me take her." He easily lifted the carrier up on the stainless steel examining table and cautiously opened the crate door.

Agnes sprang out of her confinement. Jack adroitly caught her. He shot Cora a charming grin and addressed the multi-colored feline in a practiced soothing tone. "I know how you operate, Miss Agnes."

Cora was fascinated at the young vet's kinship with animals. His calm, tolerant attention was always focused on his patients.

He stroked Agnes under her chin and smiled down at her. Agnes blinked and within seconds the tortie was purring. "I always did have a way with the ladies."

Jack weighed her before wrapping the feline for Cora to hold while he took Agnes' temperature and examined her teeth and ears. "She has no fever."

Unwrapping the tortie, the vet gently ran his hands over the cat's small frame. He listened to her heart, his contemplative attention fixed on the wall beyond them. "How long has her appetite been suppressed?

Cora caught her upper lip between her teeth, her gaze focused on Agnes' gold eyes. "I guess it's been well over a week. She's still as cantankerous as ever, but I've noticed she's sleeping more."

She raised her finger. "The day I called you, when we had the big thunderstorm? Agnes usually sticks to me like glue, wanting me to pick her up and hold her. She slept through that storm and she's never done that."

The vet nodded, his handsome features thoughtful. He consulted his laptop. "She's past due on her distemper and feline leukemia vaccinations."

Cora hung her head. "I know. She puts up such a damn fuss. Once she sees you she's fine, but…."

Jack's gaze was sympathetic. "We'll get her vaccinations caught up today and draw blood." He studied Agnes as he continued to pet her. "We'll see if there's anything to be concerned about."

Cora's heart swelled with gratitude. "I appreciate that, Jack. How's construction on Stick Pony going? Zoe says you and Ryder are working your butts off."

Jack's face lit up. "We are, but it's a labor of love. We're planning to open in August."

Cora sat in the nearby chair. "That's just around the corner."

Jack rolled his eyes. "I know, trust me. Ryder's posted a countdown on our shared calendar, complete with daily notifications. I've muted my phone, but the banners still pop up on my screen. My cousin, the whipcracker, is very detail oriented.

"I'm going to call Lisa in to give Agnes her vaccinations. Should I hold her or would you prefer to?"

"I think you held her last time. She's already mad at me, and she'll carry a grudge for the next couple of days."

Jack lifted Agnes up so he could peer into her face. "Agnes, you seriously need an attitude adjustment."

Agnes meowed and swatted at his face.

Cradling the cat, he laughed and walked over to open the door. He leaned out into the hall. "Hey Lisa, I need a blood draw, feline distemper booster and leukemia. Thanks."

Minutes later, the young assistant entered with a stainless

steel tray. She quickly and efficiently administered the two injections.

Agnes took both with little protest, but the blood draw was a different story. The vet tightened his mouth and the muscles in his arms flexed as he contained the squirming cat. Agnes hissed.

"Feisty old lady," he muttered.

Lisa left with her tray and Jack gently but firmly put Agnes back in her carrier and latched the door. The cat's low growling commenced again.

Jack shook his head smiling. "Agnes is a mature cat now and older cats have special nutritional needs. We sell a recommended brand. Once I have the test results, I'll call you."

"Thanks again for taking such good care of Agnes."

"You're welcome." Still smiling, he shot Cora a hesitant glance. "I know it's none of my business, but are you really selling The Attic?"

Cora sighed and clasped the handle of the carrier. As soon as the sign went up, she'd anticipated the rumors to start flying. She forced a blithe smile. "I decided I better take time to travel to the far-off places that I want to see in the world while I still can. I imagine I'll hear from your grandmother soon."

"I'm sure you will," Jack said with a chuckle.

Willa was a close friend, but Cora feared she would want to know more than Cora was able to divulge. Selling the shop had been a complicated decision directly tied to her efforts to find her daughter.

Jack patted her shoulder and relieved Cora of the carrier. "I'll walk you and Agnes out to the car."

❧

Trinity was emptying her third load of shredded paper and staring out the window when she spied Aunt C's vehicle turning into the driveway.

She quickly tied the trash bag and bolted from the office. "Gramps."

Her grandfather was in the dining room conferring over paint swatches with Stu. She paused on the threshold. He looked up, his expression curious.

"Excuse me, but Aunt C took Agnes to the vet today, and she just got back." Trinity took a shallow breath. "I've done three bank boxes already. Can I take a break and see how Agnes is?"

Gramps quirked a smile at Stuart. "What do you think?"

Stu shrugged. He winked at Trinity and spoke in a teasing tone. "Take a break."

Gramps motioned with his finger, his light eyes twinkling. "Come here, young lady." He enveloped her in a bone-crushing hug and kissed the top of her head. "Go. I'll text you when we're going to eat."

"Thanks. She grabbed her phone from the office and sprinted across the street. The sign was on and she entered. There was no light coming from the kitchen, so Trinity headed into the shop.

"Look who's here, Agnes." A welcoming smile split Aunt C's face.

The tortie was already curling her body around Trinity's legs, purring. Trinity squatted and ran her hand over the cat's arched back. She missed her own kitties. "What did the vet say?"

"Well, he didn't find any suspicious lumps, which relieved me. He got her caught up on her shots and suggested we change her diet so I bought her a bag of special food."

Trinity rose to her feet. Aunt C's anxious expression tore at her heart. Impulsively, she walked over to the woman and gave her a big squeezing hug like the one Gramps had just given her. "Agnes will be okay."

Aunt C's arms went around her and Trinity breathed in lavender and vanilla.

"Thank you, sweetie. I needed that." She stepped back and brushed Trinity's cheek with the back of her fingertips.

"Anytime, Aunt C. Sometimes I need a hug when I'm feeling down."

Aunt C's warm brown eyes searched her face.

"What's the matter?" Trinity grinned. "Are my teeth green or something?"

The older woman smiled and a veil of secrecy dropped over her expression. "No," she replied in a soft voice. "You just reminded me of someone, that's all."

"Who?" Trinity leaned back against the glass counter. Sometimes Aunt C's elusive responses made her wonder what she was thinking.

The bell over the door rang announcing a customer. Cora swept into the hall. "Good morning. Welcome to Aunt Cora's Attic."

Agnes leapt up on the counter and curled up in her bed. Trinity scratched the cat under her chin. "I'm glad you're okay. I'm getting attached to you."

She was getting attached to Aunt C, Stu and Spencer as well. She'd gone online and checked out the local high school already. She hoped with all her heart Mom liked the house and the shop.

Spencer didn't exactly compare to San Francisco, but the mountains were cool. There was hiking, shops and history, all stuff Mom liked. Denver really wasn't that far away. This community was the best of both worlds.

Once Aunt C's customer departed, she startled Trinity with a warm, spontaneous hug. "Thank you for coming over here and cheering me up." She laughed and rolled her eyes. "Are you sick of lemon cookies yet? I volunteered to bake three dozen for the Friends of the Library tea tomorrow afternoon."

She grabbed Trinity's hand and tugged her toward the living area.

"Can you stay and help me? You're smart enough to follow my recipe if another customer comes in."

The kitchen was in its usual chaotic state that would drive Mom nuts. Trinity regarded the hodge-podge of catalogs stacked on the counters. How could she tactfully offer to clean up Aunt C's kitchen before Mom's pending arrival?

Aunt C bustled around clearing space for them to work. "I need to pass the legacy of my lemon cookies on to someone, and it might as well be you."

Trinity smiled and read the hand-written recipe on the creased index card. She opened the fridge and gathered the butter and other ingredients. There was going to be no better time to take the plunge and bring up the subject on her mind.

"I'm thinking we might want to start staging the house and the shop. I know the realtor gave us a list of personal items to pack away and other tasks we needed to do. "

"My realtor had plenty to say about staging." Aunt C put the sugar and flour canisters next to the butter. "She more or less came out and said that next to dropping a bomb on the place and starting from scratch, I should hire a professional house cleaner."

Her voice was no nonsense and matter of fact. Trinity took that as a good sign to continue. She came over to stand next to the older woman and measured out the flour. "I'd have to clear it with Gramps and Stu of course, but I could come over for a couple of hours during the afternoons and help do some staging for you. I mean, I'm sure my mom is going to want to buy the place, but just in case she doesn't, it would help with other buyers."

She looked up to find Aunt C's gaze focused on her, the woman's expression wistful and tender.

Aunt C gently brushed Trinity's hair and hugged her again. She released her and said nothing, but Trinity felt Aunt C's gesture was like when her mother wanted to tell her she loved her and didn't use any words.

"Sweetie, I'd love to have you help me. Talk to your grandpa and see what he says."

Cora sighed and gnawed on her lower lip. "I really hope your mom likes my shop. Is she really flying out here to look at it?"

Trinity nodded enthusiastically. "Yes, this Saturday. She sent me and Gramps her itinerary yesterday."

Aunt C shot her an encouraging smile. "Well, I think that's a good thing. We'll have to save a batch of these cookies for her."

Trinity grinned as she grated lemon peel. "Definitely. She rolled her eyes at Aunt C. "Mom will do this whole song and dance about how she's got to watch her sugar, but she's got a thing for cookies."

A half hour later, they slid the first fragrant sheet out of the oven and set it on the rack to cool. Trinity's phone pinged.

She checked the screen and sighed. "Gramps says its time to eat. I've gotta go."

Cora was gingerly munching on a freshly-baked cookie without the icing. Her eyes widened and she nodded. "No problem. I'll get them frosted and freeze a half dozen for your mom."

Trinity's heart swelled with fresh gratitude. She gave the older woman a quick peck on her soft cheek. "Thanks, Aunt C. Thank you so much."

A spontaneous idea occurred to her. She twisted her hands and slanted Aunt C a hopeful glance. "My nana died when I was little, so would you like to be my adopted nana?"

Aunt C stared. Her eyes welled with tears.

Trinity threw her arms around the woman and laid her

cheek against Aunt C's soft shoulder. She was reminded of Mom. Pressure built in her chest, and her eyes stung with tears of her own. "I'm sorry. I didn't mean to make you cry."

Cora's arms tightened. She patted Trinity's back. "Sweetie, I'm not crying because I'm sad. I'm not sad at all. I can't explain how I'm feeling. I'm surprised, but very happy."

Backing away, Trinity nodded. She understood. She didn't like to push people about their feelings. She hated when people pushed her.

"Okay. I'd better go." Out of the corner of her eye, she glimpsed the cookies on the cooling rack. The enticing tart fragrance of lemon filled her nostrils.

Cora laughed and wiped her face with her apron. "Go ahead. They should be cooled enough. Take three. I need the rest for the tea."

Trinity snatched three warm cookies, her heart singing with happiness. "Thanks, I will."

The kitchen timer sounded as she stepped outside.

ora slid the cookie sheet out of the oven. She smiled, remembering Trinity's hugs, and her heart warmed at the memory of the child asking her if she wanted to be her adopted Nana.

The gluey dough clung to the spoon and her fingers. Cora turned her focus to carefully spacing the sticky mounds filling the cookie sheet. She wiped her itchy cheek on her sleeve, thankful she'd had a break in customers long enough to slide the last batch of dough into the oven. Setting the timer, she transferred the cooled cookies to a plate to be frosted.

She washed her hands and sat at the cluttered table with a cool glass of water. Trinity had been called back to Jesse's house for lunch. Cora should probably eat something herself, but a nagging feeling of familiarity she couldn't explain overrode her hunger. She couldn't make sense of the crazy idea that kept popping into her head.

Agnes meowed and jumped into her lap. The tortie pushed her head beneath Cora's clenched fist, kneading Cora's lap with her paws.

The cat's needle-sharp claws penetrated Cora's apron.

Agnes was usually forbidden to be anywhere near Cora when she was preparing food, but today was an exception. Her tortie's purring and affectionate warmth eased her puzzlement.

Cora lifted the cat and nuzzled Agnes' furry triangular face. "Your friend, Miss Trinity, wants me to be her adopted granny. You can imagine how that went down." Smiling, she absently stroked beneath the feline's chin. "Every time I see that child, I have the strangest ideas."

Agnes squirmed out of her grasp and jumped to the floor. She strolled over to her bowl and sniffed at the new food.

Cora's heart lifted and she gave a lighthearted laugh. "You're hungry."

The timer went off. Brushing off her apron, Cora hurried over to the sink and washed her hands again in hot, soapy water. She glanced down at her feeding cat. "I don't cotton to cat hair in my cookies."

Another of her grandma's proverbs that seemed to pop out of Cora's mouth these days.

She switched off the oven and set the baking sheet on the cooling rack.

The bell over the front door signaled a customer. Cora sighed, untied her apron and draped it over the nearest chair.

❦

Murphy and Stuart sat in the kitchen, devouring hot, crispy chicken, and chasing it with ice-cold beer.

Trinity burst into the room and stopped on the threshold. She grimaced, wrinkled her nose and said. "Gross. Don't you remember when I got sick on fried chicken?"

Obviously he'd forgotten. Murphy put his fork down and rose to his feet. "I'm sorry, pookie."

"I'm the one who got lunch this time. I didn't know." Stuart looked concerned.

Trinity strode over to the table and dropped a cookie on each of their plates. Murphy caught a pleasant whiff of lemon.

"Where's the icing?" Stuart asked, but was already eating his.

Trinity pinched her nose and furiously fanned her hand in front of her face. "Aunt C's going to frost them. She's freezing a half dozen for Mom."

Murphy's mind drifted across the street. He still owed Cora an apology over the way he'd acted yesterday. Since then Trinity's idea of asking Cora out had taken root in his mind. Spending the afternoon with Cora in her cozy, but chaotic kitchen sounded much better than going back into that dusty oven of a garage to sort more junk.

Trinity tapped him on the shoulder. "Gramps."

"What?" Murphy looked up at the distorted nasal sound of her voice. She was still pinching her nose.

She stuck out her free hand, palm flat. "Can I please have some money so I can bike over to the Cold Slice for a sandwich? I can't eat here. The smell is making me want to hurl."

Murphy reached into his back pocket. "My wallet's upstairs in the bedroom."

"I've got it." Stuart held out a twenty dollar bill. "There. Keep the change."

Trinity took the twenty, her hazel eyes wide. "Seriously?"

"Better take him up on it." Murphy shot Stuart a teasing grin. "That'll teach you to pick the menu."

Trinity stepped behind Stuart's chair, wrapped her arms around the man's neck and planted a kiss on his cheek. "Thanks, Stu. You didn't know."

His granddaughter had just dished out to him a big slice of humble pie. That would teach him to keep making wisecracks.

She glanced back over her shoulder with a cheeky smile.

"I'm taking one of the bikes. Oh, and Gramps, I think you should go over and help Aunt C finish baking the cookies."

The back door slammed shut. Murphy swigged his beer. He shot Stuart a tolerant smile. "Give that girl an inch and she takes a mile. No wonder Shannan wanted me to bring her along."

Stuart gnawed on what was left of his drumstick. "Well, I for one am glad you did. Trinity's a bright spot in this whole dismal scene. She's a sweetheart and a breath of fresh air."

Murphy thought back to Sunday's excursion to Olde Town and their meal at Pearl's. They'd had a great time together. He hadn't laughed so hard since before Nan's death. He agreed with his friend. Trinity's vitality was contagious.

"Murphy."

"What did you say?"

Stuart pointed at his cookie. "I said. Are you going to eat that?"

Murphy stared down at the cookie lying on his plate. "I don't know. I haven't finished my lunch yet."

Stuart shrugged and gave him a cheerful smile. "Okay. Just thought I'd ask."

Murphy drank the rest of his beer. "Eat the cookie. I'm going across the street to help Cora finish baking."

He tossed his paper plate and chicken bones in the trash and washed his hands. "If we're lucky, I'll bring some back with me."

Hopefully, Cora would accept his apology and agree to go to dinner with him. They had their differences, she was a nerve-wracking distraction and threatened to blow his life off-course, but she filled the lonely, hollow place in his soul vacated by Nan's death.

Murphy recalled the vulnerable set of Cora's pink-tinted lips, her enormous brown eyes. He sensed she owned a similar yearning that echoed his, and he didn't want to waste this second, God-given opportunity. Hadn't this been what he'd been wanting since he'd fallen in love with her years ago? The realization simultaneously excited and terrified him.

❧

Murphy crossed the street, hands fisted deep in his pockets. He wouldn't give Cora time to object. No, he'd make it a casual invitation. It wouldn't do to come right out and ask. Cora didn't like surprises, at least if he remembered correctly.

The sign reminded him that her shop was open. There might be customers. He didn't see any cars, but that didn't mean anything. He hoped they could have a few minutes alone in the kitchen without interruption.

The foyer was redolent with the sweet buttery fragrance of baking cookies. Cora came bustling out of the sliding door to his left. She was occupied with untying her apron.

Tendrils of hair framed her flushed face. "I'll be right with you." Her voice was light and breathless. She wore another baggy top over a long skirt, but in Murphy's mind, she was the same quiet girl with beautiful, soul-filled brown eyes.

"Murphy."

He flexed his fingers in his pockets. "Trinity suggested I come over and help you finish baking."

Wait for her response. You don't need to command every situation, he counseled himself.

Her narrowed gaze widened, then relaxed. The corners of her mouth lifted and she turned, beckoning him to follow.

"Smells good," he said.

Cora graced him with her brilliant smile and his heart expanded.

Her smile immediately lapsed into a frown. "Oh crap, I left my apron in the hall. I'll be right back."

Murphy wandered around the kitchen, soaking in the

room's cluttered details. The yellow walls reflected the lemony fragrance.

Lord, there was Grandma Binney's lazy susan, with the same cob of corn butter dish, salt and pepper shakers.

The maple table and chairs, the old stove and that behemoth of a refrigerator still stood in the same places.

"I've made a batch of icing." Cora came rushing into the room, tying the apron around her, giving shape to her figure previously hidden beneath the baggy clothing. She'd always been tall and willowy, like a graceful Aspen.

He opened his mouth to say something and told himself to keep it shut and wait.

She gazed at him, her warm, chocolate gaze assessing. "I don't want you to get your clothes dirty."

Before Murphy could protest, she'd plucked an apron out of one of the drawers and stepped behind him, tying it securely around his waist. "There, that shouldn't emasculate you too much."

Her musical laugh reminded him of one of Mozart's merry concertos. The back of his neck felt hot.

"Very funny," he muttered. He turned around and lightly chucked her under her chin, as he occasionally did to Shannan. Only this didn't feel the same. His intention was more than affectionate. He wouldn't be surprised if she reached over and slapped the crap out of him.

She didn't. Her features softened. Her stiff posture relaxed. She lifted her hands and clasped them over her heart.

The two of them stood frozen like that for he didn't know how long. It was the bell over the door that broke their silent connection.

"I have a customer." Cora waved toward the shop. "The icing is on the counter. Find a knife and you can frost the cookies on the table."

As she disappeared into the hallway, Murphy gazed after

Cora, his heart still pounding, his hopes rising. He'd been surprised at her friendly reception and stunned at her response to his playful touch.

He opened drawers looking for a spatula or something he could use to frost the cookies. The drawer by the stove contained an assortment of serving and cooking utensils. Murphy pawed through them until he located what he needed.

He turned and scanned the cluttered counter. Counters of chaos, he nicknamed them in his mind. Grinning to himself, he located the mixing bowl of frosting still in place beneath a large stationary mixer, similar to the one Shannan kept in her kitchen for baking Christmas cookies.

Casting a quick glance over at the door, Murphy scooped up a generous dollop of frosting on his index finger and stuck it in his mouth. He closed his eyes savoring the sweet and tart lemony taste.

Humming slightly under his breath, he dipped the spreader in the frosting and carefully frosted his first cookie.

By the time Cora returned, Murphy had iced an even dozen. He glanced over at her with a self-satisfied smile.

She crossed her arms and smiled back. "You look like Agnes after she trots in with a dead mouse in her mouth."

Murphy pulled a face. "Like my granddaughter would say, 'Eww.'"

They both laughed.

Sudden unexplainable anxiety filled his chest as Cora came over and examined his handiwork.

She nodded and tied her apron back on.

Murphy stole an appreciative glance. She still had curves underneath all those clothes. His long-dormant physical reaction pleasantly startled him.

Cora wasn't stupid. Her gaze met his, and she blushed.

"You did a nice job. I like the way you leave a swirl in the frosting. I didn't know you possessed an artistic streak."

His face warmed. Picking up another cookie, he studiously applied his new technique. "There's a lot you don't know about me."

"I know for a fact you've been eating the icing."

He licked his lips and grinned. "It's good stuff."

Cora transferred another batch over to the frosting area. "Since you're doing such a bang-up job, I'm going to let you finish frosting while I clean up."

Now would be a good time to take the plunge and ask her. Murphy sucked in a breath. "What are you doing tomorrow night?"

Cora set the canister she was holding on the counter. She turned and stared at him. "Why?"

He shrugged, frosting his thumb more than the cookie. "I'd like to take you out for dinner. I acted like a jerk yesterday. You've been so helpful with Trinity. I know you were there for Jesse and Stuart—-"

"Is that why you really want to take me out?" Her voice was soft.

Murphy gave her a guilty smile. "Nope. I was afraid. What I was really going to say, until I opened my mouth and all the stupid words tumbled out was, I'd like to take you out for dinner so we could talk and get to know each other again."

Cora nodded, and her expression became distant. She toyed absently with the silver chain around her neck.

Remembering Davey's ring, he tensed his jaw. He shouldn't have asked. He shouldn't have hoped.

"Murphy," she trained her focus back on him again. "This isn't because Trinity—-"

"Partly," he admitted, but hastened to add, "but it's mostly because I've wanted to for most of my life."

Cora stared down at the floor for a long minute. Finally she looked deep into his face, her eyes searching his.

He wanted to rush her. Yes or no. Just get it out and get

the suspense over with. Instead he waited. His heart thumped against his ribs. This was agony.

She raised a hand to her hair and looked at him doubtfully. "Are you sure? It's just dinner and getting to know each other to us, but Trinity is going to jump to conclusions, along with half the town."

His patience worn paper-thin, Murphy blew out the breath he'd been holding. "I don't care. I wouldn't be asking you if I wasn't sure. Are you sure?"

There. The ball was in her court. He couldn't stand the suspense any longer. He snatched up a cookie and the spreader, but instead of frosting the cookie, he dipped the spreader in the icing and stuck it in his mouth. He glared at her as though daring her to do something about it.

She laughed until she snorted. Covering her mouth, she laughed harder. "You look like the rascally boy Grandma Binney caught eating her freshly-made plate of fudge."

Her mirth was contagious. Another memory flooded his mind. "That wasn't half as bad as the time I caught the garter snake and accidentally let it loose here in the kitchen. I can still see Grandma standing on the chair with her hands on her hips, threatening both of us with certain death and a ferocious paddling if we didn't find that reptile and take it back outside where it belonged."

Murphy laughed until his sides ached. "Oh, it's hilarious now, but it wasn't funny at the time."

He piled up the dirty dishes and walked over to the sink where Cora stood. "I was worried about getting you in trouble because I knew Grandma Binney would paddle you, and I was terrified because if Grandma told my dad like she'd threatened, I'd get my butt paddled too."

Cora ran water and added dish soap. Her head was bent, exposing the vulnerable nape of her neck.

Murphy experienced a sudden longing to press his lips there, to wrap his arms around Cora and convince her that they both deserved to find happiness. They had the rest of their lives to explore these long-buried feelings.

She shook her head and sighed. Turning to face him, she surveyed him with desolate eyes. "Murphy, I…."

His stomach sank. It wasn't like this was a new sensation. He'd experienced disappointment before, many times. At least he'd had the guts to ask her in the first place.

Murphy managed a crooked smile of resignation. "Hey, I thought it was worth a shot. It would really be a simple meal between old friends, Cora. I wasn't planning to ply you with alcohol and seduce you."

He checked his watch. "I'll finish the rest of these cookies and then I'd better go. Trinity should be back at the house—-"

Cora moved to wrap her arms tightly around him and tipped her face up to his. "Are you going to give me a chance to get a word in edgewise?"

Murphy closed his eyes, luxuriating in her fragrance and the sensation of her warm body comfortably pressed against his.

God, he'd been lonely. He'd been missing this. Trinity hugged him, Shannan did too, but this was a deeper connection. He'd needed a woman's touch—-no scratch that—-Cora's touch for a long, long time.

She stirred, her warm breath gusting against his ear. "Murphy, I'm scared. If I tell you something, will you promise not to hold it over my head for the rest of my life?"

Cora leaned back, her gaze probing his, her tone dead serious.

He nodded, careful to stay still. He wanted her to keep holding him as he was holding her. He wanted to offer up himself to her as a shield, a haven of mutual trust and reassurance. "I promise."

She took a deep breath. "I'm so scared."

What had her so upset? The uncertainty in her eyes troubled him. Murphy inched his hand up and tenderly stroked her cheek with his thumb. "Why are you scared, Cora Rose?

Cora's eyes drifted closed. She relaxed against him, resting her head on his shoulder.

He rubbed her back lightly, tracing her vertebrae. As long as he'd known her, Cora Rose had always projected a brave front, yet she was as vulnerable as any of them. He studied the delicate shell of her ear, the silvery strands of her braided hair crowning her head.

He pressed his lips to her temple.

She sighed and tightened her hold. "I worry about the future. I have a plan, I've taken steps to implement my plan, but there are parts of my plan that I have no control over. Does that make any sense to you?"

Cora stared up at him, her dark eyes wide, reflecting his own misgivings.

Murphy nodded, his gaze drifting down to her pale lips. He resisted the fierce urge to kiss her, concentrating instead on the small space between her furrowed brows. She needed him to listen.

Cora flung her arm out, indicating the room. "This kitchen! The house! The realtor told me I need to de-clutter. I'm normally a decisive person and frankly when I look at the chore, I don't know where to begin.

"I really don't want to hire a stranger to come into my house and tell me what I should or shouldn't do. Trinity offered to help me, but I know she's busy assisting you and Stuart."

Releasing him, she stepped back and shook her head. "I haven't changed much. I still babble away like an idiot, but I think dinner with you would be nice." She stared down at the floor and bunched the skirt of her apron in her hands. "Scary, but nice."

Murphy ached to regain their fragile connection. He forced a weak smile and plunged his hands in his pockets.

"Scary? Why scary? I've thought of myself in a lot of ways before, but scary has never been one of them."

"Not you. Never you, Murphy." She laughed, but her eyes were deep pools of uncertainty. Her expression grew distant. "I haven't been out to dinner with a man, since David."

Murphy couldn't help himself. He softly snorted and stared down at his shoes. Davey again. Always Davey.

She moved in close and gripped his shoulders. "Murphy, I know it's time to move on and I'm terrified that it's too late and I'm too old."

His heart beat faster. Hope rose in his chest. "It's not too late, Cora Rose. It's not too late for either one of us."

He cradled her face between his hands, and this time, lowering his mouth to hers, he kissed her.

Her mouth was petal-soft, and so warm. He wanted to keep kissing her, but he raised his head.

"You look like I'm going to slap you," she teased, but her cheeks were flushed and her lips were parted.

He rubbed his jaw with a relieved grin.

Cora cast a shy glance up at him. "That was a nice kiss, Murphy. Would you kiss me again?"

"With pleasure." Dipping his head, he claimed her lips with his. Cora moved closer, reestablishing their pleasurable contact, but the mounting pressure of her mouth on his whipped his comfort level to an urgent sensation Murphy hadn't felt in a long, long time.

Desire. Intimacy.

The bell over the entrance rang and they sprang apart.

The tingling pressure of Cora's mouth lingered. Murphy didn't dare look down.

Her fingertips covered her mouth, but her brown eyes mirrored exactly how he felt. "Excuse me," she whispered, and was gone.

Murphy exhaled and smiled in amazement. He whistled

as he finished frosting the rest of the cookies. Sounded like a gaggle of geese out there in the shop. She'd be a while.

After washing the few dirty dishes, Murphy located a stubby pencil. Tearing off a sheet from a nearby tablet, he scrawled, 'Pick you up at 7.'

CHAPTER TEN

*T*he next morning Cora stared into the mirror over her dresser. Her eyes widened in horror. She was going out to dinner with Murphy tonight and, like her cluttered kitchen, she didn't know where to start.

She combed her fingers through her hair and lifted it off her neck. She definitely needed to wear it up, but not in her habitual braided coronet. Oh dear, that was exactly the way Grandma Binney had worn her hair.

Leaning forward, she scowled, examining the fine lines around her eyes. She hadn't paid much attention to her looks in years.

Opening her robe, she gazed down at her nude figure. She was a little thicker around the middle, but she still had a waist. Her boobs had always been on the small side, which turned out to be an advantage. Most women her age complained of their sagging breasts.

It was her hair and her face that she needed to work on before tonight.

Remembering yesterday afternoon, Cora touched her lips with her fingers and smiled. Murphy was a good kisser.

Second to David?

Frowning, she pulled her brush down the length of her locks, separating them to braid. It wasn't fair to compare the two. By today's standards, David had barely been beyond the brink of manhood. She'd been older, but not much more than a girl herself.

What she'd felt for Murphy yesterday was calmer than her heady, youthful passion for David. Maybe she was lonely, but Cora sensed a deep connection with Murphy.

She'd perceived his silent devotion the minute she'd laid eyes on him standing in her hall bearing the cookie tin.

Yesterday afternoon she'd read the caring expression in his gray eyes, his genuine distress at her worries. She'd appreciated how he'd tenderly kissed her temple and listened without comment.

Cora's deeper connection with Murphy was her love for his precious granddaughter.

She sighed and her stomach knotted with apprehension about tonight's engagement. She would call Clips and Curls as soon as the salon opened and see if Claudia could squeeze her in this afternoon. Cora liked the idea of having her hair done similar to the way she'd worn it at last fall's Halloween gala, or at least a style that would be both flattering and more youthful.

Maybe Trinity would go with her. After all, the girl had offered to help stage her house. Staging a woman for her first date in decades could prove to be equally as challenging. This really wasn't a date, Cora reminded herself, but it certainly felt like one. She had work to do. Regardless of tonight's occasion, her Grandma Binney days were over.

❦

To Cora's relief, Trinity had accepted her request with gleeful excitement. Gramps had already told her and Stu about their dinner plans tonight. She'd love to go to the salon with her and she'd be over after lunch.

The bell over the door rang promptly at one o'clock. Naturally, Cora was helping a last-minute customer who seemed to have all afternoon to do nothing other than examine every fricking china figurine in the shop.

Trinity burst into the room, her kohl-lined eyes wide with anticipation. Spying the customer, she slowed her pace and approached Agnes, curled contentedly in her bed. She stroked the feline, while darting furtive glances at the browsing customer.

Apparently, Agnes was not in the mood to endure Trinity's feverish attention. The cat hissed, leaped down from the counter, and slowly walked toward the living quarters.

Trinity gripped Cora's arm. "I'm so wired," she whispered.

Cora gently extricated her arm from the girl's hold and squeezed her hand. "So am I."

They walked over to the window. "We need to leave. What time is your appointment?"

"We have a half hour. The shop isn't that far, but I've got a bad case of the nerves. Claudia is on vacation so Robyn will be doing my hair."

Trinity giggled softly. "Gramps is a wreck. Stu and I worked all morning while Gramps went shopping. We met him for lunch at Itza Burger and he hardly ate anything." She clutched Cora's arm. "Trust me. That's not Gramps. He even gave me the rest of his chocolate shake."

"Excuse me. I'd like to pay for these. Do you have a box I can put them in?" The customer regarded them with a reproving expression.

Cora hastened over to the glass counter. "Certainly."

She eyed her stack of boxes on the floor. Tearing off several sheets of tissue paper, she carefully wrapped each Victorian lady, nestling them against each other in the sturdy container.

"I'm so glad I came in. I collect these, and they're the six that I don't have."

Cora's earlier irritation evaporated. "There's a story behind this set. I picked them up at an estate sale. The sister of the deceased had discovered them packed away in a hat box."

She processed the credit card transaction and ushered the woman to the door with a warm smile. This was the part of the business she would miss. The shared delight when a customer discovered a treasure that reminded him or her of their childhood, or a customer found a desired object they'd been searching for.

"Aunt C." Trinity was at her elbow, flashing her phone in Cora's face to show her the time.

Cora's case of the nerves came rushing back. "I know. I know. Let's pray I can find my keys."

❦

Her ancient, but serviceable Subaru transported them to Valley View Mall in minutes. She parked in a slot directly in front of the salon. Trinity was out of the car before she had a chance to shut off the engine.

She was getting her hair trimmed, styled and nothing more, Cora told herself. She'd known Claudia for years and trusted the owner's judgment. Robyn wouldn't be working at the salon, let alone taking Claudia's customers unless she was qualified. The thought did nothing to slow Cora's racing pulse. She couldn't shake the premonition that Trinity was going to talk her into something more.

Cora inhaled a calming breath and entered the colorfully-decorated salon. Trinity had already engaged the stylist in conversation and Cora's sense of foreboding blossomed.

The tall, auburn-haired woman looked up from Trinity's phone. She walked toward her, hand extended, beaming a welcoming smile. "Cora. Hi. My name is Robyn. It's nice to meet you."

The stylist's warm brown eyes were sincere behind the black lenses of her glasses. Cora responded with a smile of her own and briefly clasped the woman's smooth hand. "It's nice to meet you too."

She arched a brow at Trinity. "What were you showing Robyn?"

Trinity laughed. "Don't look so worried, Aunt C. I told her you were considering a new look, and we were checking out a couple of trendy styles."

"I was thinking of putting my hair up like Claudia styled it for the Halloween Ball at the Lodge. She did a beautiful job. I received more compliments." Cora tentatively smoothed the braids pinned on top of her head and sighed. "I should've brought a picture. Claudia would know exactly what I'm talking about."

Cora folded her arms across her chest and fixed Robyn with a resolute expression. "I know I need a trim." She narrowed her gaze at Trinity. "And a trendy style with my hair up."

Robyn pursed her coral-tinted lips. Her glance flitted to Trinity. "What about the lowlights?"

Cora gaped at Murphy's precocious granddaughter. "Lowlights?"

Unfazed, Trinity responded matter-of-factly. "Lowlights blend seamlessly with your natural hair color."

Cora frowned. "I didn't come in for lowlights."

Trinity enveloped her in a sweet-smelling hug.

"Let me show you what I'm thinking. My mom tried lowlights last year and she loves them." Trinity cast Cora a sly look. "She swears they make her look and feel...." She paused. "Twenty years younger."

"Excuse me, I've got to answer the phone." The stylist gave Cora a reassuring smile that included Trinity. "I've got

some ideas that you might be interested in, but in the meantime, why don't you take a look at the pictures on Trinity's
phone and see what you think?"

"You're not the guinea pig," Cora muttered, wandering
over to the coffeemaker. Sipping her freshly-made brew, she
looked on as Trinity scrolled through selected photos.

"These are the styles I thought would be really cool on
you—-and really flattering." Her hazel eyes reflected an
energy and enthusiasm that lifted Cora's heart as well as her
hopes.

Cora sighed and settled down in the chair. She sipped her
coffee and closed her eyes. "Okay, Robyn, show me your
pictures." She pinned a fierce look at Robyn and Trinity's
reflections in the mirror. "But I refuse to be coerced if I don't
want to do it."

"Of course," said Robyn, her sincere tone reassuring. The
stylist unbraided and gently combed her fingers through
Cora's hair.

Trinity nodded and showed Cora a photo. "No worries,
Aunt C. This cut would look awesome on you and would
knock Gramps' socks off."

❦

Murphy stuck the biodegradable carton containing his left-
overs in the refrigerator. He grabbed a soda for Stuart and
one for himself to settle his edgy stomach. Stuart had found
some boxes of kids' junk in the basement that he wanted
Murphy to look through. Murphy had immediately thought
of his slingshot and couldn't wait. Working for a couple of
hours would hopefully absorb his attention and burn off his
nervousness until it was time to shower and shave.

Clutching a can in each hand, he cautiously descended
the steep stairs into the 'bowels of the house,' as Jesse had
referred to their basement when they were kids.

Murphy handed a soda to Stuart. "Jesse and I used to play down here." He popped open his can and took a long, cold swallow. The sweet, sparkling liquid felt good going down. "I'd get engrossed in building my block city, and Jesse would creep over to the main bulb hanging over the play area and pull the chain, leaving us in the dark.

"Scared the crap out of me." Murphy shook his head, smiling at the memory. "I'd scream bloody murder, bringing Mom rushing down the stairs. That was always followed by a dressing-down for Jesse. 'You're the oldest. You should know better.'"

Stuart gave a rueful laugh. "Growing up, I heard that old chestnut often enough." The tall, lanky man leaned back against the anchored shelving unit. "How old were the two of you?"

"I was about five," Murphy said, taking another swallow. "Jesse would have been nine or ten. He was quiet, even then, but he loved to push my buttons."

"Really?" Stuart shot him a humorous look. "He said the same thing about you."

Murphy grinned broadly. His stomach was feeling better. "Let's put it this way, I probably pushed his buttons ten times more often than Jesse pushed mine."

He and Stuart barked with hearty laughter and tapped their soda cans together.

"Anyway, to finish the story, Mom draped her arm over my shoulders, and led me upstairs for cookies and milk to calm down. Jesse wised up after he'd gotten busted a couple of times." Murphy set his soda aside on a shelf and pointed. "Are these the boxes you're talking about?"

Murphy grunted as he hefted one of the boxes Stuart had indicated and trudged up to the kitchen. He set the dusty carton on the table and lifted the flaps. Carefully wrapped in plastic bags, salvaged from the dry cleaners, he discovered their old Lionel train set. "Cool."

Grinning, Murphy dug through the tracks and located the old transformer. Hopefully the rest was in Stuart's box.

Stuart appeared, lugging the other carton, and set it behind Murphy on the counter. "This is all of it, I think."

They connected the passenger car, the coal car, the grain car and the red caboose to the black locomotive. Murphy grinned at Stuart. "What do you think? Should we call it a day and play trains?" He shrugged. "I have about three hours before I need to shower, shave and get ready."

Stuart laughed, a boyish glint in his eye. "Are you kidding? I used to belong to a model railroad club. However, as long as this train has been packed away, we should plug in the transformer and see if it even works before we go to the trouble of setting up the track."

Murphy nodded. Another interesting facet to Stuart's personality he appreciated. "Let's do it."

He set the square black box on the counter and plugged the cord into the outlet. Nothing. Not so much as a click. Murphy sighed. "Well, as Trinity would say, 'that sucks.'"

Stuart took the device from Murphy and wrapped the cord. "I've worked on a couple of transformers. Once I get a little time, I'll check this one out and see if it's fixable."

"Thanks." Murphy detached the train cars and placed them back in the carton. "Did Jesse share your interest in model railroads?"

Stuart slid the box containing the tracks off the table and set it on the floor. "Not really. Jess was more of a spectator. He liked to watch the trains run through towns and tunnels." His expression thoughtful, Stuart rinsed out the dishrag at the sink and wiped down the tabletop. "He loved riding trains. We'd frequently ride the Georgetown Loop Railroad and we once took the Rocky Mountaineer train from British Columbia to Alberta. The scenery was magnificent."

Murphy stacked his box on top of the one already on the floor and brushed off his dusty hands. He glanced at his watch, then at Stuart cleaning the counter. "Let's grab a couple more sodas and sit outside. I'd love to hear more Jesse stories if you're up for it."

Stuart's solemn face brightened with a smile. "I'd like that."

❧

Murphy checked his reflection in the mirror one last time. His hair had looked scraggly around the edges, so he'd zipped over to the barber shop for a last-minute trim. The guy had done a nice job.

His pulse picked up a pleasant tempo. He slipped his keys and wallet into his pocket. Palming his phone, he scampered down the stairs, whistling *Wichita Lineman*.

Both Trinity and Stuart were poised at either side of the door. Stuart flashed him a broad grin.

Trinity's hazel eyes critically scanned him up and down.

Murphy flung his arms out at his sides. "What?"

Frowning, his granddaughter walked up to him, reached up, and undid the top button of his shirt. She tugged his collar out of his sweater and fanned it out. Stepping back, she narrowed her gaze.

"What? Will you say something? The suspense is killing me."

"I like the jeans. And you bought the right color."

Murphy rubbed his hot neck. "I called Stuart."

"The sweater's a nice touch. It gives you a preppy look." Trinity bunched up the garment around his waist.

He promptly pulled it down again. "That feels weird."

Trinity sighed and rolled her eyes. "Well, now it looks weird, but okay."

Murphy turned to Stuart. "What do you think?"

He crossed his arms, eyes wide. "I'm staying out of it."

"Yeah, right. I see whose side you're on." Murphy blew into the palm of his hand.

"Your breath is fine, Gramps." Trinity's eyes danced with amusement and her gaze dropped. "What's with the boots?"

Murphy studied the pointed toes of his newly-purchased footwear. "What's wrong with them?"

His granddaughter's eyes grew large and she giggled. "Nothing." She covered her mouth, her slender ringed fingers newly tipped with red.

He raised his brows, and she read the question in his expression. "Aunt C and I got manicures."

"Are you teasing me?" Murphy extended one booted foot. "I tried them on at the western store, and they were a perfect fit." He folded his arms and drawled in his best John Wayne imitation. "This is about as close to a cowboy as I'm gonna get."

She stared at him for a long minute and then burst into an endearing trill of astonished laughter. "Gramps, I was surprised you bought the boots. They look fine with the jeans, but who were you trying to imitate?"

He chuckled and ruffled her silky curls. "Never mind."

"You mean you haven't introduced Trinity to 'The Duke?'" Stuart asked in mock horror. Walking over, he clapped Murphy on the shoulder. "You clean up good, Murph. Go have fun, but be back by ten."

He and Trinity looked at each other and burst into more peals of mirth. "Don't worry about Trinity. We decided to eat at Pearl's tonight. Wait." Stuart's eyes grew enormous and he winked at Trinity. "Tell me you're not taking Cora to Pearl's for dinner."

"Bite me, Stuart," Murphy said with a tight smile. His stomach was knotting up.

He paused outside on the porch and stared across the street.

Murphy gripped the rail and bowed his head. His heart pounded against his ribcage. Was Cora as nervous as he was?

❦

Cora stood in the foyer, wringing her freshly-manicured hands. Agnes curled her body around Cora's bare legs, as though fascinated with her mistress' exposed flesh.

Trinity had talked her into a dress and out of wearing panty hose. Apparently nylons, as Cora still referred to them, were as outdated as she was. The breeze on her legs was a novel, but unsettling sensation. Usually, if she wasn't in a long skirt, she was in a full-length nightgown.

Cora raised her hand to her throat. The second reason she felt naked was because she'd taken off David's ring and left it lying on top of her dresser. It had been a last-minute decision, edged with guilt and regret, yet it needed to be done, at least for tonight. With the scoop neckline of this dress, the ring would have been too obvious, and Murphy would have noticed.

She had high hopes for tonight. She pictured a quiet, romantic dinner with Murphy, the two of them holding hands and getting to know each other all over again….

The doorbell buzzed.

Cora inhaled a deep breath, grasped the knob and opened the door. Her breath stalled in her chest, and her heart threatened to burst. Murphy looked hot, as Trinity would say.

He offered her a shy smile. "Hi."

"Hi yourself," she said. To break the awkwardness of the moment, she took a daring leap of faith and planted a quick kiss on his smoothly-shaved cheek.

Murphy wrapped his arms around her and pressed his lips softly to hers. Not only did he look good, he felt good. He smelled like lime and spice.

He released her too soon, but the look in his eyes promised more kisses to come. "You smell like flowers and you taste like mint."

Murphy lightly fingered her shortened tresses and grinned. "I like your hair."

"Trinity and Robyn's idea, not mine." Breathless, Cora shrugged. "In the end, I decided I was changing my life everywhere else, I might as well change my hair."

Murphy cupped the back of her head and kissed her again. His warm mouth lingered against hers. She hadn't felt passion like this since…. Cora was kissing Murphy, not David. She pressed closer and parted her lips.

Murphy broke contact. He tipped her chin until she met his questioning gaze. He started to speak, stopped and looked away.

Cora sensed his hesitancy. "Say it." She turned his face back to hers. "Ask me." Her voice held a desperate edge. "Ask me, dammit," she whispered.

His miserable expression hardened. He inhaled, his nostrils flaring. "Are you kissing me or are you kissing Davey?"

She smiled and caressed his smooth cheek. "I'm kissing you, Murphy Webster. I'm kissing you."

CHAPTER ELEVEN

*M*urphy's phone chimed, a reminder that their dinner reservations were in fifteen minutes. They reluctantly stepped apart and Murphy helped Cora into her sweater before escorting her to the Prius.

"I hope you don't mind eating at the Golden Grille." Murphy reached over and squeezed her hand. "I know the chef at the lodge is world-famous, and it's not that I can't afford it, but tonight I don't want to think about the Spencers or the past." His callused fingers grazed her cheek. "How about tonight we live in the present? I want to hear about your plans, your dreams." He chuckled and shook his head. "Boy, do I sound corny."

Cora swatted his arm. This sweet side of Murphy was a side of him she'd rarely glimpsed. She wanted to get to know this side of him. "I love corny. I'm considered eccentric, you know."

He laughed. "You sure as hell don't look eccentric right now. I'd bet the locals will fall out of their chairs when we walk in. Either that or they won't even recognize you."

Murphy's gaze dropped. "I'd forgotten what beautiful long legs you have."

His sexy tenor thrilled her. Her face warmed, and she looked out the window. She'd forgotten the pleasure of being desired. This evening promised to exceed her expectations.

❧

Murphy slowly backed into a parking space in the restaurant's lot.

"I like the Golden Grille." A brilliant smile lit Cora's face and her voice was warm with pleasure.

Murphy leaned over and kissed her cheek. He couldn't get enough of touching her. "I'm glad."

He laughed as he opened his door. "Trinity and Stuart asked me if I was taking you to Pearl's. They teased me mercilessly and enjoyed every minute of it."

Cora extended her hand and her shiny nails caught the early evening sunlight.

Murphy helped her out of the car. "Trinity said the two of you had manicures. What color is that?"

She regarded her splayed fingers. "*Hazy Mauve*. I don't know why I bought a bottle. I'll probably never wear it again."

Her brown eyes smiled into his. "I wanted clear, but Trinity insisted this was the perfect match for my dress."

Murphy laced his fingers with hers and grinned. "She can be pushy, a lot like—-"

"Her grandfather," they said in unison, laughing.

Inside, the restaurant was dimly-lit with candles at every table. Soft music played in the background and the atmosphere was redolent with the rich beefy smell of spices.

Murphy rested his hand at the small of Cora's back as they were shown to their booth.

"Will this do?" the maitre'd asked.

Murphy nodded and slipped the man a bill. He'd specifically asked for a secluded spot, where they could dine in privacy. "Thank you."

The maitre'd smiled and handed each of them menus. "Your server will be right with you. Enjoy your meal."

A young man, impeccably attired in black slacks and a white long-sleeved dress shirt, immediately appeared with a full tray. He set two tall glasses of water on the table, followed by two large wine goblets. "Shall I open the bottle, sir?"

Murphy nodded again and glanced at Cora.

"Wow," she mouthed, her expression awestruck. His heart swelled with masculine pride at Cora's pleasure. He wanted everything to be perfect.

The server poured a small amount into Murphy's goblet. The vintage was perfectly balanced with a hint of chocolate. He nodded his approval.

Raising his glass, Murphy touched it to Cora's. "To tonight and to new adventures."

Cora smiled. "To tonight and to new adventures."

She swirled the ruby-red liquid, inhaled and took a sip. "Oh my, this is good."

He had a case of it already stowed aboard the *Stargazer*. "It's my favorite. I'm glad you like it. It's bottled at a little known winery in the Alexander Valley."

"Aunt Cora?"

Murphy looked up to see a striking young redhead standing at their booth.

"Mandy. Oh my goodness." Cora scrambled out of the booth. Laughing, she embraced the expectant woman.

"I'm sorry about the other night at the schoolhouse. I was so preoccupied with getting the photos for the paper, I didn't take time to talk to you and Jesse." Mandy's smile faltered. "I was shocked to hear about Jesse's death." She turned her kind smile on Murphy. "You must be his brother. I'm sorry for your loss."

Cora looked at him sympathetically and squeezed his arm. "Murphy, I'd like to introduce you to Miranda Elliot. Miranda Spencer Buffet Elliot, Jakob's granddaughter."

Murphy stood and briefly shook Miranda's slender hand. He smiled and courteously said. "Would you like to join us?"

The young woman's smile widened. "That's kind of you to offer, but I wouldn't think of intruding."

She turned to Cora. "I almost didn't recognize you. I love your hair and that dress is beautiful. Before I forget, I talked to your realtor yesterday, and she said she's had some out-of-state inquiries regarding the shop. She wants to put your listing up on Zillow, but...."

Cora frowned and shrugged. "I know. I need to clean and de-clutter the rooms before I can stage them."

Miranda laughed. "It can be an overwhelming task, but I know some great people who de-clutter for a living, and you'd be putting those people to work."

"There you are." A tall athletic man strode up to Miranda and possessively slipped his arm around her shoulders.

"Declan, look who I ran into. It's Cora and Jesse Webster's brother, Murphy."

The man's eyes widened in surprise and appreciation. "Wow." He kissed Cora's cheek. "You look great."

He extended his hand to Murphy. "Declan Elliot. Nice to meet you."

The young man's handshake was brief and firm. He looked at his wife with a tender expression. "We're expecting."

"Congratulations," said Murphy. His plan of a quiet dinner for two was unraveling.

Cora rested a hand on the younger man's sleeve. "I'm so happy and excited for both of you. Mandy had told me the two of you were expecting, but that was months ago." She shrugged. "Time has a way of slipping away from me. The shop keeps me so busy, I rarely get out."

She reached over and clasped Murphy's hand with hers. A warm feeling of connection blossomed in his chest. "Murphy and I are enjoying a nice quiet meal and catching up with each other."

Miranda sighed. "I know what you mean. The *Herald* keeps me so busy, I don't know whether I'm coming or going. I get there in the morning and before I know it, it's five o'clock and time to go home. Speaking of which, we've bought a beautiful old Victorian not far from you. Declan and I are renovating it before we move in."

Murphy nodded and listened politely. Cora's soft, warm grip contained his restlessness.

"Before we leave the two of you alone to catch up, I want to remind you both that next week is the annual Fourth of July celebration, and nobody does Independence Day like Spencer."

Murphy remembered. As kids, they'd loved the festivities, especially the culminating fireworks ceremony.

"Grandpa has contributed some special fireworks this year, and he and Willa are grand marshals in the parade."

Murphy saw a shadow flit across Cora's face. She was thinking about Davey. He could see it. He could almost read her mind. This young woman's grandfather was Davey's older brother, and the fireworks were traditionally shot over Lake Louise. No, they definitely would be skipping the fireworks if he had anything to say about it.

Cora squeezed his hand as though she'd read his thoughts. "I'm not a big fan of the fireworks, but I love the parade and I'm looking forward to the VFW band's annual concert in the park."

She smiled at Murphy. "If I remember correctly, you're a fan of John Phillips Sousa."

Murphy nodded. He'd always enjoyed the concerts at Brook Park. "I am."

Declan tenderly gripped his wife's shoulders. "Mandy,

sweetheart. Our meal has been served." She looked up at him with a beatific expression. "I know. I know." She held out her hand. "Murphy, nice to meet you. I saw the notice you posted in the *Herald*. Again, I'm sorry for your loss." Her gaze took in Cora. "For both of your losses."

Cora embraced Miranda. "I can't wait to see the baby."

"You'll be one of the first people I call." Declan gave her a big hug and released her. "Oh, and don't forget the car show over at the fairgrounds. Murphy, if you like cars, it's one of the best in Colorado."

Declan grinned indulgently. "C'mon Mandy, love. It's time to eat."

The young couple left to enjoy their meal.

After they slipped back into the booth, Murphy reached for Cora's hand, eager to recapture the intimacy between them. "Miranda is Jakob's granddaughter?"

Cora nodded, raised her goblet to her lips with her free hand and took a swallow. "Miranda is Dierdre's daughter."

She made a face and rolled her eyes. "The last thing I want to do is discuss Jakob Spencer's family tree."

She sobered and crushed his fingers with hers. "Murphy, I don't want to talk about the Spencers." Her voice took on a low desperate edge. "Any of them."

Cora's expression was sincere. She meant what she said, but Davey, as Murphy had called him from the first day they'd become friends at school, remained an unseen presence between them.

"Murphy."

Her tone was low, but sharp. Her nails penetrated his sweater and dug into his arm. "Dammit, Murphy. Listen to me. I want to spend this night with you, catching up, sharing this wonderful experience. I don't want to talk about Jakob or David or any of the Spencers the rest of the night."

She drained her glass of wine and held it out to him. "I'd like a refill please."

Murphy poured her more wine. He touched his glass to hers and smiled. Cora was right. This night was about the two of them.

❧

They left the restaurant an hour and a half later, full, but tipsy. Murphy escorted Cora to the car. They'd eaten a substantial meal, including cherries jubilee and coffee, but he definitely had a buzz.

Cora clung to his arm. She was weaving, her slight weight dragging him, pulling him off-balance. Her cheeks were flushed, her brown eyes shiny. "Murphy, where's my hair? My hair's all cut off."

She tripped and giggled. "I shouldn't have drunk so much wine. I hardly ever drink, except when I'd eat dinner with Stuart and Jesse…."

Cora stopped, halting their progress, covered her mouth and gave him a horrified look. Her eyes pooled with tears. "I'm sorry."

"It's okay, Cora Rose." Murphy tenderly wrapped his arms around her long, slender body and buried his face in the hollow of her neck. He rubbed her back in a soothing gesture and smiled wryly. "Next time we have wine, sweetheart, remind me to cut you off after two glasses."

He couldn't resist his impulse. He briefly pressed his mouth against her tender skin.

She shivered in his embrace and pressed closer, so close he could feel her hipbones against his.

He wanted to kiss her, but he'd better not. The better idea was to get her into the car and take her home.

"Cora honey, you have to help me out here. Walk, sweetheart."

She giggled and dragged on his arm. "I love it when you call me honey and sweet…."

He steadied her and, once he felt she'd regained her balance, he trudged on until they'd reached the vehicle. Opening the passenger door, he gently poured her inside. Sighing, he carefully skirted around the pothole at the back of the car and got behind the wheel.

Cora was looking at him with a voracious expression. Her hair was tousled, her cheeks pink, her mouth tempting.

He loved her mouth.

"Murphy. Let's make out."

He'd love nothing better, but making out in a parked car in a public lot was not the romantic setting he'd imagined. He tucked a wayward strand of hair behind her ear. "Not here, sweetheart."

Cora leaned over and traced his mouth with her index finger. "Why not?"

Before he had time to react, she withdrew and sank back against her seat, her fingers to her lips, her eyes staring straight ahead. "Oh my. I'm horny."

She rolled her head toward him, her brown eyes enormous. Leaning over, she kissed him. She really, really kissed him, and he responded with all the strength and vigor of adolescence.

Thank heavens for the console between them. Three quarters of him wanted to take her here right now in the parking lot of the Golden Grille.

The smaller part of him, which he called reason, urged him to stop and think. Think of the consequences.

For one thing, Cora meant more to him than a means of satisfying his need. For another, and he'd had plenty of experience over the years, Murphy knew she would wake up tomorrow morning with an upset stomach, a throbbing headache and vague memories of stuff she'd wished she hadn't said.

Without a doubt, Cora would suffer the headache and the

nausea, but he definitely didn't want Cora Rose waking up tomorrow with any regrets.

As gently as he could, Murphy pulled away, bracing his hands on her shoulders. Damn, even in her current state she was beautiful.

"Sweetheart," he gentled his tone.

She shook her head, her eyes closed. "No, no, no. Don't say you don't want...me."

"Honey. Honey, that's not it. That's not it at all. There's nothing I want more, but...."

Murphy racked his alcohol-soaked brain for something persuasive. He fell back on his legal arguments. "But, believe me when I say this."

He lost himself in the dark depths of her eyes. "I don't want to have casual sex in a car, like a couple of randy teenagers."

Moving closer, he tenderly kissed her petal-soft lips and pulled back to look into her face. "Honey, I want loving you to be something special."

Cora nodded. She understood. He could see that, but her eyes still pooled with tears, and one slowly slipped down her cheek. Frowning, she swiped it off her face and closed her eyes. "You're right. I know that, but I'm afraid."

She was a bundle of emotion, emotion that frightened Murphy. He was terrified that what she'd say next would tear down all the fragile connections they were building.

Sighing, she sank back against the seat and turned her head away.

Murphy reached out, but instantly pulled his hand back. Was she thinking about Davey? He gazed at Cora, moved with his tender feelings for her. And what if she was? Setting his jaw, he reached over and, threading his fingers in her hair, turned her face to his and pressed a fervent kiss against her lips. "Let's get you home."

Cora's brilliant smile was all the response he needed. She hadn't been thinking about Davey. His stubborn, insecure pride had raised its ugly head. He suspected Davey was more a specter hanging inside his mind than Cora's. Murphy started the car and, careful to miss the pothole, turned out of the lot.

CHAPTER TWELVE

*A*gnes licked Cora's face and kneaded her chest. Cora opened her eyes and stared up at her bedroom ceiling. Her mind was fuzzy. Her head ached and she felt like crap. What time was it? She swept the cat aside and sat, holding her head. The sun was horribly bright.

One glance at the clock galvanized her. "Shit. Shit. Shit. Shit."

Ignoring the shooting pain in her head, Cora rolled to her feet. The room spun. She sat back down again.

A couple of deep breaths later, she stood and, with slow deliberate movements, dressed and shuffled down the hall to the bathroom, holding on to the wall for support.

She winced, squinting in the unflattering yellow light. There wasn't time to waste, and she was grateful for her shortened hair. All she had to do was run a brush through it. She cut her toothbrushing regimen in half and was good to go.

Bustling through the kitchen, she unlocked the front door and switched the sign on. Ready for business.

Not really. She peeked out the window, relieved to see

her walkway and the street deserted. Time. She needed time to get her act together before her first customer showed up.

Coffee sounded horrible, and food sounded worse. Aspirin and orange juice sounded better.

By the time her first group of customers walked through the door, Cora had fortified herself with both. She told herself she'd have time to process last night's dinner with Murphy later after she closed. Today was Friday. The tour buses would be in town, so traffic in the store would be brisk.

Her stomach gurgled throughout the day. Between waves of tourists, she sipped ginger-ale, munched on saltines and popped aspirin every four hours. A couple of times, she'd peeked out the window at the house across the street and wondered how Murphy was feeling.

The last customers left at six. Cora locked the door and switched off the sign. Her stomach had settled, and she realized she was hungry. She hadn't eaten anything all day except a sleeve of crackers. Soup and more crackers sounded good.

She'd had a profitable day. She was in the shop tallying her receipts when the doorbell buzzed.

She hoped it was Murphy but then again, she hoped it wasn't. She hadn't had time to process everything that had happened in the last twenty-four hours. Cora smoothed her hair and smiled as she opened the door.

A cooling breeze tinged with the scent of pine bathed her face. Murphy stood on the porch holding a bouquet of yellow roses wrapped in green floral paper. He flashed her a wry smile and shrugged one shoulder. "Here I am again. May I come in?"

Speechless, her heart racing, Cora took the flowers and headed into the kitchen. She stood on her toes to grab a vase out of the cupboard.

Murphy slipped his arms around her. "I'm sorry I got you drunk."

Why did he have to be so sweet? Why couldn't she forget David entirely and love Murphy the way he deserved to be loved?

Afraid she might drop it, she gripped the vase with both hands. She set it down on the counter and turned to face him.

Before she had a chance to say it wasn't his fault, he kissed her. She was a grown woman for goodness sake, but her thoughts deteriorated at that point. All she could think about was the gentle, smooth friction of his mouth against hers and the desire that stirred deep in her belly.

He stopped kissing her, his concerned gaze searching her face. "I felt like shit this morning. How about you?"

Cora nodded, her palms flat against his chest. His heart was pounding as hard as hers. She looked back behind her at the flowers.

"Thank you for the roses. They're beautiful."

"Yellow signifies friendship, Cora. I want us to be friends first. I mean, I know we're already friends, we've been friends since we were kids—-"

She put a finger over his mouth, her heart swelling with tenderness. "I know what you mean."

Thinking of the night before, she blushed. "Did I really?" She stopped and stared down at the floor. "Did I really tell you I was horny?"

She couldn't look at him, but she sensed he was smiling in the affirmative. "I did, didn't I?"

"You did." His voice was laden with laughter, but he was obviously doing his best to contain it. He tightened his arms around her and she sagged against him, reveling in the secure sensation.

He nuzzled her neck. A bolt of pleasure rocketed all the way down to her toes.

"If it makes you feel any better, I was horny too. I just didn't say it." He convulsed with laughter and she joined in.

"You're such an ass." She intoned it as an endearment and smiled to soften her words. "Are you hungry? I don't have much to offer in the way of food. Frankly, I haven't felt much like eating today, but I'm hungry now."

"Me neither." Murphy cradled her hand, toying with her fingers. "I was thinking, only if you felt up to it, we could go to Pearl's and grab some chili and onions." His teasing grin and the twinkling light in his eyes gave him away.

"Murphy Webster, shut up. Let me see what I have in the pantry."

Following her, he reached over her shoulder and grabbed the can of chicken noodle soup. He whistled a merry tune under his breath as he snagged the open box of saltines. "How about I cook tonight?"

Cora chuckled and followed him with a jar of applesauce. "Only if you clean up after yourself."

He shot her an approving look. "Nice. Where's your can opener?"

She pointed to the appliance behind the phone book. "It's the electric one over there."

He raised his brows and said nothing, which was good, because she knew what the neat freak was thinking.

She sat at the table while Murphy stirred the soup and hunted in the cabinets for bowls.

"Warmer, warmer, cool, cold, warmer again."

She was tempted to tell him where they were, but she enjoyed watching him move. Why hadn't she noticed how handsome he was before? She knew why. Because compared to David, Murphy Webster had been a slight, scrawny kid. Because from the first moment she'd laid eyes on David Spencer, she had never seen anyone else.

Stop it, she told herself. Why couldn't she put David out of her mind? He'd been gone nearly fifty years. She knew why. As soon as she'd started her search on the Internet, hunting for reputable sites that reunited parents with their adopted children, David had crept back into her mind and into her dreams.

Murphy sighed and rested his hand on the back of her bare neck. "It's like he's sitting here in the kitchen with us, isn't it?"

Cora met his tortured gaze and tears stung behind her eyes. "Murphy, I want…"

He smiled sadly and gently combed his fingers through her hair. "I know. You have friendly feelings for me, but you want Davey back. I miss Davey too. I loved him and I'd do anything to bring him back, but I'd want some things to be different."

The soup in the pan hissed. Murphy walked over to the stove and stirred it. He kept his back to her. "I'd want him to love someone else. I'd want you to see me instead of Davey. I'd want you to like me as much as I've always liked you."

She sprang to her feet and went to him. She wrapped her arms around his solid chest and laid her head against his broad back. "Will you let me get a word in edgewise? I admit that a lot of what you said is true, but honey, David isn't coming back. After years and years of living with the ghost of a boy, barely a man, I'm finally coming to realize that I need to look ahead, not back."

She gripped him more tightly. "Wasted years. I wanted to call you when Jesse told me that Nan had died. I kept telling myself to wait until you came back to town to visit Jesse. I even wrote you a letter and stuck it in a condolence card. I still have it upstairs."

His hand stilled on the spoon.

She closed her eyes and listened to his heart, felt the rise and fall of his breathing. "I asked Jesse for your address—-"

Murphy turned around and kissed her. He slid his hands down her back and over her hips. She smelled lime and spice and chicken soup. She parted her lips and matched his deep kiss.

At a faint chime, Murphy stilled and broke the kiss. "It's my damn phone. I'll read it later."

Smiling against his mouth, Cora drifted her hands lower, curling her fingers around his belt.

Murphy cupped her butt and she froze.

"Too much?" His face was flushed, his breathing labored.

She grimaced and kissed him lightly on the lips. "I'm sorry. Not too much. Too fast." She smiled what she hoped was a tender smile into his gray eyes which had darkened considerably. "I didn't mean to get you all hot and bothered and then stop."

She smoothed a lock of hair off his forehead. "I meant to thank you for last night. I was drunk, and you could've had your way with me."

She'd meant it to be playful.

Murphy's gaze turned bleak. "Yeah, I had hoped the evening would have played out differently." His arms dropped to his sides. He turned his attention back to the roiling soup, stirring it so vigorously the liquid slopped out on the stovetop. He shook his head. "I'm sorry."

She turned him back to face her. "Murphy, nothing is perfect. I think our expectations were too unrealistic."

She sighed and gently relieved him of the spoon. "We have a lot of the past to work through. Both of us. If we're patient—-"

"We don't have the time to be patient, Cora. I could drop dead tomorrow. Jesse did."

Murphy's mouth turned down. His jaw tightened. He lifted his bleak gaze from hers and swallowed. He cupped his hand over his eyes.

She held him as he wept. She held him and her heart wept for him too. This big strong man who'd once been a scrawny, skinny boy. Beneath his light-hearted, teasing exterior, beat the heart of a gentle, loving person.

She wanted to give Murphy Webster all the love he

deserved, give him her heart unreservedly, without any doubt.

Could she?

❦

Trinity rolled off her bed when she heard the front door open. She crept down the hall to the top of the stairs in time to see Gramps head into the dining room. Headed for the liquor cabinet, no doubt.

It wasn't that Gramps drank all the time, but he'd had at least one scotch every day since they'd boarded the plane in San Francisco.

Since they didn't live together, she wasn't sure how much he drank at home, but his drinking was worrisome.

She been dying to find out how his date with Aunt C had gone. Gramps had slept in, so she and Stu had worked alone in the basement until lunch.

She'd knocked on his bedroom door and asked him if he'd like to come to Pearl's with them.

"No thank you." His emphatic reply had ended on a groan.

Trinity sighed and descended the stairs. Mom had texted her. She'd had to delay her flight again. Bummer. Trinity had heard that Spencer had an awesome Independence Day celebration. She'd been jazzed that her mother would be in town to celebrate with them.

Mom may have texted Gramps about her postponed arrival, but it would give Trinity an excuse to talk to him. Hopefully, he was feeling better by now and the scotch had mellowed him out.

One lamp lit the room. Gramps was sitting on the couch in the shadows, his stockinged feet resting on the coffee table. Instead of a scotch, he was drinking a soda. "Hello, pookie."

She plopped down on the cushion next to him and kissed him on the cheek. "Hi, Gramps."

He'd looked like he'd been crying.

He took a sip and gave her a wan smile. "What's up?"

She laid her head on his shoulder. "You smell like soup. Is that what you and Aunt C had for dinner?"

"Chicken noodle. What did you and Stuart have?" Transferring his soda to his other hand, he slipped his arm around her.

Trinity snuggled up to him and smiled. "A half-sausage, half-veggie pizza with stuffed crust. We ate the whole thing."

Gramps laughed. "Sounds good."

His voice lacked conviction. He patted her leg and sagged back against the couch, crossing his ankles the other way.

Obviously, she was going to have to lead the conversation since he was not in a talkative mood. "Mom had to reschedule her flight. I wanted her to be here for the Fourth."

Murphy nodded and sipped his drink. "I know, pookie. I'm sorry. I know you're disappointed."

He kissed the top of her head, but he looked tired and sad. She should wait for another time to bring it up, but the suspense was killing her. "Gramps, I haven't had a chance to talk to you. How did it go last night?"

He drank more soda and sighed.

"Gramps?"

"Pookie, Cora and I have a lot of time to account for. It's complicated."

"'It's complicated,' is an adult way of saying you don't want to talk about it," Trinity grumbled. She got up on her knees and peered into her grandfather's face. "You look sad."

He grimaced. "I am sad, pookie. I lost my brother. I didn't get a chance to say goodbye or tell him I loved him."

She wrapped her arms around his neck and hugged him. "I'm sorry, Gramps."

He kissed the top of her head and squeezed her hard.

"Thank you, pookie. I'm sorry too." Releasing her, he rose to his feet. "I think I'll go upstairs and get some sleep."

"What about Aunt C? Are you two still friends?"

Gramps looked at her as though she'd grown two heads. "Of course we're still friends."

"Did you kiss her goodnight?" The words tumbled out before she could stop them.

Gramps rolled his eyes. "What do you think?"

Trinity grinned. "I think you kissed her. I think you kissed her more than once."

Gramps actually grinned back. He came over and pecked her on the cheek. "Don't stay up too late. We still have more work to do."

"I won't. What's with the soda instead of the scotch?"

Gramps arched a brow. "I'm recovering from too much wine last night. I don't always drink scotch."

Trinity decided not to push the issue. "Stu and I are almost finished in the basement. We figure another day down there, and then we'll go through Great-Grandma's cedar chest that's in my bedroom."

Murphy nodded.

"Gramps, I forgot. Would you believe I found a couple more bank boxes filled with files under the stairs? I thought I was done."

"This old house has a lot of nooks and crannies." He smiled down at her. "Sounds as though you and Stuart got a lot done. Thanks for all your help."

"I love you, Gramps," she said, and gave him a bear hug.

He hugged her back. "I love you, too, Pookie. Don't stay up all night playing with your phone."

CHAPTER THIRTEEN

*A*fter applying her favorite lipstick, Cora checked her appearance in the mirror. She and Trinity had picked up nearly two-hundred dollars in cosmetics and face creams at the local health food store.

"They're all organic and these companies don't test their products on poor defenseless animals," Trinity had stated in an earnest voice.

Cora smiled and smoothed her hair. She was getting used to the shorter length and she liked the lowlights.

She examined her khaki-colored capris, as Trinity called them. She'd urged her to buy the white ones, but Cora had objected. They'd show everything she dripped on them.

Cora smoothed the red, white and blue blouse, blanketed with stars over her hips.

Trinity had suggested the princess-seamed garment because it sparkled. "That way you'll dazzle Gramps."

The girl was as bossy as she was charming.

Agnes yowled, garnering Cora's attention back to the present. The cat trotted ahead of Cora as she headed downstairs to the kitchen. Her tortie's appetite had returned, and she was as demanding as ever.

"I'm going to be gone until late tonight, so I'm going to give you some crunchies to tide you over." She shook out enough dry cat food to fill a small bowl. Agnes paused to sniff the nuggets and went back to nibbling her new soft food with added protein and amino acids.

"Have at it, old girl." Cora stroked her kitty and rubbed behind her ears. It had been almost a week since Jackson had called to tell her that the tests had been negative. "I'm glad you're your old self."

She glanced up at the clock. "I still have a few minutes before Murphy gets here."

The shop was closed for the holiday, and she had the whole day to spend as she wished. Her heart picked up a faster rhythm. She wanted to spend the whole day with Murphy.

As had been her habit for so many years, her hand crept up to her chest, where she'd worn David's ring. She hadn't put it back on since her dinner with Murphy. "I've got a hot date, Agnes. If you'd told me a month ago that I'd be dating the boy I grew up with, I would've told you you were nuts."

She scowled down at her tortie. "Agnes? Are you even listening to me?" Laughing she brewed a fresh pot of coffee and set two places at the table.

They had developed a fresh exciting routine. Murphy had been coming over for breakfast the past two days. After sharing a meal, he'd returned to Jesse's and worked on the house with Trinity and Stuart.

Both afternoons, Trinity had bounced over after lunch to pack boxes for Stuart and Murphy to take to the storage compartment Cora had rented.

The darling girl had suggested staging the shop after the kitchen, but Cora had put her foot down. "Absolutely not. The shop is a piece of me, and it is what it is. Your mother, or whoever buys this place, can wait until I've left in a cloud of dust and then do whatever they want."

Trinity had thrown up her arms in defeat, her beautiful hazel eyes laughing. "Okay, okay, whatever."

Now Cora gazed around her kitchen. Trinity was good. She'd accomplished in only two afternoons what Cora had been working on since she'd listed the place almost a month ago. The clutter had disappeared and the yellow formica countertops gleamed in the morning light streaming in through the pristine glass over the scrubbed sink.

The doorbell buzzed, reminding her that she'd forgotten to unlock it before she made the coffee.

She opened the door. Murphy walked in bearing a broad smile and carrying a white bag. He brought the fresh, cool mountain air in the house with him. "I went down to the pancake breakfast and got us a couple of orders to go."

He chuckled and led the way into her kitchen. "I didn't even have to wait long. Those Catholic ladies know their business. All I had to do after I forked over my money was head over to the take-out table and pick them up."

Cora poured mugs of coffee and rustled up an ancient bottle of syrup from her pantry. She peered at the label. "It's expired."

Murphy waved and grinned boyishly. "They gave me a handful of butter and syrup packets. Sit down, my love and we shall feast together."

A rusty giggle sprang from deep in her chest. "Is this how the whole day is going to go?"

He took the chair across from hers and reached for her hand. His expression was solemn and tender. "It's going to be a great day, Cora Rose, from beginning to end."

The butter didn't melt into the lukewarm pancakes, the scrambled eggs and bacon weren't as piping hot as she liked them, but sharing breakfast with Murphy more than made up for it.

She looked across the table at Murphy, intently eating his

pancakes. She wanted to believe. No, she would believe that today was going to be a great day from beginning to end.

❧

Murphy stole glances at Cora as he munched on a piece of bacon. His heart expanded. He loved starting his day with her. He'd gotten used to her bobbed hair with its silvery color and blended streaks. He loved her new wardrobe that showcased her gorgeous, long legs. Even her tailored slacks emphasized her slim curves, her waist, and especially her ass.

She'd caught him staring a couple of times and given him a dirty look. Once, he'd dared to protest. "I can't help it, love. I'm a man. We like women's butts, especially nice looking butts like yours."

She'd turned beet red and dropped her gaze.

He'd slid his fingers under her chin and smiled into her deep brown eyes and stolen a quick kiss. "I like everything about you."

Cora tapped her index finger against the top of his hand, her expression teasing. "I said, what are we doing after breakfast?"

Murphy reluctantly stopped thinking about the alluring curve of her hips and sipped his coffee to *buy time*. "I thought we'd grab some fishing gear and hike up to this lake I know and catch some trout."

Cora lightly smacked his arm and rose from the table. "Will you please get serious, at least until we get out the door?"

He followed her movements as she dumped her empty take-out carton into the trash. He loved her legs.

She intercepted his gaze and, instead of frowning, she actually arched a brow and winked at him.

His face got hot and, dammit, she made him look away first.

She made up for it by coming up behind him and reaching over his shoulder to grab his empty carton.

He snagged her wrist and pressed kisses to whichever parts of her flesh he could find.

Her trembling response immediately triggered his desire to pull her onto his lap and kiss her everywhere she'd let him.

As though the creature had read his mind, Agnes climbed up onto his lap, its needle-sharp claws digging into his leg. "Owwwww."

Reflexively, he swept the animal off his lap. He stood, nearly knocking over his chair and uttered a string of curses.

The cat ran off somewhere, and Cora followed.

He was in trouble now. He walked from the brightly-lit kitchen into the dim foyer. There went the day he'd so carefully planned.

Cora cradled the cat against her chest, swaying softly. The animal lifted its head and stared at him as if to say, 'you're in deep shit now.'

Murphy wanted to go over and make nice with Agnes, but he wasn't sure how Cora would react.

She gently put the cat on the floor. The animal promptly vanished into the dark depths of the shop. Cora slipped her arms around his neck, tipping her sweet mouth up to his. "She's fine. I know how sharp her claws can be. She's done that to me, too. Agnes has at least seven of her nine lives left."

Cora cupped the back of his head and kissed him. "I don't know what I did to deserve a second chance with you Murphy, but I'm not going to waste valuable time thinking about it."

Did she mean what she'd just said? He hoped so.

"I am sorry," he whispered against her lips. "I don't want to hurt your cat. I don't ever want to hurt you."

Cora cradled his cheek, her brown eyes thoughtful. "I don't think you could. I'm the one most likely to do that because—-"

"Shut up." He stopped her with a loving kiss. He checked his watch. "I hate to stop making out, but it's time to go."

She held his hand as they walked down to the Prius parked at the curb. "Where are we really going?"

He grinned. "It's a surprise."

"You know I don't like surprises."

He chuckled and opened her door. "I know. That's what makes this one so fun."

❦

Cora folded her hands in her lap and stared out the window. She took a quiet, calming breath and told herself to be patient and let life unfold, rather than wrestling with it. "Are we really going trail-riding? I thought you were kidding, but we're heading the right way."

Murphy glanced down at her shoes and made a face. "Naw, I just said that to put a burr under your saddle."

He was enjoying drawing out the suspense much too much. "You're going to milk this for all it's worth, aren't you?"

He laughed and nodded, his handsome profile brightly lit by the morning sun.

She lightly punched his arm. "That's for being such a rogue."

"Ow," he said, grinning.

They passed the sign indicating Matt Chandler's outfitting establishment and Cora shrugged. "Okay. I give up. I'll wait and see what you've got up your sleeve."

"That's my girl," he said, his attention focused on the steep, curving incline of the road.

"Don't sound so smug."

The stunning beauty and majesty of the Colorado Rockies never failed to move her. She couldn't imagine living anywhere else. She cast a surreptitious glance at the man next to her.

What was going to happen to their relationship when Jesse's estate was settled and Murphy returned to San Francisco?

Cora didn't want to confront the desolate prospect of not having him around to share meals with, to talk to, to laugh with. She would miss his corny jokes…She'd miss his touches, his kisses. She enjoyed his instinctive ability to stir the gossamer threads of desire.

She didn't want to lose anyone else.

She couldn't think about his leaving. She refused to look too far ahead. Today was enough.

Murphy stopped the car behind a line of other vehicles, most of them with out-of-state plates.

"Rocky Mountain National Park?" She turned to look at him and hope blossomed in her chest. "Murphy, this is a wonderful surprise. I haven't been up here in years. It's so close, but it's no fun coming alone."

She leaned over and kissed his cheek. "I forgive you for teasing me this morning."

He regarded her quizzically as he pulled his wallet out of his pocket. "Is that your way of saying, thanks, I love it?"

Cora nodded and sank back against her seat, smiling in anticipation of spotting wildlife. "Can we stop at one of the gift shops?"

He laughed and shook his head. "You, too? You fit right in with Shannan and Trinity. Always shopping."

She smiled. "I'm really looking forward to meeting Shannan. Trinity said she'll be out in little over a week."

Murphy nodded. He opened the window and handed a bill over to the young man in a National Parks uniform.

The kid handed Murphy a map and a receipt. "Thank you, sir. Enjoy your visit."

Murphy winked at Cora and said. "We plan on it."

As they navigated the winding road through the park, Cora spotted two eagles soaring above the treetops.

Murphy obliged her by stopping at one of the gift shops on their route. Cora led him outside the building onto the jutting overlook. The weather was warm with a light breeze. A distant herd of Elk grazed in the valley below.

He stood behind her, gently caressing her shoulders. Cora leaned back against him. "This was a lovely surprise. Thank you."

Murphy stroked her hair and kissed her temple. "I'm glad you liked it. I have a few more surprises up my sleeve."

The low, husky inflection in his voice promised companionship, intimate conversation and shared touches. Cora turned and gazed up into his warm gray eyes. "I can't wait."

Murphy broke out in a broad, boyish smile that melted her heart. "I thought you didn't like surprises?"

Cora cupped the back of his neck and lightly kissed him. "You've changed my mind." Releasing him, she opened the small crossbody bag she wore over her shoulder to retrieve her phone. "Let's take a selfie and send it to Trinity."

Murphy stared. He raised a brow and laughed. "From a romantic kiss to a selfie?" He shook his head in disbelief. "Woman, you never cease to amaze me. Hand over your phone."

Cora gave Murphy her phone and led him over to the spot she had in mind. He lifted the phone until both their faces were framed on the screen and snapped three shots. Cora chose one and sent it to Trinity, who immediately responded.

You and Gramps look cute! Stu and I are at the parade. The high school band was pretty good!

By the time they drove out of the park toward Spencer, vehicles were strung on the highway, bumper to bumper.

"I'm glad we came early." Cora sighed. "Sometimes, I'm very selfish. I hate to share this park. I know people only want to soak up the beauty of these mountains, but it's almost like they're trespassing."

Murphy reached over and stroked her cheek softly. "You love this part of Colorado don't you?"

She leaned back and turned to look at him. "I do. You grew up here, too. Don't you miss it?"

His expression grew thoughtful. "There are times when I do. Especially, when we first moved out to San Francisco. I really missed the seasons." He shrugged and shot her a wan smile. "Now I'm in love with the ocean and the Golden Gate."

She nodded, a tight band of dread constricting around her chest. She kept her anxious thoughts to herself and made a decision. Whatever tomorrow held, today would be good —-if she had anything to say about it.

❦

Murphy's attention drifted from the bumper to bumper traffic as they crawled their way into town. "Are you getting hungry, Cora?"

She smiled at him. "Keep your eyes on the road, please. I'd feel terrible if you wiped out a couple of tourists while gaping at me. I don't know if there's a place anywhere in this town that won't be crawling with people. Why don't we go back to my house? I can fix something for us to eat."

Murphy stole another quick glance at her. "I have a better idea." He grinned in anticipation. "We're going on a picnic."

"A picnic sounds fun, but again, where are we going to find a nice quiet place to eat?" Cora craned her head around to glance behind her. "Where's the food?"

"Trust me, everything's taken care of."

She wrinkled her nose. "Well, aren't you the clever one? Another one of your surprises?"

"You're catching on fast." Whistling under his breath, Murphy turned off Valley View Road onto her street. Minutes later, he pulled into Jesse's driveway.

"The picnic is a surprise from Trinity and Stuart."

Cora shook her head, and her brown eyes shown. "The two of them are thick as thieves. Trinity's been good for Stuart." She clasped Murphy's arm, kissed his cheek and rested her head on his shoulder. "She's been good for me too."

Murphy's heart swelled with love. His precious granddaughter bringing them together had been a blessing for all three of them, but his mind was presently occupied with Cora and her repeated displays of affection throughout the day.

"Right this way, madam." Escorting her along the side of the house, he reached over and unlatched the gate. "After you."

Stuart had told Murphy he and Trinity had set up a romantic picnic area in the backyard, but Murphy wasn't prepared for what met his eyes. "I wasn't expecting this."

"Oh Murphy." Cora's voice was soft and filled with delight.

She walked over to the old trestle table that had dominated the yard when he and Jesse were growing up. It was now draped with a red linen tablecloth. A blue plastic vase containing red, white and blue carnations with a couple of sprigs of baby's breath sat in the middle of the table. On the ground next to the nearest bench, a sturdy old-fashioned basket on top of a rugged steel cooler completed the picnic tableau.

Cora dazzled him with her brilliant smile. Her eyes sparkled. "It's beautiful."

Murphy grinned. He'd have to do something special for those two co-conspirators.

The basket contained plates, napkins and silverware,

along with two champagne flutes. Murphy narrowed his gaze. "After our last experience, I'm not entirely sure we should drink alcohol, especially this early in the day."

Cora lifted the green bottle out of the cooler and read the label before handing it to him. "This is safe. It's sparkling cider."

Murphy peeled off the protective sleeve and opened the bubbly drink while Cora finished setting out the cooler's contents.

"Looks like they cleaned out the deli. Olives, foccaccia sandwiches, pasta and potato salad," she said, accepting the glass of fizzy beverage he handed her.

Murphy laughed. "I'm going to need a nap after all this food."

Cora didn't say anything. She looked at him thoughtfully, unanswered questions in her gaze.

He put his hand on the back of her bare neck, his voice soft. "Why don't we take a nap after this? The band concert doesn't start until six and it's going to be a late night."

Her hand covered his and she gazed up at him. "I'd like that. We can go over to my place."

Sitting next to each other on the bench, they ate their lunch and sipped sparkling cider.

Cora opened the white carton with the distinctive *Cupcakes from Cookie's* label. "Murphy, wait until you taste these. There are cupcakes, and there are cupcakes. These delicious treats are works of art, but I think we should eat them later."

She graced him with a shy smile.

Pleasurable heat flooded his chest. Murphy reached over and tucked a shiny lock of Cora's hair behind her ear. "I think the cupcakes can wait."

They cleared the table and set the decorations inside on the kitchen counter.

Cora placed the vase of carnations next to the cupcakes.

He followed her as she walked around the house, her arms folded, her expression sad. "It's starting to look like someone else's house."

Murphy's heart sank. "I know. Our family heirlooms and Jesse's personal stuff are gone. All that's left is the attic, and a few odds and ends in the bedrooms and the basement. I'll notify the realtor when we're done, and the house will be on the market."

"Are you sure you don't you want to hang onto it? After all, you'll need a place to stay when you visit." Cora looked at Murphy, her eyes brimming with apprehension. "You will come to visit, won't you? Jesse said you meant well, but you always seemed too busy."

Murphy pulled her into a tight embrace. He swallowed the hard knot of regret that rose in his throat. *I'm sorry, Jesse.*

His shameful disregard for his brother's feelings need not be repeated with this living, breathing woman in his arms. His-round-the world voyage seemed a distant vision compared to Cora Rose.

Murphy raised his head to meet her anxious gaze. He tenderly stroked his thumb over her furrowed brows. "I won't make the same mistake with you that I made with Jesse. I will come back to visit you, Cora Rose. I will stay with you, wherever you are."

She relaxed against him. The tiny smile lines around her eyes deepened. She pressed her soft lips against his in a firm kiss. "See that you do, Murphy Webster. I will hold you to that."

Closing his eyes, he nuzzled her neck and gloried in her shivery response, her heady scent. He sought her lips and kissed her deep, then deeper, until she uttered a soft pleasured groan.

"Come on." He tenderly cupped her nape, his voice husky. "Let's go take that nap."

CHAPTER FOURTEEN

*T*rinity followed Stuart inside Jesse's house.

"Hello?" Stu called out, his gaze drifting in the direction of the stairs. He arched a brow and looked at Trinity.

Trinity made a face. "What? No way."

"You are incredibly intelligent and incredibly naive, girl. Do you think they only kiss?"

Trinity looked at him with an astonished grimace. "I don't want to think about it at all. Eww. That's worse than thinking about my mom and dad."

Stu sighed and strode into the kitchen. "So, did the stork drop you down a chimney?"

Trinity trailed in after him, checking her phone for messages. "I know where babies come from. I just don't want to know all the personal details about my parents doing it, that's all."

Stu closed the door to the fridge, and lifted the lid on the cooler. "It looks like they ate almost everything. The cupcakes are missing so, unless they're upstairs eating cupcakes in their birthday suits, I'd wager they're across the street."

Trinity crossed her arms and slumped against the counter. "Well, so much for meeting them at the car show."

A sympathetic frown creased Stu's brow. "Trinity, honey, I know you're disappointed, but your grandfather didn't make any promises. I think he and Cora want to spend as much time together as they can."

"I know. Aunt C's been good for Gramps. It'll be interesting to see if she can take his mind off his precious boat. He used to talk to me and Mom more before he fell madly in love with the *Stargazer*."

Stu edged closer to her. "Really? What kind of boat?"

"It's a sailboat. He calls *Stargazer* his sweetheart."

Trinity loved being out on the water. The few occasions Gramps had taken her out on the sailboat had been exceptionally awesome. She'd begged him to go out under the Golden Gate into the open sea, but he'd balked. Another time, he'd promised.

She wouldn't hold her breath on that one. She wandered over to the fridge and surveyed the assortment of beer, soda and take-out cartons. "There's nothing good in here to eat."

Stu reached over her shoulder and snagged a soda. "How in the world can you possibly be hungry? You've been eating non-stop all day."

Trinity grabbed an apple out of the crisper drawer. "I just am."

"That's because you've been eating nothing but crap." He sat down at the table and swigged his drink.

Trinity rinsed her fruit under the faucet. "Mom says crap is okay on special occasions."

"You're missing your mom, aren't you?" Stu's face was kind, his expression concerned.

"I wish Mom was coming this Saturday instead of next weekend." Smiling, Trinity flashed her screen at him. "Look, Mom sent me a pic of Binx curled up on my bed. She said he misses me."

The older man nodded and dutifully looked at her cat. "Binx like the black cat in the Halloween movie *Hocus Pocus*? Makes complete sense."

"Yes, except my Binx isn't possessed," she declared emphatically.

He handed the phone back to her. "And you miss him too."

She pecked Stu on the cheek and took the chair next to him. Crunching the sweet, crisp fruit, she smiled and swallowed. "You're a very perceptive man."

"You're a very special young lady." A fleeting look of sadness crossed his face. He sipped his soda and looked around the kitchen. "I'm going to miss this house." His gaze dropped to his hands, and he twisted the white gold band on his finger.

Trinity remembered how she'd felt after losing her nana. "I'm sorry, Stu. You miss Jesse, don't you?"

He cleared his throat. "Yeah."

She turned her half-eaten apple in her hands. "I miss my nana. I miss her hugs and the times we spent baking apple pies together." Trinity closed her eyes, picturing her grandmother's big kitchen and the sweet aromas of cinnamon and sugar. "Every Christmas, Nana took me and Mom to see The Nutcracker." Trinity bit her lip and sighed. "Death sucks, big time."

Stu squeezed her hand. "I know, honey, but your nana and Jess wouldn't want us to mope around. Years ago, Jess and I were sitting under orange umbrellas on a beach in Sorrento. I remember it vividly. Jess reached over and gripped my hand so tightly I thought my fingers would break. He looked at me with his gorgeous blue eyes and said if he died before me, I was not to brood, like I have a tendency to do." Stu gave a sad chuckle. "Jess said, 'Remember all the good things about me, remember all our happy times, like this, and most importantly live each day to the fullest and don't take life for granted.'"

Trinity nodded. Holding Stu's hand made her feel better. It reminded her of the happy times when her dad was home. It reminded her of his hugs. They'd made her feel safe—-loved. That had been before he had traveled so much.

Stu gave her hand a final squeeze and sighed. "Okay, enough talk of death. It's the Fourth of July, remember? Let's hit the car show. We'll stuff you full of soft-baked pretzels and cotton candy. Later we'll check in with your grandpa and Cora to see what their plans are."

Trinity sniffled. Impulsively, she threw her arms around the comforting older man. "I love you, Stu."

The tall man hugged her back, and dipped his head to smile into her face. "I love you too, honey."

She'd only had Nana and Gramps her whole life and she'd missed having two sets of grandparents. Now, she had Aunt C and Stu, as well.

It was true. Spencer was beginning to feel more and more like home.

❧

Cora woke first. She blinked awake. The rectangular window of her bedroom still reflected light. What time was it? She glanced over at her clock on the nightstand and spied Murphy's watch.

She smiled and clasped her hands over her stomach. Her body felt fluid. Sex with Murphy had been amazing. He might be impatient at times, but as a lover he'd been tender and anxious to please her.

Details flooded her mind with images and sensations. She turned her head and reached out to brush her hand against Murphy's bare back and hesitated.

He snored softly. She didn't want to wake him. Instead,

she committed to memory his masculine form, barely concealed beneath the cotton sheet, and the sun-bronzed tint on the back of his neck just below his precisely clipped hairline.

Cora frowned at the scar that traveled diagonally from Murphy's right shoulder down to his waist. A souvenir from Nam was all he'd offered as she'd gently traced the white ridge of flesh.

Smiling, she recalled his tender kisses, his tentative caresses, his whispered questions. *Is this okay? Do you like this?*

After their picnic, they'd walked hand in hand across the street, up the stairs and into her bedroom.

Murphy's gray eyes had taken on the color of Thompson Creek on a stormy day, his intention transparent. What had come next had been deliberate, unhurried.

On edge at the prospect of intimacy with this man, even though she'd known him most of her life, Cora had licked her lips and confided in a breathless voice. "My heart is pounding so hard I'm afraid I'm going to crack a rib." She'd rubbed her arm. "Where did I put the cupcakes? They should probably go in the refrigerator—-"

Murphy had silenced her with a soft kiss, nuzzled her throat, which created shivers along her limbs, and she'd forgotten all about the cupcakes.

Afterwards, they'd talked. Really talked. She'd confided her fear of the future, her uncertainty about what she'd do, where she'd go.

He'd listened, his head propped on his elbow, his smoky eyes intent, occasionally reaching out to touch her hair, her shoulder. She'd naturally snuggled into his warm embrace.

Now Murphy turned and pressed his lips against the sensitized flesh of her nape. Cora shivered. She rolled over and faced him. "You were snoring your head off a minute ago."

His face colored, but then his gaze narrowed. "Tease."

He dove under the sheet. Taking his time, he rained slow
kisses on her most sensitive parts, lightly skimming his
fingers below her navel, along her inner thigh. She gasped,
closed her eyes and arched her back. Every muscle in her
body tightened. A scorching wave of pleasure coursed
through her like a bolt of lightning. Cora convulsed, covering
her mouth with her hand as she cried out.

"Who are you afraid will hear you? We closed the door so
Agnes couldn't interrupt us." Murphy grinned, his face
flushed, his eyes dancing.

She could hardly raise her arm to swat him. Her body
sank deeper into the down mattress cover. Brimming with
ecstasy, Cora gazed up into his face. Physical intimacy with
Murphy was wonderful, but what she treasured most was his
company and their conversations; sharing their feelings,
trading laughs and memories of Grandma Binney.

Cora had expressed all the unanswered questions
weighing heavily on her heart except the search for her child.
Murphy had no idea she'd had a baby let alone given her
daughter up for adoption. And if she told him, he'd immediately know who the baby's father was. Her stomach knotted
at the prospect of Murphy's response. How would her
shocking revelation affect their budding relationship?

Murphy planted a gentle kiss on her lips. "What's going
on inside that beautiful head of yours?" He smiled, but his
tone was quiet and laced with suspicion. The foolish man
suspected she was thinking about David and she was, but not
from Murphy's defensive perspective.

Cora's heart pounded. She would tell him. She had to.
Trust was imperative if she was to totally commit herself to
this relationship. She felt as though she was leaping off a
sheer cliff into an empty void. Closing her eyes, she pulled as
much breath into her lungs as she could muster and spoke
before she could think twice. "I have something I want to tell
you."

Murphy's smile disappeared. He stared at her, his gaze wary.

She swallowed and fisted her hands. "Years ago, I got pregnant and I put my baby up for adoption. I've engaged an online detective agency to find her."

❦

Cora's confession had the same heartrending, suffocating impact as Stuart's revelation that Jesse had been gay.

"Davey's?" There was no doubt in his mind that his best friend had been the baby's father.

"Yes." Her dark eyes were enormous in her pale face. He could feel her pounding heart below her breast.

Murphy rolled over on his back and flung an arm over his head. He closed his eyes, struggling to understand, willing himself to set aside his conflicted feelings to reassure her. He'd wasted enough opportunities in the past with Nan and Jesse. This was his chance to prove to Cora how much she meant to him.

"Murphy?" Her emotion-choked voice jolted him out of his self-serving thoughts.

He turned on his side and gently kissed the lone tear trailing down her cheek. "I'm sorry, Cora Rose. I can be such an ass sometimes." He smoothed her hair away from her face. "When did you find out you were pregnant?"

"Shortly after David's death, I went to a clinic in Longmont." She tensed and squirmed against him. "Please, hold me Murphy. Please."

Murphy curled his body around hers, spoon-fashion. He squeezed her hand. "Is that better?"

She nodded and breathed a relieved sigh. "I didn't know what to do. I couldn't tell David's father. He had never accepted me and had done his best to separate us. Jakob was busy with his own family and his business."

Murphy remembered Davey's anger at his father's repudiation of Cora. *My bastard of a father thinks shipping me off to a school back east is going to make me forget the only girl I've ever loved? What a crock.*

Cora sighed and laced her fingers with his. "I couldn't tell Grandma Binney. She thought I was an angel and I couldn't bear to disillusion her. As soon as I started to show, I told her that my mother wanted me to come down to Denver for the summer."

Murphy kissed Cora's shoulder. He remembered when Cora had left to visit her mother. He and Nan were preparing to move to San Francisco.

"I wanted to keep the baby, but my mother convinced me that adoption was the best solution for both the baby and me." Cora inhaled deeply and stiffened against him. "I should have stood up for myself, but I was so damn young and scared. Look at all the single moms today."

"Sweetheart, that was over forty years ago. Times were different. Society was different." Murphy kissed the back of her head and rocked her gently.

"I remember sneaking into the law office through a back door. By then I was very pregnant. My hand shook so badly, I could barely sign my name."

She turned in his arms and pressed her flushed cheek against his bare chest. "But I did. I signed my baby's life away and my mother witnessed it. For years, when I'd see little girls in the shop or around town, I'd wonder where my little girl was and what her life was like."

Murphy stroked her hair. He grieved for the young, frightened Cora, pregnant and alone, forced to give up her baby, and he grieved for the mature Cora he presently held close to his heart. He was reminded of all the nights he'd held Nan in his arms, trying to comfort her and ease her distress. "You've engaged an online detective agency?"

"Yes. I checked the ancestry websites first, but nothing

turned up so I googled finding children given up for adoption. I thought about trying a free website, but I wasn't comfortable with putting my personal information out on the Internet."

Cora sighed. Tugging free from his embrace, she scooted up and propped her head against the pillows. She clutched the sheet over her chest and her hopeful gaze searched his face. "I check my emails twice a day and I still haven't heard anything from the agency, but it's only been a couple of weeks. I know that the search takes time." She raised a bare shoulder and shot him the ghost of a smile. "You know me. I never could wait for anything."

Murphy caressed her cheek. "I don't know, Cora Rose. You've been waiting to find your child for years."

Cora covered his hand with hers, her anxious gaze probing his. "Murphy, I had to tell you, but I was afraid of how you'd react. It's important to be honest with each other if we're to have a healthy relationship."

Her expression saddened. "Now that Jesse is gone you're the only person who knows what happened."

"You told Jesse?" Murphy eased his hand from hers and scratched his head. Since arriving in Spencer, it seemed as though he'd been hammered with one startling revelation after another. He was filled with regret at how disconnected he'd been from both Jesse's and Cora's lives. But, this was not about him and his feelings.

This was about Cora. She'd trusted him with her secret and she needed his support. Murphy extended his thumb to smooth the deepened lines between her brows. "Sweetheart—-"

Cora flashed him a weak smile and sat up. She reached for her robe at the foot of the bed. Standing, she wrapped the garment securely around her body and knotted the belt. "You had married Nancy and were living your own life in San Francisco. I had nobody to advise me. I'd consulted Jesse as my friend and as my attorney. I'd wanted to determine what rights I had."

Crossing her arms, she cupped her elbows with her hands and stared out the window.

Murphy climbed out of bed. He walked up behind her and gently grasped her shoulders. "I'm glad Jesse had been there for you." He rested his chin on the top of her head. "From now on, I want to be there for you."

Cora turned and faced him. Her solemn brown eyes softened. "Thank you," she whispered, and pressed her soft lips against his.

Murphy slipped his arms around Cora and cradled her close.

She ended their kiss and tilted her mouth in a teasing smile. "After we both get dressed, what other plans do you have in store for us today?"

Murphy chuckled. "I hate to disappoint you, but I'm afraid we'll have to forego the auto expo if we want to grab a bite to eat before the band concert."

Cora's smile broadened and she winked at him. "Honey, I'd rather hike to a mountain lake at the break of dawn than go to the auto expo."

Murphy laughed and threaded his fingers between the soft layers of her hair. He kissed her. "I'll text Trinity and Stuart and tell them we've changed our plans." He kissed her again, his lips lingering on hers. "What about the band concert?" He nuzzled her throat and slipped his hand inside the lapel of her robe, John Phillips Sousa's rousing marches all but forgotten.

Cora lightly smacked his wayward hand and retreated out of reach. Her pink cheeks gave her away. "We're going to the band concert. I'll pack ham and cheese sandwiches, fill the thermos with coffee, and we'll bring the cupcakes for dessert. Would you mind going across the street and grabbing the basket we used this afternoon?"

"Yes, ma'am," he said.

Murphy frowned as he took the stairs down to the kitchen. He struggled to process the ecstasy of making love to Cora, followed by the stunning disclosure that she and Davey had had a child together. He needed time to sort through his muddled feelings.

Cora was right. He didn't want to keep any secrets from her either. After the heartache of giving her child up for adoption, how would Cora feel about what he and Nan had done?

❦

The afternoon sun was hovering barely above the mountain peaks when Cora and Murphy spread their colorful blanket on the lawn in front of the old-fashioned bandstand in the park.

"I'm glad we came early." Cora settled cross-legged on the blanket and, looking up at Murphy, patted the place next to her. He removed his shades and squinted. "Me too. I don't think there's a single inch of ground in this town that isn't crawling with people."

He lowered himself next to her, bracing his arms behind him.

She was learning the look and feel of his lean body. "How do you stay so fit?"

His gray gaze bored into hers. He reached over and tapped her chin. "I watch what I eat and I drink a little scotch now and then."

Laughing, she snatched his hand and threaded her fingers through his. She traced the pattern on the blanket. "Time's been good to you."

She plucked at the stitching under her finger and lifted a shoulder. "All of this is so new to me, but this afternoon was...."

He scooted closer and cupped the back of her neck. "This afternoon was special, Cora Rose."

The noise level of the crowd was a low din, everyone else obsessed with their own private conversations.

She unpacked their sandwiches. A fusillade of fire-crackers split the air, followed by the loud boom of a cherry bomb. Cora flinched and uttered a startled curse. "I'm glad I wasn't pouring the coffee."

Murphy grinned. "It's all part of the holiday experience."

Cora handed him the thermos. "Since you have nerves of steel why don't you pour the coffee?"

Sitting beside Murphy on the blanket, she ate her sand-wich and sipped coffee. The VFW band was assembling inside the gazebo. The concert was the perfect ending to a perfect day.

Murphy ate without comment throughout their meal, his attention directed elsewhere, as though he had something on his mind. When Cora offered him the box of cupcakes, he chose one with an absent smile and quickly consumed the delicious dessert.

An uneasy sensation stirred in the pit of her stomach. "Murphy, you're awfully quiet." She rubbed his arm. "You practically swallowed that cupcake whole. What's wrong? Is it about what I told you this afternoon?"

Murphy planted his hands on her shoulders. "I have something to tell you. After you told me about your preg-nancy and how important honesty is in a relationship, I real-ized I need to be honest with you."

He sighed. "Okay, here goes. I married Nan because she was pregnant. The baby was mine. I was responsible." He dropped his gaze. "I'm sure you heard the rumors around town. Nan's family arranged a private Catholic ceremony in Boulder."

Cora covered his hand with hers. The rumors hadn't

interested her. She'd still been recovering from the shock of David's tragic death.

"After the wedding, we moved to San Francisco. Our baby died in the womb. Nan was distraught. She had to endure a long, painful labor and deliver a stillborn child."

"Oh, Murphy. I'm sorry. Nancy was one of the sweetest people I knew."

Murphy slid his grip from Cora's shoulders and bowed his head. "She was. She didn't possess a selfish bone in her body and she was fiercely devoted to Shannan and Trinity."

He closed his eyes and scrubbed a hand down his desolate face. "Trust me, it was a grueling experience." He slipped on his sunglasses even though the sun was no longer in their field of vision.

Cora's heart ached for them. At least she had given birth to a healthy baby.

Murphy cleared his throat and shifted on the blanket next to her, pulling his legs up under his chin. "She became clinically depressed. I was afraid I'd have to commit her somewhere, Cora. I worried that she'd commit suicide while I was at work. I was on guard twenty-four-seven.

"A few weeks later, one of the partners at the firm I was interning at called me into his office. He knew of an unwed mother who was giving up her baby for adoption. We went through all the legal channels and that's how we got Shannan."

Cora's breath hitched and she stared at him. "Shannan? I always assumed Shannan was yours and Nancy's."

"Make no mistake, Shannan was ours, maybe not biologically, but in every other way possible. She saved Nan's sanity, and my sanity for that matter. She saved our marriage. Shannan was, and is our daughter in grace."

"Of course she is. I didn't mean it like that," Cora assured him.

Murphy found her hand and gripped it painfully. His eyes

were hidden behind the dark lenses, but the set of his mouth was rigid. A muscle in his jaw twitched. "Cora. This is important. It is imperative that you tell no one about Shannan. I can't stress that enough."

She rubbed his arm. "Honey, I won't tell anyone."

"Especially not Trinity, or Shannan when she gets here."

"What?"

He removed his glasses and leaned forward, his earnest expression punctuating his words. "Nan and I...back then; things were a helluva lot different than now...you know that."

Cora's heart tightened with dread.

"Don't look at me like that," he said.

Who was she to judge him and to judge poor Nancy for doing or not doing whatever they'd done?

"After losing the baby, Nan clung to the idea that Shannan was hers. Even though...."

Murphy bowed his head and blew out a long breath. "Our baby had been a boy.

"When I initially brought up the idea of telling Shannan, once she was older, that she was adopted," Murphy rubbed his mouth, "Nan was still recovering. She said some mean, hateful things. Things I knew she wouldn't have said if she'd been in her right mind. Once she'd improved, I didn't have the heart to bring up the subject again. I was afraid I'd trigger a relapse."

His anguished expression touched Cora's heart.

"The upshot is we never told Shannan she was adopted. Right or wrong, what purpose would it serve now, except to hurt her?"

Cora knew Murphy was looking for reassurance. He and Nancy had given Shannan both a mother and a father, a loving home and a secure life.

She couldn't look at him. She couldn't look at him because her heart and her mind belonged with that poor girl, alone and frightened, forced to give up the one thing that probably truly belonged to her. That baby had been alive and moved inside her for months.

The barked orders of the leader announcing the advent of the Color Guard and the opening ceremony preceding the concert saved Cora from having to respond.

CHAPTER FIFTEEN

*T*rinity woke up the next morning. The sun was already well above the horizon. It was nine-thirty and she was starving. Her dry mouth tasted gross. She padded down the hall to the bathroom. The door to Gramps' room was still closed. When had he and Aunt C arrived home?

Downstairs in the kitchen, she snagged a glass out of the cupboard and filled it from the tap. In spite of all the sunscreen she'd applied yesterday, she was sunburnt and her leg muscles were sore from pedaling the boat out on Lake Louise.

Well. Stu wasn't here and Gramps must still be in bed.

What she was really craving was caffeine and sugar. Trinity sighed and rummaged through the cupboards.

She spied the cookie tin on the counter. Trinity popped the lid. Two left. There was a jar of instant coffee, but she'd only drink that if she was desperate and could drown it in tons of milk and sugar.

Aunt C usually had the coffee pot on in the morning. Trinity smiled. Perfect. She'd take the tin back, have a cup or two of coffee and find out how Aunt C and Gramps had enjoyed their day together.

After locating a pen, she scrawled a quick note on a napkin and left it on the table in case Gramps or Stu wondered where she was. She doubted they'd get much work done today anyway. Her mind made up, Trinity jogged upstairs to take a super quick shower.

Less than a half-hour later, she stepped into the brilliant mountain sunshine and trotted across the street.

The door was still locked. Trinity remembered today was Sunday and the shop didn't open until noon. She knocked on the door.

The door opened. Aunt C's eyes widened. "Trinity."

"I was wondering if I could bum a cup of coffee with milk and sugar. Gramps is still sleeping and I don't want to wake him up. He gets grumpy when I do that. Just for future reference."

Aunt C's face turned pink. She gave Trinity a faint smile and led the way into the kitchen. "I can use another cup myself."

The table was set for two. Trinity's smile broadened. "He's upstairs, isn't he?"

Aunt C's complexion deepened. She grabbed a mug and poured coffee about halfway. She set it down in front of Trinity. "Milk's in the refrigerator. Sugar's on the table."

"Hey, it's not for me to judge." Trinity heaped two spoonfuls of sugar into her coffee.

Aunt C served herself and sat across from Trinity. "I don't want to talk about it." Her eyes were dead serious.

Trinity gingerly sipped and nodded. She didn't want to embarrass Aunt C any more than the woman already was. She wasn't sure how Gramps was going to react. It might be better to drink her coffee and go back across the street.

She checked under the table and the floor around Agnes' bowls. "Where's Agnes?"

Aunt C brought her mug up to her lips, and then set it on the table instead. "This morning, when I came downstairs and she didn't run into the kitchen, I went into the shop. She was still curled up in her bed sleeping, but she responded when I stroked her. Agnes always runs out to meet you when you come over. Now I'm worried about her all over again."

Trinity's stomach knotted. She set down her cup and cookie. "Let me go check." She gave Aunt C a weak smile. "Sometimes our cats eat something they shouldn't."

Sun slanted in through the open windows shining directly on the glass counter and Agnes' bed. The pressure in her chest eased. Agnes was probably enjoying the extra boost of heat. "Agnes, kitty. It's time to wake up."

Trinity paused. The tortie was still curled up in her bed. Her eyes were closed, but her mouth was partially open, like she was panting.

Something wasn't right.

"Agnes, kitty?" She pressed her hand to her mouth and took a step closer. The cat's position never changed. She didn't move.

Trinity's eyes filled with tears. A hiccup hitched in her chest. It hurt to breathe. She slowly reached out her hand and touched Agnes' multicolored fur.

Instead of the cat's body being warm and yielding, Agnes was stiff and cold. Trinity snatched her hand away and heard a wail that she realized came from her. "Noooooooooo."

Aunt C must have been right behind her. "Trinity, sweetie."

"Agnes is dead!" She threw her arms around the tall woman and buried her head against her chest.

"Oh, Agnes." Aunt C hugged Trinity tightly, her voice thick with tears.

Trinity raised her head to look up at the older woman. "Why? Why, did she have to die now? We were just becoming frie—-friends." A fresh wave of grief washed over her. "Where's Gramps?"

But it wasn't her grandfather that she wanted. It was her mother. She missed her. She raised her face to look at Aunt C again. "I want my mom. I want her here. Now."

"Sweetie. Your mom's coming." Aunt C smoothed her hair, like Mom. It helped a little.

Trinity cried because Agnes died. She cried because she missed Mom. She missed Dad, who was always away. She missed her kitties and her room where she could watch the afternoon fog sweep in through the Golden Gate.

❦

Eventually, with Murphy's help, Cora was able to persuade Trinity to go back to the kitchen. She led the girl over to a chair. "Sit down, sweetie. I'll get you some tissues and some fresh coffee. Okay?"

Trinity nodded. She looked at Murphy and the tears started all over again. "Gramps. Agnes died."

Murphy's careworn face creased with sympathy. "I know, pookie. I'm sorry."

Rising, he took a handkerchief from his pocket and gently dabbed her face. Trinity wrapped her arms around his neck. "It sucks. I want Mom."

Murphy glanced up at Cora and gave her a wan smile.

"I know you want your mother." Murphy kissed the girl's cheek and smoothed her tousled dark hair. "As soon as you calm down a little—"

Cora cleared her throat and shook her head.

He gave a helpless sigh. "Why don't you wait and call her in a little bit."

Dumping out Trinity's cold coffee, Cora grabbed the eggs and bacon out of the refrigerator. She peeled off slices and slapped them into the cast iron skillet.

Trinity's chair scraped against the linoleum. She wrapped her thin arms around Cora's waist and hugged her. "I'm sorry, Aunt C. I know you raised Agnes from a kitten and how much you loved her."

Cora's throat closed and her eyes welled with unshed tears. Gazing into Trinity's beautiful hazel eyes, Cora was once again struck with the notion that this precious child had been sent to her.

She shook her head. Somehow, she'd lost Agnes, but she'd gained Trinity. Smiling, her heart expanded with love. Forgetting her loss for a moment, she kissed Trinity's forehead, catching the girl's faint fruity fragrance. "Thank you, sweetie. Why don't you wash up and I'll fix breakfast?"

Without makeup, Trinity looked younger with her damp lashes and freckles sprinkled over the bridge of her nose.

"How do you want your eggs, Trinity?"

"Scrambled please. Only can you make them kind of soft, not runny though, just soft and fluffy? That's how my mom makes them."

The girl shuffled off to the bathroom and Cora grinned. She cracked eggs into a blue ceramic bowl and whipped them into a frothy blend.

Before she could stop him, Murphy rose from the table and enfolded her in his arms. "I'm sorry, love."

She knew he cared, and she was glad he cared, but right now, she couldn't let herself think about Agnes. She forced a smile and pecked a kiss on his cheek. "I know. Thank you for that." Squirming out of his embrace, she turned her attention to the frying bacon. "How do you want your eggs today?"

"Cora. Don't shut me out."

She swallowed the lump of grief rising in her throat. She couldn't look at him or she'd break into a thousand tiny pieces. "I'm not. I can't think about the cat right now."

Murphy sighed and headed back to the table. "I'll take my eggs the same as Trinity's."

"That I can do." Cora wiped a tear from her cheek, grateful the shop opened later today. She'd ask Murphy if he would dig Agnes' grave after breakfast.

❦

Murphy took the slippery, wet plate Cora handed him and dried it with the dishtowel. He stared out the window at the old, gnarled apple tree. "Remember, how Jesse used to climb almost to the top of that tree and toss down apples for us?"

Cora nodded. "We'd wait until Grandma Binney and her church ladies were busy with their Bible study."

Murphy chuckled and stole a glance at her profile. Something about the contour of her jaw struck him as familiar. He dismissed the odd thought. After all, he'd spent the last week with Cora, so her face was becoming recognizable. He set aside the plate he'd dried and took the next one Cora handed him.

The fleeting impression was gone. Her eyes begged him to continue, to talk of other things.

He wanted to gently pull her away from the sink and console her, yet, he sensed she was taking comfort in the mundane task and the hot, soapy water.

Murphy took the plate she held out. "That's right. I forgot about your grandma's Bible study. We got away with it for a few weeks, until one of the ladies happened to look out this window and snitch on us. That's one of the few times Jesse actually got in trouble."

Cora's hands were bright pink from the hot water. He felt the heat of the silverware through the thin cotton material of the towel.

"You were such a scalawag, Murphy. You were staring down at your bare toes while Grandma was bawling out Jesse. I saw the sly grin on your little mug."

She lifted her hands out of the sink and flicked water in his face, her brown eyes dancing. "That's for Jesse."

Startled, Murphy blinked. After he wiped his face with the towel, he snapped the linen cloth against her trouser clad hip, causing her to yelp. "You little tease."

"I made a little casket for Agnes." Trinity's small voice cut through the hilarity.

Murphy turned. His granddaughter stood on the threshold of the kitchen. Trinity might be fifteen, but at this moment, she looked like she had when she was five, and her pet guinea pig had died.

"Let's take a look." He might not be able to comfort Cora, but he could hug his granddaughter.

Trinity set the cardboard box on the table and returned his hug.

Cora looked inside the container. Her lips tightened. She raised her hand to her throat and met his eyes.

"Stu helped me," Trinity said.

Murphy examined the box, now transformed into a make-shift casket. He picked up a tattered stuffed mouse. "What's this?"

"Agnes' favorite toy," she replied in a reedy voice. Sniffing, she raised her tearful eyes to Cora. "Don't you think Agnes would like that?"

Cora nodded with an encouraging smile. "She would."

Murphy rubbed his granddaughter's thin arm. "Where'd you and Stuart find the pretty pink satin?"

Trinity looked guilty. "Actually, we found the material inside Great-Grandma's cedar chest. You don't mind, do you?"

Murphy fingered the cool, silky fabric. Mom had always loved to sew. "No, pookie. I don't mind at all." He gave Trinity a tender smile. "I think your Great-Grandma would like that."

Cora cleared her throat. "I'm going out back to find a spot."

The screen door slammed against the back porch.

Trinity wiped her nose with Murphy's handkerchief. "Is Aunt C mad at me?"

"No, pookie, she's not mad at you, or at me. Cora's always handled her grief privately." He recalled yesterday afternoon and how she had confided her search for her baby and his heart turned tender.

Trinity handed him the box. "Would you please put Agnes in her casket? I want to remember her purring and batting me with her little paws."

"Of course."

"Thanks. I'm going to text Stu. He said he'd help you dig Agnes' grave." She rolled her eyes. "Stu loved Agnes, too. I know he said he'd wanted to shoot her, but he really didn't mean it."

A smile tugged the corners of Murphy's mouth. He begged to differ, but for Trinity's sake, he nodded and headed toward the shop.

CHAPTER SIXTEEN

*T*rinity's loving gesture of making the casket for Agnes had nearly undone her. Cora stood beneath the apple tree, bracing her back against its solid trunk. She plucked a green leaf and crushed it to a pulp. She lifted it to her nose and breathed deep. She looked up into the interior branches and saw the small green fruit that would soon be a pale red come late August. She picked one, barely the size of a golf ball. The sour taste made her wince, but it distracted her.

Cora pressed the heels of her hands against her eyes and exhaled. She wished Murphy would come out. She wanted the comfort of his arms, his reassuring deep voice.

He'd silently respected her wishes. He'd read the looks she'd given him since they'd discovered Agnes. Yesterday afternoon, when she'd poured out the story of giving her baby up, he'd listened with compassionate silence and had shared his own tragic experience afterward.

Murphy was healing her. Cora realized that what bound them together was real, not forced by circumstances. What bound them together, warts and all, was love.

She heard the screen door squeak open and slam.

Hurriedly, she wiped her face and dried her hands on her pants.

He didn't call out. He knew. He came directly to the apple tree. He reached out to her. She took hold of his warm hand, and he pulled her against his chest.

Cora closed her eyes. She heard the calm beating of his heart, felt the rise and fall of his chest, inhaled lime and spice. The soft caring touch of his lips reassured her.

Not long afterward, the screen door banged again. Trinity and Stuart walked across the yard, Stuart toting a shovel.

Murphy raised his head and his arms tightened around her. "That's the shovel Jesse and I always used to dig up worms in the back yard for fishing."

Cora sighed and reluctantly released him. She squared her shoulders and led Murphy by the hand over to the open area in the garden that she'd picked out. She offered him a wan smile. "Agnes used to like to lay out here in the sun."

Murphy squeezed her hand and kissed her cheek. "I bet she did."

Cora gently tugged her hand free from his grasp. "I better fix my face and open the shop."

Trinity caught up with her. The sweet girl said nothing, but her fathomless hazel eyes reflected her shared sorrow.

Cora wrapped her arm around Trinity's shoulders. "Would you feel up to working with me in the shop today? I think having you with me would really help." She sighed. "Otherwise…."

The girl slipped her arm around Cora's waist and nodded. "Sure. Working with you would help me too. Aunt C?" Trinity gazed up into Cora's face.

Cora smiled. "What, sweetie?"

"Is it okay if Stu or Gramps puts all of Agnes' stuff away, especially her bed?" The girl closed her eyes and blew out a long breath. "I think that would make being in the shop easier, for both of us. And after the shop closes, could we have a little service for Agnes before she's buried?"

Cora swallowed another surge of emotion and wrapped Trinity in a caring embrace. "Good idea, sweetie. We'll definitely have a little ceremony for Agnes after we close. I need to freshen up before we open. Why don't you ask either Stuart or your grandpa to go into the shop and get Agnes' bed."

Trinity was a godsend. She brightened up the shop with her smile and the customers adored her. Business was brisk and the day passed quickly.

After locking the door, Cora and Trinity joined Murphy and Stuart outside in the backyard. Cora clasped her hands tightly and looked on as Murphy knelt on the ground and carefully placed Agnes' makeshift casket into the ample hole he and Stuart had dug.

Trinity referred to the screen of her phone and performed a short service. She grabbed a handful of loose dirt from the pile next to the grave, and her solemn gaze swept over the three of them.

Cora plunged her hand into the moist, dark soil, taking comfort in its earthy fragrance. She dropped her handful on the box, wincing at the finality of the sound. "Ashes to ashes. Dust to dust."

Trinity was next. "We'll miss you, Agnes, kitty. May you enjoy frolicking with your other cat friends who've crossed over the rainbow bridge."

Stuart cast his handful following Trinity. "I'm sorry we didn't get along. Rest in peace."

Murphy held his fist out over the opening. He opened his fingers and the dirt cascaded down on top of the box. "Rest in peace, Agnes. You gave Cora much joy." He paused and glanced at his granddaughter. "And Trinity too."

Cora smiled into his sympathetic gray gaze. Considering

that her cat's last act had been sticking her claws into Murphy, his words were kind.

Her smile faded. She couldn't imagine her life without Agnes. Her spirited tortie had been an essential part of her daily routine. Maybe the cat had sensed the winds of change when Cora had put the shop up for sale.

❦

Murphy grunted and lifted another heavy shovelful of dirt. They were almost done filling in the cat's grave.

Stuart wiped his brow with his handkerchief. "I'm getting too old for this crap. And to think I'm doing this for that damn cat." He raised his eyes heavenward. "Jesse, I know you're laughing your ass off at this ironic turn of events."

Murphy leaned on his shovel and looked at the lean silver-haired man. Stuart's face was beet red with exertion.

Stuart sighed and scooped up another load of dirt. "Jesse was an agnostic." He gave Murphy a wry smile. "I'm sure you knew that."

No, he hadn't known much about his dear brother at all, Murphy mused sadly. "So, Stuart, are you religious?"

Stuart nodded and groaned as he lifted his shovel and turned it over to let the dirt loose. "Yeah, I was raised Catholic." He grinned and plunged his shovel back into the mound. "That says it all. It's so flipping ingrained. I even went to Sunday mass after I realized I was gay, before I met Father Tom at my parish church and made one holy helluva confession."

For some reason Murphy found that hilarious. He laughed and heaved a final load of dirt into the hole. "One holy helluva confession." He gave Stuart a companionable smile. "That's rich, man. I love that. Yeah, our parents nearly came unglued when Jesse told them he didn't believe in the Methodist Church, or any church for that matter."

Murphy used his shovel to level the dirt. "I became Catholic when I married Nan. So we shocked them twice. Dad more than Mom." He sighed with relief and grinned at Stuart. "I think we're finished. I'm parched. Let's go get something cold to drink."

They trudged up the steps to the back porch. Stuart leaned his shovel inside the doorway. "Don't let me forget this."

Murphy propped Cora's shovel next to it. "Oh, don't worry, I won't. I'll wash and oil both of them as soon as we get back to the house. I'll clean Cora's as best I can."

He shook his head with a fond smile. "I'll skip the lecture I was going to give her."

They stomped toward the kitchen and Stuart sniffed appreciatively. "I think I smell cookies."

Murphy tagged behind and made a detour into the bathroom to wash his hands. "I'll take anything to drink as long as it's cold."

Trinity and Cora served them tall, frosted glasses of iced tea with the cookies. Afterwards, Trinity and Stuart headed across the street, each bearing a shovel.

Cora put her hand on Murphy's arm as he was turning toward the door. He slid his hand beneath her soft hair and cupped the warm skin of her nape.

She closed her eyes and sighed deeply. "I love it when you do that."

He grinned and pressed a gentle kiss on her forehead.

She wrapped her arms around his neck and kissed him softly. "Thank you."

"You're welcome, Cora Rose. Thank you for asking Trinity to help you in the shop today. She loved working with you and it took her mind off the cat's death."

"Murphy, will you?" Cora stopped and lowered her head. She straightened her shoulders and lifted her face to his.

"Will you please come over later? I don't want to be alone tonight."

Murphy tugged her against his chest and kissed her. She smelled sweet, like the inside of a bakery. He didn't want to think about what he smelled like. "I'll be over after I take a shower."

"Murphy."

He smiled down and tucked a lock of hair behind her ear.

"Murphy, I love you."

Her brown eyes had grown enormous, her lips were slightly parted, her expression utterly transparent.

He couldn't talk. His throat was too tight. Pressure built behind his eyes. The only time he'd witnessed her face this way, heard her voice this tender had been with Davey. How many times had he fantasized about this moment? Tilting her chin, he reverently pressed his lips against hers. Gazing into her lovely face, he smiled. "I love you, too, Cora Rose. I've always loved you."

Murphy meant every word he'd said, but the unbidden image of the *Stargazer* rose in his mind. How could he commit to his relationship with Cora Rose and follow his dream of sailing around the world? Cupping the back of her head, he kissed her again. He would persuade her to come with him.

CHAPTER SEVENTEEN

*C*ora sat at her kitchen table and absently sipped a steaming cup of herbal tea. She gnawed on her lower lip. She'd taken a long, hot bath, hoping it would soothe her frayed nerves and pass the time until Murphy arrived.

Clad in her long nightgown and light robe, Cora looked down at her bare feet and breathed a sad sigh. Agnes would've been curling her warm furry body around her legs and licking her toes. Tonight, without the cat underfoot, the kitchen was too quiet and too empty.

Shannan's approaching arrival signaled Murphy's departure. He would be leaving soon. This afternoon Cora had declared her love for him, and he'd professed his love for her, but would their devotion for each other be enough to maintain a long-distance relationship?

Checking the time, she rose from the table and wandered out into the foyer. She'd left the front door unlocked in case he'd arrived while she'd been in the tub.

Footsteps echoed on the porch. The knob turned, and the door swung open. Murphy stepped inside, gripping a green gym bag. He dropped the bag, opened his arms and gave her a broad smile. "Come here, my love."

Cora laid her head on his shoulder and closed her eyes. She held the man she loved in her arms. She kissed his warm lips and his minty breath gusted over her face. She refused to think ahead and dwell on their inevitable separation. At this moment, all she wanted was one more night with Murphy.

"You smell good, Cora Rose."

She cherished the low tender note in his voice. Smiling, she inhaled his calming scent of lime and spice. "So do you."

He cradled her cheek, his gray eyes probing. "You told me you loved me. I didn't dream that, did I?"

Cora covered his hand with hers. "I do love you, Murphy. The only dream I want to have tonight is the very real dream of you lying beside me." She kissed the inside of his callused palm and laced her fingers in his. "Let's go to bed. I don't know about you, but I'm exhausted."

Upstairs, Cora turned back the covers while Murphy used the bathroom. She removed her robe, laid it carefully at the foot of the mattress, and crawled beneath the sheets.

Murphy came through the doorway wearing plaid pajama bottoms and a v-neck t-shirt. He laid his bag just inside the door and switched off the lamp.

Moonlight streamed through the open window, and the sound of the night breeze was a comforting lullaby.

The mattress gave beneath his weight.

Cora smiled and stretched her arms above her head. "I'm glad you like having the window open. I love the fresh air and I sleep better."

He turned toward her and his breath heated her face. "I sleep better with fresh air myself."

She scooted closer. Slipping her hand beneath his shirt, she rested her palm above his beating heart. "Thank you for coming over tonight. How's Trinity doing?"

Murphy sighed. "She's okay. Stuart's staying over." He

lifted Cora's hand and pressed his warm lips against each one of her fingers. "Stu's a good man. I'm glad he and Jesse found each other."

Cora smiled into Murphy's face. "Me, too."

Her earlier anxious thoughts returned. She rose on one elbow and gazed down. "So, after you take care of Jesse's estate, how long until you head back to San Francisco?"

Murphy's eyes were liquid in the moonlight. He sighed again and turned his head toward the window. "I don't know, Cora." He combed his fingers through her hair. "I used to think I'd be on the next flight out of Denver as soon as everything was taken care of. Actually, I'd even considered appointing Stuart as executor so I could leave sooner."

Cora was grateful Murphy had changed his mind and stayed. She was curious about his life in San Francisco. She needed images that she could picture in her mind after he'd returned home. "Tell me about your house."

Murphy laughed softly. "What do you want to know?"

She rested her head on his chest and closed her eyes. "I want to know whatever you want to tell me."

"I live in what they call the Avenues. It's the same house Nan and I bought when we first relocated." He chuckled wryly. "It was once termed a modest bungalow before housing prices skyrocketed. Shannan grew up there."

"Do Trinity and her mother—-live nearby?" Cora skimmed her fingers over the roughened texture of his skin. She wanted to memorize each detail for the future. For the alone times to come.

Murphy's chest rose and fell when he laughed. "They live in a much nicer, upscale Victorian. Shannan and Pat, when he's not overseas, have social obligations."

Cora nodded. She really didn't want to talk about Nan, or Shannan or even Trinity tonight. "So, what do you do now that you're retired? How long has it been?"

He trailed his fingers down her shoulder and inside the

lace-trimmed strap of her nightgown. Gooseflesh stippled her skin.

"Almost two years. I had a rough time at first, so I signed on for some pro bono work in the panhandle. It's taken me that long to get organized, tie up loose ends and buy my boat."

"Your boat?" Cora raised her head and looked down into his face. "What kind of boat?"

Murphy's teeth shone faintly in the moonlight. "She's a hybrid, a sailboat. She's a beauty."

He cupped his hand at the nape of her neck. "Almost as beautiful as you."

Cora would miss his kisses. She appreciated how they started feather-soft, and then became stronger, demanding her hungry response.

He groaned and nuzzled her jaw, her ear. "We can talk later."

She gave a soft, breathless laugh. "You'll fall asleep later. Tell me her name."

Murphy stroked her body, the curve of her hip. He hitched the nightgown up her leg, slid his hand under the fabric and stopped. "She's the *Stargazer*, the only other woman in my life besides you."

"The *Stargazer*." Cora pronounced it on a sigh, because his gentle, questing touches were igniting a deep, pleasured response in the pit of her belly.

She would miss these few intimate nights they shared together, miss the heat and strength of his body, miss the gratification he gave and she returned.

His daughter was flying in the day after tomorrow, and her arrival would change everything, not only because of Murphy, but because of Trinity. Cora envied the bond that anchored them together. *A family.*

She lay awake long after Murphy had drifted off. She'd missed an opportunity. She'd wanted to tell him again she loved him before his daughter arrived and everything changed.

❦

The next morning she was awakened by the robust aroma of fresh-brewed coffee. Dressed in jeans and a red shirt, Murphy sat on the bed holding out a steaming mug. "Rise and shine, beautiful."

Her eyes felt tired and gritty. She'd been awake most of the night, her thoughts troubled. She would be alone soon and she needed a plan.

She smiled and propped herself against the pillows. "Thanks." Accepting the cup, she cradled its heat gingerly. "How long have you been up?"

Murphy's gray eyes appeared thoughtful. He sipped his coffee. "I've been awake since sunrise. I lay next to you for a long time and watched you sleep."

Cora raised a hand to her messy hair. "Good Lord, why would you want to do that? I must look like a frightful mess. Did I snore?"

He laughed. "A little, but it's cute, and I won't ask you because I know I snore. Stuart texted me and said he and Trinity were going to Pearl's for breakfast and then they were planning to finish up in the basement."

He shrugged and gave her a crooked grin. "We might be done earlier than I expected. Stuart is still planning to have a celebration of life for Jesse, probably early next month."

He set down his mug on her bedside table and tilted her chin, holding her gaze, his gray eyes solemn.

Cora's spirits plummeted. Murphy would give her the good-bye speech. Wrap up the last few weeks in a tidy summation like one of his court cases.

"Cora Rose, look at me, please."

Embarrassing tears filled her eyes. She'd known this was coming.

His thumb swept the tear from her cheek. He took her cup and set it down beside his. When he spoke, his voice was soft. "I've been thinking."

She closed her eyes and nodded. She had a pretty good idea what he'd been thinking.

"Shhhh. Honey." He gently wiped her face with his soft handkerchief.

Cora couldn't bear to think of him leaving and the thousands of miles that would separate them. She wrapped her arms around his neck. Agnes was gone. Murphy would go back to his boat, and Trinity and her mother would return to San Francisco. Shannan wouldn't want a shop in this small Colorado town. Too much of a contrast from an exciting, vibrant life on the west coast. With Jesse gone, there was no reason for Stuart to stay in Spencer.

Buck up, Cora. She lifted her head and met Murphy's concerned gaze. "I'm fine. I'm still thinking about Agnes, that's all."

Liar.

He gently gripped her shoulders and studied her silently for a long moment. "I've been thinking. Would you consider coming to San Francisco with me?"

She read the apprehension in his eyes. His question was unexpected.

"San Francisco." She let the reality of his suggestion penetrate her consciousness.

He clasped her hands in his. "Yes, San Francisco. It's in the state of California."

Cora rolled her eyes and smiled. "I know where San Francisco is." She looked down at his hands, the veins standing out against his tanned skin. "For how long?"

Murphy's complexion deepened. His gaze shifted from

hers and a corner of his mouth lifted. "For as long as you can put up with me."

Cora felt torn. She was dedicated to finding her child. Yet, she couldn't bear to think of stepping out in her new life without Murphy. She forced a light laugh. "Be careful what you offer. I can put up with you for an awfully long time."

He grinned, and she was reminded of the mischievous boy she'd grown up with. "That's what I was hoping you'd say."

"I know Trinity will be overjoyed." Cora slanted him a wary glance. "What about Shannan?"

"Shannan will be happy for us." Murphy's confident tone was encouraging. "She's wanted me to find someone since a few years after her mother died."

His face turned serious. He brought both her hands up to his lips and kissed them. "I have something else I need to ask you, Cora. When you told me yesterday that you loved me, I spent the rest of the afternoon thinking about my love for you and how important our relationship is to me."

Murphy sighed. Releasing her hands, he rose from the bed and paced the floor. "Remember last night when I told you about my sailboat, the *Stargazer*?"

Recalling how his face had lit up at the mention of his boat, Cora's stomach tightened with apprehension. The breeze drifting in through the open window was still cool. She climbed over the mattress and reached for her robe. "Yes."

He stared down at her, his gray eyes pleading. "I haven't brought up my travel plans because in all honesty, I'd envisioned sailing around the world alone."

What? Cora bolted to her feet and clutched her robe at her chest. "Sailing around the world alone? Murphy Webster, what in god's green earth are you talking about?"

An exasperated sigh escaped him. He held his palm up to stop her. "Cora Rose, please sit down and hear me out."

Tying her robe, she sat on the edge of the bed, making an effort to understand his bewildering statement. "I'm listening."

Murphy flashed a crooked smile and sat beside her. "I've realized that I want to share everything with you, including sailing around the world aboard the *Stargazer*." He gently turned her face to his. "I love you, Cora Rose. Will you consider sailing with me to Hawaii, the South Pacific, and New Zealand?"

His hopeful, earnest expression deeply touched her. What he didn't know was she'd already planned to visit those places, but to share those desired experiences with this man that she loved was a dream realized.

Cora's heart yearned to say yes, but first she had one more important and urgent issue in her life to resolve. "Murphy, I love you. I want to say yes, but even if I sell the property and follow you to San Francisco, I won't leave the country. I don't want to be halfway around the world when the agency locates my child."

❧

A weight settled on his chest. Murphy nodded. He clasped his knees and stared down at the floor. He couldn't blame her for wanting to find her child. How could he insist she set aside her dream for his?

He wouldn't.

Cora grasped his hand, her brown eyes sincere, and her voice firm. "Honey, this is about my child. This isn't about David."

Murphy ruefully smiled to himself. How could it not be about Davey? Davey was the child's father. That was biology. But Murphy wouldn't argue with her. He wouldn't argue with her because he loved Cora Rose and he wanted her happiness.

"I know." He planted a gentle kiss on her lips and tucked her hair behind her ear. "I know how important finding your child is to you, and I understand you want to be available when the agency contacts you.

"And if you're willing to sail with me, I would be willing to wait until your child is located and matters between the two of you are resolved to your satisfaction."

He shrugged and gave her his most persuasive grin. "I can still take lessons and we can sail on short trips up and down the coast. We can wait for news of your child together. So, will you come to San Francisco and someday sail away with me?"

Cora laughed and gifted him with her brilliant smile that melted his heart. I've always wanted to travel to the South Seas, and I'd rather be out on the open seas with you than cooped up in an airplane." She rose and sat on his lap. Looping her arms around his neck, she leaned over and soundly kissed him. She rested her forehead against his. "If you will wait with me, my darling, I will wait with you."

CHAPTER EIGHTEEN

*T*rinity checked her phone and glanced out the window at the industrial landscape along the Interstate. The airport was about two hours away. "I'm glad the weather is good. Spencer looked beautiful this morning with the sun rising behind the mountains, don't you think, Gramps?"

"Yup."

Her grandfather was apparently preoccupied with thoughts of his own. She glanced at his profile against the morning sun streaming in through the car window. "You look younger today, Gramps, and extremely handsome."

An incredulous expression crossed his features and he turned to her. "Where in left field did that come from?"

"I think it's because you're in love."

Gramps glanced from the road over at her and grinned. "I think you're right, pookie." He laughed and shook his head. "About the I'm-in-love bit. I'm not so sure about the younger and more handsome bit."

Trinity slipped her phone out of her pocket and glanced at the blank display. No new notifications. She couldn't help checking. She was so tense.

She was happy for Gramps and Aunt C, but she was still sad about Agnes. Mom had repeatedly assured her that her kitties at home were as healthy and playful as they'd been when she'd left.

"Trinity."

"Yeah, what?"

"Check your phone and then check mine will you? I want to make sure we don't receive any last-minute texts from your mother, saying she missed her flight, or cancelled her flight, or such."

Trinity made a show of looking at her phone screen. "Nothing on mine."

She picked up Gramps' new phone and smiled. "Mom sent you a text. She says, 'Can't wait to see you either, Daddy. Love you. Heart emoji.'"

Gramps smiled and then returned his attention to the road. The wrinkles lining his forehead had smoothed out. "Even though your mother is a grown woman, she'll always be my little girl."

"I suppose." Trinity wished her dad felt that way about her. Maybe, after they'd moved to Spencer, Dad could change jobs and they could spend more time together.

She gripped her phone more tightly. She needed to distract herself from thinking and worrying so much. "Gramps, is it okay if I play a game on my phone for a little while? I have my earbuds."

Her grandfather's eyes never left the road. "I suppose, but I'll need you to help me navigate when we get closer to Denver."

Trinity smiled. "Thanks, Gramps."

It was a relief to take her mind off stressing about her mother's first impression of Spencer, the shop and Aunt C. She wanted Mom to love Spencer and the shop like she did, and hopefully make Aunt C an offer on the spot.

Trinity knew her mother well enough to know that Mom was hard to read and never made quick decisions.

Plugging in her earphones, she swept her finger over her screen. Now that she thought about it, Mom was a lot like Aunt C that way. Hard to read. Trinity was not sure what to expect. She didn't even want to think about her mom not liking the shop or not approving of Aunt C.

Mom might have raised her eyebrows at Aunt C's long skirts and baggy tops, but she looked entirely different now, and when she smiled at Gramps, she looked positively beautiful.

They stopped for gas and a potty break. Gramps got his coffee and Trinity got a soda for her queasy stomach. They pulled out of the station and back onto the busy Interstate.

She checked her phone screen and navigated Gramps' next connection to bypass the large mile-high city and connect directly to the airport.

Her grandfather frowned and slowed down as he navigated the car around the curving exit ramp.

A network of tracks and graffiti-clad rail cars nestled beneath the elevated highway. Large cement warehouses with colorful graphics dotted the landscape. Off to her right, the tall buildings of downtown Denver nestled in a soft cloud of stagnant air.

"I meant to ask you how you and Stuart did on the basement."

"The basement is finished. Stu even looked in the dark, creepy places, like under the stairs and in the storage room that he said was probably a fallout shelter."

Gramps laughed. "That was your great-grandma's root cellar. It was the designated place to go if we were under attack by the Russians."

Trinity stared. "Seriously? If we get nuked, fallout shelters aren't going to save us."

Her grandfather sipped his coffee and kept his eyes on the

road. "Things were simpler back when I was a kid. You're right. Our nuclear capability and that of foreign nations is greater and more deadly."

"Anyway, it was a dark, creepy room full of spiders, and Stu said there probably were even some snakes down there." Trinity shuddered. "We still have the attic and great-grand-ma's cedar chest to sort through. Mom might want to look through the chest and see what her grandma saved."

Gramps checked the rear-view mirror and sighed. "Dammit. That guy's going to drive right up my ass."

Trinity sighed and plugged in her earbuds. Gramps was stressing out about the traffic and she didn't want to hear it. She wanted to focus on maintaining a positive attitude. The Universe tended to reflect one's thoughts and feelings, and she wished with all her heart that everything in her life today reflected the positive.

Inhaling a deep breath, she thumbed a message to Mom. Her mother would read it after her plane touched down.

Welcome to beautiful Colorado, Mom. Can't wait to see you!
Kissy-face emoji, heart emoji, cat emoji

* * *

Murphy scanned the curb at arrivals. He drove slowly, looking for his daughter.

"There she is, Gramps!" Trinity's voice was high and shrill with excitement.

All the curb space was already taken with a knot of vehicles. Murphy sighed and angled the car over as close as he dared to the vehicle in the front. He refused to circle around again. It was about a ten-minute trip.

Trinity was right. There was Shannan. Tall and beautiful, dressed smartly in slacks and a tailored jacket with one of her ever-present neck scarves.

He got out. The cool air smelled of exhaust and echoed with the sound of engines accelerating and idling.

He hugged his daughter and hefted her carry-on into the back of the Prius.

Trinity had moved to the rear seat.

"Thanks, Dad." Shannan kissed his cheek and turned to look behind her.

"I got your message, pumpkin. Thanks."

Glancing in the rear-view mirror, Trinity's face positively glowed. Murphy grinned happily. Sometimes the two of them were at each other's throats.

He glanced over at his daughter. He'd missed her, too. "Are you hungry?"

She turned her large, brown eyes to his and smiled. "A little. My flight left so darn early, I slept most of the way. I really haven't had much time to work up an appetite, but something to take the edge off would be nice."

Murphy turned his attention to the highway. They'd stop along the way and grab a bite before heading back to Spencer.

He had to admit he was a little apprehensive about Shannan meeting Cora. Sometimes with women, it was hard to tell. Recently, Shannan had been after him to socialize more, but he wasn't sure how his daughter would react to the news that he'd fallen in love. Truth be told, he was feeling completely out of his element.

Driving, he was content to listen to his daughter and granddaughter catch up, until their conversation melded into a pleasant white noise.

His memory returned to the past two nights he'd spent with Cora. Murphy hadn't realized how starved he'd been for affection. How badly he'd craved a woman's touch. The pleasure he took in Cora's kisses and caresses, and the pleasure of kissing and caressing her in return.

Shannan's voice and her accompanying question startled
Murphy out of his pleasant thoughts.

"What's this about Trinity telling me you're in love?"

Murphy stole a fleeting glance at his daughter's mildly
curious expression. His face heated and he laughed. "It's
crazy, but it's true. I've known Cora practically my whole
life, and as we've gotten reacquainted one thing naturally led
to another."

He glanced in the rear-view mirror and winked at his
granddaughter.

Trinity grinned back at him, her hazel eyes twinkling.

❧

Cora paced around the shop and wished a customer would
come in so she could think of something else besides the
gaping empty space on the counter where Agnes used to
sleep. She hadn't realized how often she'd confided in her
beloved tortie. Now, she had no Agnes to tell her worries to.
In spite of Murphy's confident assurances, she dreaded
Shannan's arrival.

What would the woman think of her? What would she
think about her too-cluttered shop, her too-cluttered
kitchen, even though she and Trinity had packed and
straightened and thoroughly cleaned the room?

Cora frowned and strode over to an arrangement of
china. She straightened the stacked plates and turned all the
cup handles in the same direction.

Sighing, she rubbed her arm in a soothing motion as she
walked throughout her displays, inspecting them with her
newly-developed critical eye.

She smiled and wandered over to the window and gazed
out. Her garden was probably one of the highlights of this
place. The roses were in bloom. She closed her eyes. She
could almost smell their sweet perfume from here. Shannan

couldn't help but love the garden. Cora swallowed and her gaze moved to the gnarled apple tree. Shannan was Murphy's daughter, and probably a large part of his life. Seriously, as Trinity would say, where did Cora fit into his life?

Murphy had assured her that she'd fit in seamlessly between his daughter, his granddaughter and the *Stargazer*. He'd asked her to join him on a cruise around the world. He'd said he'd wait, but after checking her email this morning she still hadn't heard anything from the agency about her child's whereabouts.

The bell over the entrance rang, jolting her out of her thoughts. Cora took a deep breath and fixed a welcoming smile on her face.

Trinity appeared, practically towing a tall, slender woman toward her. "Aunt C, this is my mom, Shannan. Mom this is Aunt C."

The first feature of Shannan's that Cora noticed were her expressive brown eyes, highlighted with artfully applied cosmetics. Trinity had been right. Her mother was excellent with makeup.

Shannan gave her daughter an indulgent smile and kissed her cheek. "Thanks, pumpkin. I can take it from here."

She walked confidently up to Cora and extended her hand. Cora noted her French-manicured fingers. "I'm Shannan Thompson." She smiled and gave a lilting laugh. "Trinity has told me so much about you and your shop, I feel as though I already know you."

Cora shook Shannan's hand and smiled in return. "Your daughter has brought a burst of fresh air into my life."

She glimpsed Murphy standing behind Trinity, his hands resting on his granddaughter's shoulders. His smiling gaze was meant to reassure her, but so much depended on what Shannan thought.

The elegant woman was cordial enough, but Cora couldn't tell what she was thinking. Cora had acquired a wealth of experience with people over the years, and first impressions were vital in the business world. "Trinity tells me you have a fondness for antiques and that you've been looking for a shop of your own."

Shannan nodded. "I've always loved the history behind antiques and the cultures they reflect. Antiques play a large role in my decorating business. Many of my clients prefer collectibles to modern objects."

Cora watched Shannan move gracefully around the shop, noting the displays. She paused in front of the window overlooking the backyard. "Oh!" Her voice held a note of delighted pleasure. Shannan turned to face her. Trinity had drawn close to Cora's side. "You were right, pumpkin. The garden is gorgeous."

Her lovely brown eyes gazed into Cora's. "I'd love to look outside if that's okay with you?"

"Of course." Cora straightened her shoulders and led the way to her kitchen.

CHAPTER NINETEEN

*M*urphy grinned and gave Cora a quick thumbs-up as he trailed Shannan and Trinity through the kitchen and out the back door to the garden.

Cora had lifted her chin in response. The only indication that she was a bundle of nerves was her telling habit of rubbing her hands together.

Trinity led Shannan over to Agnes' grave. The two of them were occupied in a discussion and oblivious to him. Cora needed reassurance and he longed to hold her.

Murphy doubled back and slipped his arms around her. He buried his face in the familiar hollow of her neck. The holy place, he liked to think of it. "Shannan loved the fresh flowers in the hall. The shop looks nice and I don't even recognize the kitchen."

She gave him a breathless laugh. "The flowers were Trinity's idea."

Lifting his head, he gently rubbed his thumb over the space between her brows and whispered, "Don't worry. It's all good, Cora Rose."

She nodded and closed her eyes for a long minute. "I suppose I should make a pot of tea."

He winked and reverently pressed his lips to hers. "I suppose you should."

Minutes later, while Cora brewed tea and set out a plate of cookies, Murphy peeked out the back door.

Shannan and Trinity stood under the apple tree. His daughter caught sight of him and waved him over.

Murphy rubbed the back of his neck. Shannan was going to ask for his advice. He didn't mind, but he longed to return to the previous two days, when it had been only him and Cora eating breakfast in her kitchen, watching the rising sun filter through the trees and the world come alive.

With a deep sigh, he plunged his hands in his pockets and slowly descended the wooden steps leading down to the yard.

"Hey, Dad." Shannan glanced from him to Trinity, whose hazel eyes shone with excitement. She planted a tender kiss on Trinity's cheek and gave her daughter a quick hug. "I want to talk to Gramps for a few minutes. Why don't you ask Cora if she needs any help?"

Trinity frowned and looked to him for confirmation.

Murphy struggled to remain neutral. He'd formed a close bond with his granddaughter over the last couple of weeks, but he wasn't about to contradict Shannan. "Pookie, Cora may not need your help, but I'm sure she'd love your company."

Trinity slanted him a ghost of a smile before jogging across the lawn and up the steps.

Murphy squinted at the apple tree. They'd be finished with the house and the estate soon. He was going to miss those days and the times he'd shared with his precious granddaughter.

Shannan gripped his hand firmly. "Dad. What do you think of the price? It seems reasonable, given the condition of the interior and the shop." She sighed and looked around her. "Even though it's going to take extensive updating, I think this is the one." She shook her head. "I can't believe I'm even thinking about buying this place. It's thousands of miles from San Francisco and my business. Patrick needs the proximity of an international airport."

Murphy kissed her soft cheek and caught a whiff of her favorite musky perfume.

Shannan swept her arm around the garden. "Tell me what you think of this place as an investment." Her laugh was incredulous. "More than an investment, this would be our new home—-a plus concerning Trinity and her radical friends. Of course, I still need to talk to Patrick." A sour look crossed her face. "Although I don't know why. He's away from home most of the time anyway."

Murphy hated to see his little girl unhappy. He had opinions of his own and he'd had to bite his tongue regarding his son-in-law's extended absences. He gave his daughter a quick hug and tugged a lock of her stylish hair. "Stuart and I listed the house with Cora's realtor. She seems knowledgeable and has a good grasp of real estate values in the Spencer area. I think Cora's property is reasonably priced and the house is solid, structure wise. You'd want an inspection, along with an appraisal of course, but yes, I'd say it was a good investment."

"Thanks, Dad." She graced him with her familiar heart-tugging smile and wrapped her arms around his neck. She sighed and rested her head against his shoulder. "I've missed you, and I've missed Trinity too."

He caught another whiff of her expensive perfume. Beneath her sophisticated persona Shannan was still his doe-eyed little girl, clutching her baby doll and giggling at his lame knock-knock jokes.

Murphy gazed at his beautiful daughter and felt a pang of remorse. He and Nan should have told Shannan she was adopted. At the thought of sitting down with her and telling her now, a sick feeling of dread churned in the pit of his stomach. So much was at stake. The night he'd confided Shannan's adoption to Cora, the closed expression on Cora's face had said it all. Shannan was entitled to the truth regarding her birth.

His daughter playfully poked his shoulder. "Cora is pretty and she seems very nice. You told me you were in love, Dad, but both of you have got it bad. You can't take your eyes off each other."

Murphy chuckled and lightly pinched her cheek. He couldn't contain his grin. "Life is full of surprises. Cora has been good for me. She's brought out my better side." Remembering Nan, he sobered and searched his daughter's sympathetic features. "You know I loved your mother."

Shannan rubbed his back. "I know, Daddy, but you've been lonely, especially since you retired. You've been so obsessed with your boat and your trip. I was worried you'd stick a sailor's cap on your head, a corncob pipe in your mouth and go sailing off into the sunset, leaving us behind." She kissed his cheek. "At least Colorado is closer than the South Pacific."

His daughter was still opposed to his cruise. He was about to make her day a little brighter, thanks to Cora. Murphy crossed his arms and rocked back on his heels. "I have news for you. Cora has agreed to come to San Francisco with me and, you'll be happy to know, she's talked me into post-poning our sailing date.

"We still intend to cruise to the South Pacific, but I want to take more sailing lessons and get more experience under my belt. In the meantime, we plan to sail on shorter excur-sions off the coast."

Shannan planted her hands on her hips and tilted her head. A jubilant grin lifted the corners of her mouth. "I'm glad Cora talked some sense into your hard head. I like her better by the minute."

Murphy rolled his eyes. "Don't act so damn happy."

He thought of Trinity and her high hopes. How much she was counting on Shannan's decision. "Trinity loves it here," Murphy said. "She's gone so far as to check out the local high school and seems content with the absence of big city conveniences."

Shannan was strolling through the garden, an absent smile on her face. She bent to sniff a scarlet rose. "I know. I can tell by her texts. The mountains are beautiful, but San Francisco...."

Murphy's heart swelled with pride. Shannan had started her own business and had become quite successful. "You do have your own sphere of influence there, your friends and connections."

She chewed on her lower lip thoughtfully. "We have a great website and online presence. I could always fly out when it was necessary, and Astrid is a competent manager. The Attic has a high profile as a tourist destination in Colorado and the mountain states. I'm thinking very seriously about making an offer, but I want to see the rest of the house and talk more to the realtor."

Shannan linked her arm through his. "Let's go back inside. I'm dying to taste those lemon cookies Trinity's been raving about."

Inside the warm, fragrant kitchen, the table was set with delicate china that Murphy had never seen before. Linen napkins graced the space next to the plates, and a heaped platter of cookies dominated the center.

Trinity was frowning in concentration as she poured steaming water from the tea kettle into a second intricately-flowered teapot. "Aunt C wanted me to brew a pot of herbal tea, too. She had to help a customer. She said that I was to act as hostess until she returned."

"Shannan stood next to him, her attention wandering around the room, her voice pensive. "The shop is fine for now. Cora's eclectic displays are charming and prominently featured in brochures and the online tourist sites I researched. They appear to be a large part of The Attic's brand that I'd want to retain. Eventually, I'd want to expand into the living quarters and stagger the displays further apart to showcase particular objects." She sighed and ran her hand over the wall of metal cupboards above the counter. "But first, I'd have to gut this kitchen."

Trinity set the kettle back on the gas burner. "You should've seen the kitchen before Aunt Cora and I worked on it. Huh, Gramps?"

Murphy leaned against the counter, staring at the fancy table setting. Now that the introductions had been made and the ladies seemed to be getting along, he was tempted to text Stuart and suggest they take in a baseball game over a pitcher of beer at the Wild Card. He smiled at his granddaughter. "You did a great job, pookie. Cora said she couldn't have done it without you. She told me what a hard worker you are."

"She is a hard worker." Cora came bustling back into the kitchen. She breezed past him and he inhaled a tantalizing trace of her flowery scent.

"The tea's brewing," Trinity declared, gazing at the three of them. She flashed the screen of her phone. "I set the timer."

"Perfect." Cora indicated a chair. "Shannan, if you'd like to take a seat." Cora's beautiful dark eyes rested on him. "Murphy."

Murphy winked at her and sat down at the table in his accustomed spot. He cautiously lifted the small, fragile cup from its equally fragile saucer. "Where'd you get the fancy dishes?"

Cora flashed him a shy smile. "Grandma Binney gave them to me for my hope chest."

The words were barely out of her mouth when the bell over the door rang, announcing more customers. She glanced apologetically at Shannan. "This time of year business is pretty brisk. Go ahead with your tea, and I'll join you as soon as I can."

"That's a good thing." Shannan rose. "Do you mind if I go with you and browse while you assist your customers? I'd like to get an idea of the clientele and foot traffic."

Murphy caught the momentary frown of anxiety that passed over Cora's face, but she recovered with a confident, gracious smile. "Of course."

The two women walked out of the kitchen, leaving Murphy sitting at the table and Trinity standing near the stove. Trinity's timer dinged. She sighed and silenced her phone. "Tea's done. You want some, Gramps?"

Her hazel eyes were cloudy with disappointment. Before he had a chance to speak, she poured him a cup. She poured herself one and collapsed onto her chair. "By the time they come back, the tea will be cold, and then another bunch of customers will straggle in." She uttered a dramatic sigh and stared up at the ceiling. "Aunt C had this all planned out. It was going to be so nice for Mom, like a little welcome ceremony."

Murphy lifted a lemon cookie from the plate and took a tangy bite. He washed it down with one swallow of tea that nearly emptied the cup. "Pookie. Trust me. Your mother will be more impressed with the busyness of the shop than this little ceremony. Not that this isn't very nice. It is. You did an excellent job, cleaning up the kitchen and acting as hostess, and I know you're frustrated."

Trinity drank her tea and gazed around the room. "Yeah, but you're right, Gramps. Mom is definitely more interested in 'possible revenue.'"

Her voice did an accurate imitation of Shannan's.

Murphy chuckled and drained his cup. This tiny thing held hardly anything, and he was afraid he'd drop it and break Cora's heirloom.

"Gramps?"

Murphy carefully set his cup down in its saucer. His granddaughter's face was tight with concern. "What, pookie?"

Trinity twisted her ringed fingers. "Do you think Mom likes the shop and the house?"

Before Murphy could phrase his reply, Trinity's expression morphed into youthful exuberance.

"I know she loves the garden." His granddaughter bounced to her feet and leaned against the sink. She peered out the window overlooking the yard. "I love it too. Mom said there was nothing in the garden that she'd change."

Trinity turned back to face him, her forehead creasing, her arms wrapped tightly around her petite frame.

He had a fierce desire to hold and protect her from all the future tragedies and disappointments life would hand her.

"Gramps."

Her exasperated tone roused him from his thoughts. He straightened and reached for another cookie. "What?"

"What does Mom think about the house? Did she say anything to you?"

Murphy rubbed his mouth. He hoped the customers would leave the shop soon so Cora and Shannan would return and distract his edgy granddaughter. "Honey, your mother is a shrewd businesswoman. She wants to take a look around, and she wants to talk to Cora's realtor."

He didn't want to tell Trinity that her mother thought this was the shop she'd been looking for, or that she was serious enough about it to contact Trinity's father. Murphy didn't want his sweet granddaughter's hopes dashed, if this fell through.

"I know." Trinity clasped her hands and heaved another sigh. "It's just that I like this place so much." She gazed around the kitchen. "I don't know how to say this, but it's as though I belong here."

"I know, pookie. I know."

He was relieved when Cora and Shannan returned to the kitchen, deep in conversation about the shop and tracking sales.

Trinity recovered her cheerful spirits. She insisted that Cora and Shannan sit down while she poured the tea.

Murphy decided he'd pass on more tea and beg off on the ladies with the excuse that he wanted to check in with Stuart.

✦

Gramps polished off his third cookie and wiped his mouth with his napkin. "If you ladies don't mind, I'm going to head back across the street and see how Stuart is coming along with the closets."

"Careful, Murphy. You're practically knocking over the chair." Aunt C was half laughing, and her face was all pink and pretty. She packed up the leftover cookies and put them in the tin. "Here, take these over to Stuart."

She arched a delicate brow as she slipped her arm through Gramps' and walked him to the front door. "Tell him they taste better with milk than scotch."

Trinity giggled and nibbled on her cookie as she watched her mother take her first bite.

Shannan nodded at her as she chewed. She sipped her tea. "You're right, pumpkin. They're yummy. Not too sweet, with a tart aftertaste."

After she'd finished her cookie, Mom stood and took her cup and saucer over to the sink.

"Cora, the tea was lovely, thank you. If you wouldn't mind, I'd like to see the rest of the living quarters upstairs."

"Of course." Aunt C's voice was pretty straightforward, but she was biting her lip as she carried one of the teapots over to the sink.

Trinity cleared her own place. "I can show Mom the upstairs."

Aunt C smiled and wrapped an arm around her shoulders. "That's kind of you to offer, sweetie, but I was going to ask if you wouldn't mind watching the shop while I show your mom the rest of the house."

Mom chimed in with an approving smile. "Cora gave you glowing references. She said the customers loved your warm and outgoing personality, and you were an asset to the business."

"I meant every word." Cora gave Trinity a quick hug before releasing her and leading Mom up the back stairs.

Trinity basked in Mom's approval and Aunt C's praise. She'd enjoyed working in the shop and had come up with a couple of ideas for promotion on social media. Another thought that she was turning over in her mind concerned her black cat, Binx. He was pretty mellow and although Agnes was irreplaceable, Trinity was thinking Binx could be the shop's new kitty.

Trinity cleaned up the kitchen and carefully washed the delicate china. She'd finished drying the last cup when the bell over the door rang.

She hoped that Mom liked the rest of the living quarters. She and Aunt C had worked extra hard de-cluttering and staging the rooms upstairs. Waiting was the hardest part of her life right now. What if she and Aunt C did all that work and got their hopes up for nothing?

Trinity squared her shoulders, fixed a welcoming smile on her face and went out to greet the shop's customers.

CHAPTER TWENTY

*C*ora leaned against her kitchen sink clutching the
PDF she'd printed. She read the letter for the
umpteenth time. She couldn't wrap her mind around what
the message implied. The detective agency had located her
daughter and had provided the woman's business address
and phone.

Someone was rapping on her door and cranking the old-
fashioned doorbell. Startled, Cora glanced at the time. Ten
minutes past. She had never heard the clocks chime the hour.
After checking her email, she'd neglected to switch on the
sign and open to the public.

Dropping the paper on the table, Cora rushed to answer
the door.

Her daughter stood on the threshold.

Shannan Webster Thompson. The name the agency had
provided. Her business address was located in San Francisco,
California.

If the agency had their facts straight, this elegant, accomplished woman was her child, grown with a daughter of her
own. Trinity was her granddaughter. That would explain the

girl's mercurial smile and her curly black hair, so much like David's.

David was her grandfather, not Murphy.

Both Shannan and Trinity were directly descended from David. Murphy would be devastated.

Shannan's smile faded. "Cora, you don't look well. Is everything all right?"

Cora clapped her hand over her mouth and fought back sudden tears. No. Everything was not all right. How could something so joyful like finally locating her baby girl tip her life upside down?

She rubbed her watering eyes. "I'm sorry. I hardly slept last night and I know this sounds silly, but I'm—-I'm missing my damn cat."

"Oh Cora, I'm sorry about Agnes," Shannan said, her voice laced with sympathy. I know the feeling. Trinity's probably told you about our cats."

Three vehicles parked at the curb. Brightly-clad ladies wearing red hats poured out in a steady stream. Cora closed her eyes. The Red Hat group from Longmont. They'd called last week to give her a head's up, and they were rapidly approaching, chattering in merry anticipation as they climbed the steps to the porch.

Shannan cradled the cookie tin against her side and brandished the realtor's folder in her other hand, a resigned expression in her beautifully made-up brown eyes. "It looks like my exciting news will have to wait, but I'd love to help you in the shop if you don't mind."

Her daughter's radiant face pierced Cora's heart. After so many lost years, this was not how she'd imagined their reunion.

Cora stepped aside and launched into her patented greeting, acutely aware of Shannan waiting her turn to follow the group inside. "Good morning, ladies. Welcome to Aunt Cora's Attic where treasures lie in wait to be discovered."

The women crowded in the hall, marveling at the shop's charming interior and examining the artfully arranged pictures hanging on the walls.

Shannan flashed Cora a reassuring smile. "I'll drop this stuff in the kitchen and be right in to help you."

She'd left the letter on the table! Shannan would be sure to see it. Please, God, she can't find out that way! Cora rushed after Shannan, only pausing long enough to excuse herself to the group's hostess.

Too late! The sheet of paper rattled in Shannan's trembling hands. She looked up from the bold letterhead, incredulity in her shocked gaze.

Cora rubbed her hands together. "Shannan, I am sorry. I didn't expect…." She swallowed and closed her eyes. "Please, forgive me."

Her voice broke. Cora shook her head, unable to continue.

Shannan's complexion paled and her nostrils flared. "Does my dad know about this?" Her fist crumpled the paper. She slowly paced the room as she read the letter again, her free hand absently rubbing her arm.

"Murphy knew I'd been looking for you," Cora said, "but I don't think he knew I was your mother. Honey, none of us did."

"Well, he definitely knew I was adopted." Shannan waved the paper, her brown eyes flashing. "May I take this copy and leave by the back door?"

"Of course," said Cora. "I'll close the shop—-"

"Please don't." Shannan attempted a smile and failed. "Please…."

Dread knotted Cora's stomach. Murphy was about to be blindsided by her equally blindsided daughter.

❧

Murphy leaned precariously on the stepladder propped in front of the closet in what had once been his bedroom. The last carton on the shelf was tucked in the far corner beyond his fingertips.

His childhood relics had disappeared years ago. Most of the items he'd cleared off the shelf had been dusty shoeboxes containing greeting cards and family photos Mom had collected. Murphy had stacked them in a clear plastic tote bound for the temporary storage unit he'd rented.

The house smelled like fresh paint and was stripped clean of Jesse's personal belongings. The movers were scheduled for the end of next week.

Murphy still hoped to find the slingshot, but his long-lost treasure hadn't turned up yet. Trinity was working in the attic, listening to her music and happy to be finished with the boring office. Maybe she'd run across the toy. God knew why he was so obsessed with the slingshot. Murphy smiled. Sentimental, he supposed.

He expected there'd be a celebration tonight. Late yesterday, Shannan had told him in the strictest of confidence that she'd talked to Pat and planned to make an offer on Cora's property in the morning. She didn't want Trinity to know until she was reasonably sure her offer would be accepted.

A door slammed. Rapid footsteps ascended the stairs. Shannan appeared in the doorway. "What are you doing? Get down off that ladder now before you break your neck."

The sharp, trembling pitch of his daughter's voice disturbed him. Murphy clutched the shelf with both hands to steady himself.

"Dammit, Shannan. What's wrong?"

"Where's Trinity?"

"Up in the attic working, why?" Murphy turned to gaze down into his daughter's pale, drawn face.

"What about Stuart?" Shannan's dark eyes were enormous. She clenched a piece of paper in her fist.

Murphy slowly descended to the floor. The back of his neck tingled, and he rubbed at the sensation. "What's wrong?"

"Where is Stuart?"

"Stuart called this morning. He'll be over later this afternoon. He had some business to attend to." Murphy opened his arms and stepped closer to hug her. "Honey, what's wrong? Has something happened to Pat?"

She held a palm up to stop him. "I'm sure Patrick is fine." Shannan's eyes filled with tears. She bit her lip and thrust the paper at Murphy. "Read this and tell me exactly what it means."

She closed the bedroom door and leaned back against it, her arms tightly folded across her chest.

Murphy took the paper and reached into his pocket for his glasses.

Shannan angrily dashed away the tear trailing down her cheek. "Where are your glasses, Dad? Or whoever you are."

"What the hell is that supposed to mean?" Murphy's pulse accelerated. He turned and snatched his readers off the dresser. "They're right here."

He read the letter. He read the letter again. Shock, guilt and fear coiled in his gut. He glanced at his daughter's stricken face and extended his hand. Shannan was Cora's child she'd given up for adoption?

"Shannan, Cora had no right to—-"

"Cora didn't do anything except look for the baby she'd given up for adoption. She had no idea that I was coming. I had to bang on the door. She was late opening the shop and was obviously upset."

Shannan rubbed her temple. "She didn't know I would go into the kitchen and see the letter lying on the table. She was as shocked as I was.

"You and Mom never told me I was adopted. Why?"

Nausea rolled over Murphy in a wave. Yesterday,

standing with her in the backyard rose as an ugly reminder. He should have told her last night when she'd talked to him about buying the shop. But, she'd been so excited and happy. "Shannan, please believe me, your mother and I never meant to hurt you. Honey, it was a closed adoption. We didn't know Cora was your mother. We didn't know who your parents were. All we knew was how happy we were when we brought you home and how much we loved you. Times were different."

Shannan's voice rose hysterically. "Didn't the two of you ever think I might find out?" She waved her arm. "With the ancestry websites and all the other information on the Internet, it never crossed your minds?"

"Sweetheart, there was no Internet when you were born. I made a promise to your mother."

"Mom is dead." Shannan's laugh bore an alarming edge. "Oh, wait, that's not true. My mother lives across the street in the house I just put earnest money down on."

❦

Trinity had been working most of the morning on the far side of the attic, grouping neatly marked cartons for Gramps and Stu to carry downstairs. Mom still hadn't said anything about buying Aunt C's house and the shop. Granted, Mom had only inspected the premises yesterday, but the suspense was unbearable.

Aunt C was as nervous as she was, especially when Mom had peppered her with questions about the foundation, the plumbing and insulation.

Earlier this morning over coffee and cereal, Trinity had confided her worries about Aunt C and the shop to Gramps. He'd hugged her and shook his head with a fond smile. "I wish Cora wouldn't fret so much."

He'd winked at Trinity over his mug. "I think your

mother is pretty serious about buying The Attic, otherwise she wouldn't be wasting her time talking to the realtor this morning."

Trinity had squealed. She'd been so relieved and excited that she couldn't help herself.

Gramps had cupped his hand over his ear and made a face. "Jesus, Mary and Joseph, Trinity Grace, you nearly gave me a heart attack." He'd sighed and sipped his coffee, his expression totally serious. "Don't you dare tell your mother I said anything." He shook his finger at her. "And don't get your hopes up in the clouds. One of the hardest lessons you'll learn growing up is you have to wait and see what happens. You can't always force life to conform to your terms."

He'd pushed back from the table, rinsed his mug in the sink, and kissed the top of her head. "Now get your fanny up to the attic and start working before she gets back."

Trinity had grabbed her phone and earbuds off the bedside table in her room on the way up. Gramps' awesome news called for her victory playlist.

The tunes were peppy and upbeat with amazing guitar riffs. Work went fast. Trinity danced to the other side of the storage space and spotted a brown corduroy jacket draped over a tidy stack of boxes labeled Christmas decorations.

The coat looked as though it had been worn and forgotten. The ribbed garment was soft and emanated a faint woodsy scent. Maybe Jesse's?

Trinity checked the inside pocket and withdrew a bulky white envelope stamped and addressed to Gramps in San Francisco. She unearthed three yellow-wrapped butterscotch candies, two paperclips, a thick rubber band and a small key attached to a circular label. DESK was printed in precise black letters. Her breath hitched in her chest.

This had to be the key Gramps was looking for. Heart racing, Trinity flung the jacket over her arm. Clutching the envelope and the key, she clattered down the narrow stairs.

She skidded to an abrupt halt. The door to the room she'd been sleeping in was shut. Mom and Gramps were arguing. A sick feeling knotted her stomach as it always did when Dad was home and her parents argued.

Retreating a few steps, Trinity absently chewed on a finger. She knew better than to interrupt, but she glanced down at the coat still draped over her arm. Mom would be pissed, but Gramps would want to know.

She took a decisive breath and rapped on the door. "Gramps, I found the key you've been looking for. And there's a letter."

Silence. A muffled curse from her mother.

Bedsprings creaked. Gramps cleared his throat. "I'll look at everything later, pookie. Your mom and I are talking."

She hesitated. Gramps sounded so sad. Had something happened between him and Aunt C? "Gramps, are you okay?"

Her mother wrenched the door open, her face ashen, her mascara smeared beneath her eyes. "If you're finished in the attic, you can start packing. I'm booking us on the first available flight to San Francisco."

"What?" Panicky tears blurred her vision. "Mom, why are you crying? Tell me what's going on. Aren't you going to buy Aunt C's? Gramps said you went to the realtor's today."

"Trinity Grace, enough!"

Her mother was losing it. *She* was losing it. "Are you, or aren't you? I want to know!"

"That's enough, I said! We'll talk about this later. Now leave us alone and start packing. I need to talk to your grandfather."

Mom slammed the door in her face.

How could everything be perfect one minute and so crappy the next? Something terrible had happened, and apparently nobody thought she counted enough to share it with.

Defiant tears sprang to her eyes. She banged once on the door with her fist. "Excuse me, how can I pack when you won't let me in the room? You can fly back if you want to, but I'm staying with Gramps."

Weeping, Trinity slipped the key inside her pocket. She carried the jacket into Gramps' room and left the garment on the bed with the envelope tucked beneath the lapel. She wiped her teary eyes on her sleeve and wished Stu was here. He always listened and never judged her. Next to Gramps and Aunt C, Stu was the person she felt closest to.

She plucked a tissue from the box on the bedside table for her nose and headed for the stairs. Mom and Gramps were still going at each other. Trinity wanted to get as far away from that scene as possible.

Aunt C might need help in the shop, but Trinity didn't feel like smiling at customers and pretending it was a nice day. She'd miss Agnes curled up in her bed on the counter and, if Mom wasn't buying the shop, seeing the place would hurt too much.

She fingered the key in her pocket and slipped inside the office. Next to Aunt C's she had spent most of her time in this room. The bare walls reeked of paint, but the muted space was peaceful.

Trinity sat on the chair behind the desk and peered at the keyhole. What could possibly be in the desk drawer? Gramps had been almost as obsessed about finding the key as he was about the *Stargazer*.

There was only one way to find out. She retrieved the key from her pocket and inserted it into the tiny lock.

❧

Murphy flinched. He'd caught a brief glimpse of his grand-daughter's stricken face before Shannan had slammed the door so hard the frame rattled. He rubbed his stomach. His gut burned like hellfire. His daughter was hurting, and it was his fault.

Poor Trinity. She'd been so excited. She'd found the key he'd been looking for. He'd heard her excitement turn to concern, then panic and end up in anger. Murphy grunted and sat down hard on the bed. He dug into his pocket and popped two antacid tablets. "What do you mean you're flying back to San Francisco? You just got here."

Shannan closed her eyes and covered her mouth. Fresh tears rolled down her cheeks. "I just slammed the door in my daughter's face. I shouldn't have yelled at her. None of this is Trinity's fault. She looked so heartbroken."

Still staring at him in shocked bewilderment, Shannan raked her fingers through her hair. "What am I going to tell Trinity?" She folded her arms protectively around herself. "I had friends who knew they were adopted. You knew their parents. How could you and Mom lie to me my whole life?"

"We didn't lie, dammit! Murphy rubbed the back of his neck, remembering Cora's silent admonition the night of the band concert. She'd said nothing, but he'd read the censure in her glance.

His heart went out to his wounded daughter. "You were less than two weeks old when we brought you home. We considered you our flesh and blood. To be truthful, Shannan, years went by while you were growing up when your mom and I forgot that you were adopted at all.

"The first year after your mother died." He shrugged help-lessly. "I missed her so much. I worked as many hours as I could because I couldn't bear to think about her. You and Trinity were what held me together."

Shannan swiped her fingertips beneath her eyes, her voice weary. "I am flying home. We've taken on a high-main-tenance client who insists on dealing with me personally. I was going to break it to Trinity after the good news. I know how badly she wants me to buy the shop. I love the shop too.

I've made an offer." Shannan dropped her arms at her sides. "Now, I'm so confused. I don't know what I want to do."

Sniffling, she looked around the room. "I need a tissue. I'm going for a walk anyway. I need time alone to think."

"Here, take this." Murphy pulled his handkerchief out of his back pocket and extended it to her, as he'd done so many times while she was growing up.

"Oh, Daddy," she whispered, her voice a poignant echo of that little girl in pigtails. Shannan snatched the folded square of white cotton and pressed it to her nose. Choking back a sob, she ran out of the room.

Murphy closed his eyes and buried his face in his hands. The sultry air coming in through the open window heralded a storm.

He tried to mouth a quick plea to Almighty God, but he couldn't find the words. Prayer had always helped in the past, but right now, even God seemed remote.

The most important people in his life were slipping away from him. The key and the slingshot were trivial. Trinity had been right when she'd told him he couldn't talk to a boat. He'd gladly sacrifice the *Stargazer* and his 'round the world voyage for Shannan, Trinity and Cora. His cherished family.

Poor pookie. He couldn't tell her why he and her mother had been arguing, but he could give her a hug and tell her that he loved her. Since he and Shannan had occupied Trinity's room, Murphy climbed up to the attic. She might have taken refuge there. Or, she might have gone across the street to Cora's.

Murphy scrubbed a hand down his face. Cora Rose. He ached to wrap his arms around her and tell her how sorry he was. He'd denied Shannan the truth about her birth and the opportunity to look for her biological parents if that had been her choice.

Trinity wasn't upstairs, but Murphy discovered a brown jacket and a bulky white envelope lying on his bed. The letter was stamped and addressed to him in Jesse's distinctive script. Murphy's throat tightened. This letter could possibly be his brother's last words to him.

Murphy slipped his thumb under the flap and paused. Not here. He slowly descended the stairs and headed to the office. For some reason the room was calling to him. He stopped short in front of the closed door and broke into a relieved smile. He hadn't thought to look in the jacket for the key, but that didn't matter because he knew where to find both the key and his darling granddaughter.

CHAPTER TWENTY-ONE

*T*rinity turned the key and slid the drawer open. Nothing mysterious or valuable there. With a puzzled frown, she pulled out an old wooden slingshot and held the toy up in the light to read the faded lettering. "*WHAM-O?*" Okay. She set aside the item on the desk and withdrew a small red photo album.

Her stomach gurgled. She glanced at her phone. Lunchtime, but she didn't feel like eating thanks to Mother. From her pocket, she fished out the three pieces of candy she'd found in the jacket and lined them up on the desk. They were the same cellophane-wrapped butterscotch discs Nana used to keep in a candy dish on her buffet.

The lock clicked. Trinity jumped and turned around.

Gramps smiled, but his eyes looked sad. "Hi, pookie-poo. I thought I might find you in here."

She immediately went to him and hugged him tightly. She closed her eyes and rested her cheek against his beating heart. "I refuse to fly back to San Francisco with Mom. She's a witch! I'm staying here in Spencer with you."

Gramps rubbed her back and kissed the top of her head. His deep, soothing voice calmed the hurt, angry, and sad feelings swirling around in her chest. "Don't be so hard on your mom, pookie."

"I can't help it. She screamed at you. She screamed at me and slammed the door in my face. You and Mom are upset, but neither one of you will tell me why. I'm not a kid anymore."

"Honey, she loves you very much. She was mad at me and took her anger out on you. She told me she was sorry for the way she treated you. You know how she hates surprises? Well, today she got the surprise of her life."

"We all did," he added, in a voice so low Trinity barely heard him.

"What do you mean? It doesn't sound like a good surprise." She stepped back and looked up at him.

He kissed the top of her head again. "I can't tell you, sweetheart. Your mom will have to tell you." Frowning, he checked his watch and strode over to the window. "She should be back from her walk soon. I don't want her caught outside in a thunderstorm."

Mom went for walks when she was upset or needed to think, and she was usually calmer after she returned. Trinity picked up the slingshot and gently tugged on the thick rubber band. "What was in Jesse's letter?"

Gramps turned back to her and shrugged with a little smile. "I don't know, pookie. I haven't opened the letter yet. I want to sit here in Jesse's office and think about him while I read it."

He noticed the old toy she held in her hand. Gramps beamed and chuckled. "Well, I'll be damned. You found my slingshot."

Trinity smiled and held the toy out to him.

"WHAM-O," she said, putting air behind the word.

Gramps pulled back on the rubber band. "I had a lot of fun with this gadget." His gray eyes twinkled. "And it got me into a lot of trouble." He set the toy down on the desk, picked up one of the butterscotch discs and arched a brow. "Where did you get the candy?"

She shrugged. "I found them in Jesse's coat. I was going to ask you if I could have one."

Gramps nodded. He sat down on the desk chair and removed the cellophane wrapper. "I say we both have one. I don't think your great-uncle would mind at all."

Trinity popped the sweet, buttery candy into her mouth. "There's a photo album in the drawer, too."

She stuck the wrapper in her pocket and examined her grandfather's troubled expression. "Is everything between you and Aunt C okay? I was going to go see her after the shop closed."

"I need to talk to Cora," Gramps said. He made a face and rubbed his stomach.

Thunder rumbled in the distance. The room grew darker.

Trinity sat on the edge of the desk and absently twisted her rings. She wasn't sure what Gramps meant about Aunt C, but she had something else pressing on her mind that she wanted to address. In his present mood, Trinity wasn't sure how Gramps would react, but she'd been stressing about him and Stu and it was better to get the weight off her chest. "Gramps?"

He shifted in the chair and gave her an uneasy look. "What?"

She sighed. "When you were home, before we came out here, did you drink scotch every day?"

Gramps looked at her. "I'd have one at night before dinner." He scratched his jaw. "Sometimes I'd have two. Why?"

Trinity leaned forward, planting her palms on her denim-clad legs. "You know how you worry about me participating in protests?"

"Yes." His gaze narrowed.

"Well, I worry about you drinking scotch all the time. I

stress about both you and Stu." Trinity straightened and folded her arms. "I looked it up and alcohol isn't the best for stomach problems."

Gramps smiled. Reaching over, he squeezed her knee. "Thanks for worrying about me, pookie."

Trinity hopped off the desk. Bending over him, she locked her arms around his neck and kissed his cheek. "It's because I love you, Gramps."

He kissed her back and patted her face with a gentle smile. "I know, pookie-pie. I love you, too."

The doorbell rang.

"Mother must be back from her walk."

"Trinity Grace." Gramps' voice carried a warning.

"What? All I'm telling her is that I'm staying here with you."

"I know you're still angry with your mother and you're spoiling for a fight. Do me a favor…." He closed his eyes and shook his head. "Give her the opportunity to speak first before you issue an ultimatum. You'll stand a better chance of getting what you want." He shot her a smile. "After all, you're not a kid anymore."

❧

As soon as the last carload of women pulled away from the curb, Cora quickly ran upstairs to her bedroom and collected her cherished scrapbook. Switching off the sign, she posted a note on the door claiming a family emergency and crossed the street to Jesse's house.

She'd respected Shannan's wishes as long as she could. All morning she'd existed in a state of uncertainty, calling on every ounce of fortitude she'd possessed to project a cheerful, helpful countenance to her customers.

Stamped in her memory was the vision of Shannan, clutching the email in her fist, the defenseless expression of betrayal on her face as she'd confronted Cora in her kitchen.

Cora still struggled to absorb the knowledge that Murphy's daughter was her grown child. The child she'd given birth to and had been searching for most of her life.

Murphy's Prius was parked in the driveway. On one hand Cora wanted to smack him upside the head for his role in her daughter's anguish; on the other hand she wanted to hold him. A tender part of her knew deep down that Murphy's motives had been based on love, but her immediate concern was for Shannan and Trinity.

A gust of cool air lifted her hair off her neck. Thunder rumbled. An afternoon storm loomed in the charged atmosphere.

Clutching the scrapbook to her chest, heart thudding against her ribs, Cora rang the bell.

Shannan opened the door, her face devoid of makeup, appearing years younger and endearingly vulnerable. She studied Cora as though seeing her for the first time.

"Aunt C." Trinity appeared behind her mother. The charming expression sparkling in her granddaughter's hazel eyes mirrored David's. Cora marveled that she hadn't noticed the girl's uncanny resemblance to her grandfather before.

Shannan gently grasped Cora's free hand. "Come in. It's just us girls." She led the way into the living room and seated her on the couch. "We're having chai tea. Would you like a cup?"

Cora nodded. "That would nice. Thank you."

Her daughter slipped an arm around her granddaughter and smiled. "Trinity, will you please help me in the kitchen?"

"Sure." Trinity slanted a curious glance at the scrapbook. "Did you bring over pictures to show us?"

Cora ran her hand over the faded cloth cover and nodded. "I did, if you and your mom want to see them."

"I do." Trinity gave Cora another of her sweet, impish grins. "Be right back."

Cora set the album beside her on the couch. She gazed around the room that had once hosted so many friendly conversations and contained so many happy memories. The walls had been painted a warm neutral color that highlighted the gleaming woodwork. The sunburst clock and Jesse's Ansel Adams photographs had been packed. All that remained was the sofa and matching loveseat grouped around the coffee table and a solitary floor lamp.

A momentary wave of melancholy washed over her followed by immense gratitude and happiness for Jesse's friendship, and the miracle of finally being together with her daughter and her granddaughter.

"I checked the weather on my phone and we're under a severe thunderstorm warning and flood watch." Shannan appeared bearing two steaming mugs of tea. She set them down on the coffee table but remained standing, her gaze curious rather than critical.

Trinity carried a mug and a small paper plate of lemon cookies. "Stu passed on these so I figure they're ours." She took a cookie and settled cross-legged on the couch close to Cora.

Cora had no appetite, but she sipped the spicy, sweet brew and smiled first at Trinity, then at Shannan. She wasn't sure about her daughter's raw emotions and how Shannan was feeling about her. "Thank you. It's been a long day and it's barely past noon."

Shannan barked a wry laugh. She curled up on the loveseat and reached for her tea. "I hear you." A contrite expression came over her face. "I'm sorry I deserted you this morning. I honestly meant to help you, and I didn't mean to snoop. The paper was on the table, and I saw my name and address. I was reading the letter when you walked in."

She dropped her gaze and drank from her mug. "I

couldn't believe it was true. My mom and dad, who I've known and trusted all my life, lied to me. I was shocked, and then I was angry."

Shannan rubbed her temple. "Let's just say my reaction this morning wasn't one of my proudest moments." She slanted a sympathetic glance at her daughter. "Poor Trinity didn't know what was going on. She thought I'd gone off the deep end."

Trinity nodded at Cora, her hazel eyes sincere. "Mom told me to pack because we were leaving Spencer and flying home to San Francisco."

Cora's breath stalled in her throat. Her tea sloshed and she covered the top of her mug with her hand. "You're flying back to San Francisco? When?"

Her granddaughter shook her head with a reassuring smile. "It's all good Aunt C—-I mean Grandma. Mom has to go back on business." Still sitting cross-legged on the cushion, Trinity clasped her knees and gently bumped against Cora. Her smile broke into a full-fledged grin. "But she has to come back here to Spencer because she's buying the shop. Right, Mom?"

Shannan nodded and focused her brown eyes on Cora's. "That's why I came over to see you this morning."

Gripped with relief and joy, Cora gazed at her daughter. "That's wonderful news. My realtor had left me a voicemail, but I was so upset at the time I ignored it."

"It's been that kind of a day." Shannan absently rubbed her arm. "After I unloaded on Dad, I went for a walk to think and to calm down." She gave Cora a self-conscious smile. "When I came back to the house, I apologized to Trinity. I told her about the email—-"

"Excuse me. That's when Mom told me that you actually are my grandmother." Trinity beamed.

Cora was happy for her granddaughter, but she yearned to smooth the worry lines creasing her daughter's brow. She studied Shannan's facial expressions, her gestures. She listened to the cadence of her voice. Her daughter shared the height and slim stature that was a hallmark of Cora's mother's family.

Shannan set her mug on the table. "I was worried about what I was going to tell Trinity. I knew she thought the world of you, but I wasn't sure how she'd react to the news about her grandparents."

Trinity shook her head. "I don't understand why Gramps and Nana had never told Mom she was adopted. I have a friend at school who knows he's adopted and he sees his biological mom every week."

Cora reached over and stroked her granddaughter's silky locks. "Life was different back then, sweetie. Certain subjects weren't openly discussed."

Trinity twisted the hem of her shirt. "I don't mean to be rude, but why did you give Mom up for adoption in the first place?"

"Trinity." Shannan's reprimand was half-hearted. She cradled her mug between her hands, her expression as questioning as Trinity's.

Out of the corner of her eye, Cora caught a brief flash followed seconds later by a peal of thunder. She set her mug down on the table and reached for the scrapbook. She curled her fingers around the cloth cover and inhaled a deep breath. "It's an honest question. In those days, unmarried girls who found themselves pregnant usually married the baby's father or gave their babies up for adoption."

David's face rose in her memory. Goosebumps broke out on her arms. Cora inhaled another deep breath and addressed her daughter. "On a stormy afternoon like this one, your father, David Spencer, died while attempting to rescue two boys out on one of the local lakes. We weren't formally engaged. David's father didn't think I was good enough for the Spencer's. I hadn't planned on getting pregnant, but I hadn't known that some prescription drugs weakened the effectiveness of the birth control pill. And that's how it happened." Her voice took on a weary edge. "There was no over-the-counter pregnancy test in those days. I suspected I was pregnant, but I didn't find out until after David's death."

Cora was stunned by the strength of her feelings of loss and pain. "At first, I wanted to keep you. You were mine. Mine and David's. A little piece of your father for me to hold onto. However, my mother convinced me that adoption was the best solution. You deserved both a father and a mother, parents who could afford to raise you in a nice home, give you a good life, and a stable environment. I needed to finish my education and become a journalist."

She sighed and gripped the album until her knuckles whitened. "I wanted you, Shannan. I wanted you with all my heart. I thought about you every day. When you were born, I heard your first cry, and I carried that memory with me every day of my life."

The soft light of the floor lamp illuminated her daughter's attentive features.

Trinity's incredulous gaze drifted from Shannan to Cora. "Seriously? Those were your only options? Your own mother made you give up your baby? That was so wrong on so many different levels."

Shannan lowered her head and massaged her temples. Her tone drained. "Trinity Grace—-"

"Honey," Cora interjected, sensing a potential argument. She ached to comfort her dazed daughter. Instead, she hugged her granddaughter and kissed her cheek. "I know from today's perspective that those limited options don't make sense."

Trinity's hazel eyes searched Cora's for a long minute. She briefly glanced at Shannan and then relaxed, resting her head against Cora's shoulder. "Did you become a journalist?"

Cora closed her eyes and inhaled her precious grand-daughter's sweet, fruity fragrance. "No. I dropped out of school and helped Grandma Binney with the shop."

She'd returned to Spencer. Her mother had remained in Denver and lived with her aunt until her death.

Trinity tapped the scrapbook on Cora's lap. "If Mom doesn't mind, can we look at the pictures?"

"I don't mind." Shannan rose from the loveseat and sat down next to Cora. Cora rejoiced in her daughter's closeness and the faint musky fragrance of her perfume.

David's high-school graduation picture was on the first page. His granddaughter had inherited his disarming smile and his curly black hair.

"Wow! David was on-fire-hot. Amber eyes are exceed-ingly rare." Trinity glanced from Shannan to Cora. "You look more like Grandma, Mom."

Shannan traced an index finger over her father's photo-graph and sighed. "Trinity bears a strong resemblance to him."

Cora nodded. "It's amazing. I don't know how I missed their likeness to one another."

She was reminded of Murphy. Knowing his conflicted feelings for her relationship with David, she experienced a fleeting twinge of sympathy.

Trinity reached over, paging through school photos, faded prom programs and corsages. She was particularly interested in the yellowed newspaper articles on David's death tucked in the back of the album.

Shannan returned to the loveseat. She curled up on the cushion and clasped her arm, her thoughts turned inward.

Thunder boomed and rattled the windows. The wind whistled under the eaves and something thudded above them. Trinity glanced up at the ceiling "I bet some of the windows are still open, especially in the attic. I better go check."

She set the album on the cushion and sprinted out of the room.

Shannan stirred. She smiled wanly at Cora. "Thank you for bringing the scrapbook over. May we keep it a couple of days? I'd like to look at it later.

"I'm sorry; right now all I can think about is my dad. I need to talk to him. He's in the office reading a letter Jesse apparently meant to mail him."

Her daughter rubbed her forehead. The corners of her mouth turned down. "I still have lots of questions. I'm shocked and confused and hurt. I was going to say angry, but I'm hurt. He's my dad, and he…." Her eyes welled with sorrow. "He kept things from me. Important things."

Cora instinctively rose from the sofa. She perched next to Shannan and grasped her daughter's cool, slender hand. "Shannan, your dad told me he had wanted to tell you about your adoption when you were old enough to understand, but your mother had some physical and emotional issues…."

Cora paused. It wasn't her place to tell Shannan about the baby that Murphy and Nan had lost, but Shannan was her daughter. She'd suffered enough because of secrets, and Cora wasn't sure Murphy would think to tell Shannan about the baby's death himself. Knowing about her parents' loss might help Shannan understand and forgive her father.

Another bright flash lit the solid sheet of rain outside the windows. A sharp crack of thunder split the air causing both Cora and Shannan to jump.

Shannan withdrew her hand from Cora's and rubbed her forehead. "You said my mother had some issues? What was wrong with her?"

Cora lowered her voice and fixed her daughter with a somber look. "Shannan, please discuss this with your father when you talk to him. I want no more secrets between any of us."

She sighed and tightly clasped her hands together.

"Shortly before they adopted you, your mother was pregnant and delivered a stillborn baby. A little boy. She suffered from a severe form of post-partum depression. Honey, your father swore to me that adopting you saved your mother's life and your parents' marriage."

Shannan stared back at her. She slowly raked her fingers through her hair and shook her head. "I'm sorry. I think I'm on overload. I'm going upstairs to lie down for a while. Would you please check on Trinity? I think she'd like to talk to you more about her grandfather."

After Shannan left the room, Cora sat alone on the sofa. The storm raging outside the house reflected the tempest of conflicting emotions raging within her. Cora couldn't blame Shannan for feeling overwhelmed. She picked up the empty mugs and carried them into the kitchen.

From the kitchen she strode over to the closed door of the office. She raised her fist to knock, and hesitated. Cora sensed that Murphy needed time alone to read Jesse's letter and process the unbelievable events of the morning. He'd come out when he was ready to have a discussion and she'd be there to talk to him. Meanwhile, her granddaughter needed her.

❧

Calming Trinity had temporarily comforted and distracted Murphy from this morning's shocking discovery and Shannan's blistering outrage. His daughter's anger was justified, but his world was as turned upside down as hers.

Shannan, the daughter he and Nan had raised as their own, was Davey's. He thought of Cora and, in spite of his good intentions, a resentful lump rose in his throat. It turned out that all his life he'd lived and loved in David Spencer's shadow.

And Trinity! From her dark mass of curly hair to her

fleeting mannerisms and facial expressions, Davey's DNA was stamped all over his precious granddaughter. The evidence had existed in front of him, but he'd been too blind to see it.

Murphy sank back in the desk chair and rubbed his temples. He'd been the only father and grandfather Shannan and Trinity had known. Davey might have fathered Shannan, but he'd raised her from infancy to adulthood. He'd walked the floor with her in the middle of the night when she screamed with colic. He'd held his breath the first time she pedaled her bike without training wheels. He'd taught Shannan how to drive, applauded at her high school and college graduations. He'd walked her down the aisle on her wedding day.

Murphy sighed and absently rubbed his irritated stomach. His heart was sore and his mind was exhausted. He couldn't stand to think about it anymore. He'd try to talk to Shannan later. Hopefully, she'd be willing to listen and forgive him.

He gazed around the room that had served as Jesse's office. He felt safe and connected with his brother in this space. The letter lay on the desk, and Murphy experienced a gentle nudge to read it, but glimpsing the nearby slingshot resurrected the vivid childhood memory of sneaking into Dad's office and opening the narrow middle drawer of the desk. Trinity had mentioned unearthing a photo album in the desk, along with the slingshot.

He retrieved the small red album and laughed. On the first page, he was treated to a bare-assed baby picture of himself, bald as a billiard ball, grinning in toothless glee. On the flipside was an identical photo of his brother. Baby Jesse sported a corona of white fuzz on his head and a prominent tooth. "Show off," Murphy said out loud.

The next photo was taken the Halloween that Jesse dressed up as Frankenstein with fake bolts sticking out from the sides of his neck. Wearing a wacky grin and a plaid winter hat with earflaps, Murphy stood beside Jesse dressed as Elmer Fudd. Murphy rolled his eyes and shook his head.

He flipped a couple of pages to a hunting picture. Their father stood in the middle, wearing a broad smile, resting a hand on each boy's shoulder. On the opposite page was the five-point buck they'd bagged. Dad had worked long hours in his law practice. He had been happiest and most approachable when outdoors, hunting or fishing.

"Those are the best times to ask Dad for permission, or make a confession." Jesse had pointed out that opportunity to Murphy at a young age.

Murphy sensed his big brother's presence reaching out to him. Jesse had left him the slingshot and those snapshots of their life growing up together.

He picked up the envelope addressed to him in Jesse's nearly perpendicular script. Once again he was weighed down with regret for missing out on the chance to share in his brother's adult years.

With his pocket knife, Murphy slit open the thick white envelope and unfolded the lengthy letter on top.

Dear Murphy,

I haven't heard from you since I left a message on your phone. It's occurred to me you may have already sailed on your voyage. Because I'm not sure when you'll get a chance to return my call, I decided I'd better write a letter of explanation to cover the enclosed documents. I discovered these days ago among Dad's personal papers in the attic.

I'm hoping this letter proves unnecessary and sooner, rather than later, you'll fly out for a visit. I'd love nothing better than to bare my soul to my little brother over a couple of beers at the Wild Card. Life has a way of sweeping us through time at an alarming rate, and none of us are getting any younger.

After reviewing the papers, I was extremely concerned at the impact this revelation would have on you, Shannan and Cora. God help me, I honestly considered tossing the whole mess into the fireplace and taking the secret with me to the grave, as our father obviously did.

As I debated over how best to tell you and Shannan, I also had Cora to consider. She'd disclosed her pregnancy and adoption to me years ago, invoking attorney-client privilege. Imagine my dilemma when I discovered the truth contained in these papers. I felt I couldn't reveal what I knew to Cora, whom I'd known most of my life and who'd trusted me, until I'd also informed both you and Shannan. My greatest fear and the reason I've agonized over what action to take was how each of you would react, particularly Shannan, as she is unaware that she's adopted! When Cora recently confided to me that she has actively engaged an online detective agency to look for her adopted daughter, I realized I needed to contact you immediately.

Murph, before you read the attached papers, I'm asking you to think back to a different era, when our society swept teenage pregnancy and adoption under the carpet. 'Good' people didn't discuss such shameful issues. If they or their family member was involved, that person was either ostracized or the matter was dealt with in secret. While I deplore this agreement and Dad's part in it, I think he and Cora's mother sincerely believed that theirs was the best solution to Cora's pregnancy at the time.

However, I still struggle to understand how Dad could continue to keep this information from all of you, even after the stigma associated with unwed mothers and babies born out of wedlock has been alleviated.

I urge you to tell Shannan she was adopted as soon as possible, regardless of your promise to Nan. I know Nan's heart was in the right place, but should Shannan find out before you tell her she'd understandably feel betrayed.

I couldn't bring myself to destroy the truth, but keeping the truth secret, even for this brief period of time, has been eating me alive.

I hope you, Cora, and Shannan can find it in your hearts to understand and forgive each other, and as difficult as it may be (even though both of them are no longer with us) to forgive Dad and Cora's mother. I know it's a cliché, but life is too short, and our relationships with those we love are too precious to harbor grudges.

Know that I love you, little brother, and I hope to hear from you soon.

Jesse

P.S. If you're reading this letter, I trust you to call me immediately so we can arrange a meeting between all of the above persons. With everyone's consent, I'd like to include Stuart, because as my lifelong partner and Cora's close friend, I feel he is entitled to be informed.

Outside, the sky had darkened to the color of dusk and rain pelted the window. The overhead light failed to dispel the gloom. The pain in his stomach was back again. Looking at the date on the letter, he realized it coincided with getting his new phone. He'd waited for Trinity to set up his new voicemail.

He'd missed the last chance to talk to his brother, and together share the burden of the adoption papers with Shannan and Cora. None of them would have been blindsided as they had been today.

Murphy examined the documents enclosed with the letter. After today's earlier discovery, he wasn't surprised. Was it coincidence or synchronicity that Trinity found Jesse's letter with the adoption papers and Cora received the email revealing Shannan as her daughter on the same day?

The ultimate shocker was Henry Webster's complicity. Murphy recalled that, at the San Francisco law firm where he'd clerked, the senior partner had been a classmate of

Dad's. Jesse had spelled it out in the letter, but reading the signatures compounded the offense. His father, who Murphy had looked up to, who he and Nan had trusted, had betrayed that trust. If Murphy had known that Cora had been Shannan's mother, would he have told Nan?

Probably not, given Nan's frail mental state at the time. Shannan had been his wife's ticket back to sanity and his own sanity as well.

He reached to retrieve his handkerchief and stopped. He'd given it to Shannan. He pinched the bridge of his nose and closed his eyes, jammed with conflicting emotions. How could he resent Davey for fathering his dearly loved child? How could he harbor bitterness toward his own father for rescuing Shannan from the anonymity of adoption in the seventies and easing their grief over the loss of their own baby?

CHAPTER TWENTY-TWO

*F*eeling hungry and rubbing his irritable stomach, Murphy left the office to discover a rain swept version of Stuart standing in the kitchen, clutching a six pack of soda.

Murphy grinned. He briefly embraced the damp man and clapped him on the back. "You're a godsend." He saw the three large pizza boxes stacked on the counter. "And you brought food."

A startled smile creased Stuart's face. He set the sodas down on the table, shed his light jacket and draped it over a nearby chair. "I'm glad to see you too. The weather is nasty out there. Some of the streets are flooded." He raised a hand to finger-comb his disheveled strands of hair. "Where are Trinity and Shannan? They're probably hungry too. I thought I'd call Cora and invite her to join us. I don't imagine she'll have too many customers until the rain lets up."

Murphy stared. Stuart had no idea what had happened in his absence. Cora's email, Shannan's reaction, Trinity's sweet concern and Jesse's revealing letter on top of his own inner turmoil rolled over him. He clenched his jaw and swallowed the unexpected emotion that clogged his throat. Snagging

the nearby package of sliced bread and a plastic knife, he
gave Stuart an abbreviated version of the morning's turbu-
lent events while he assembled a couple of turkey sandwiches. "If you don't mind, we'll save the pizza for later with
the girls. I have an important letter in the office to show
you."

They carried their sandwiches into the office along with
their sodas and a roll of paper towels.

Murphy directed Stuart to sit behind the desk. He
dragged a chair in from the kitchen for himself and sat down
facing the window. "Thanks for letting me hang out in here."
He glanced over his shoulder. "I wanted to ask your advice
before I meet with Shannan and Cora." Shaking his head, he
popped open his drink and took a healthy swallow. "They're
both forceful women, with equally strong opinions and
emotions."

"Sure," Stuart said, slipping on his reading glasses. He
pushed aside his sandwich, his attention already focused on
the area immediately in front of him. The desk chair
squeaked as he leaned forward and reached for the sheaf of
papers.

Murphy stared out the window and absently ate while
Stuart read the letter. Outside, it was still raining. The storm
drains had backed up and water gushed out into the street.
He frowned at the darkened windows of Cora's shop. Stuart
was probably right. She would reopen once the weather
cleared, but he needed to call her anyway. Murphy thought
of Cora Rose and the additional heartbreak Jesse's letter
would cause her.

The desk chair squeaked louder and papers rustled.
Stuart blew his nose and cleared his throat. He opened his
soda. "Murph, are you going to call a meeting like Jess
suggested?"

Murphy stood. He scooted his chair closer and sat across
the desk from Stuart. He directed a helpless look at the man

he'd come to know and respect. "I want to, but after this morning, I'm nervous as hell. I'm not sure if Shannan will ever speak to me again, and I don't know how Cora feels. At least Trinity still loves me."

Stuart's mouth quirked up at the corners and his sympathetic dark eyes fixed on Murphy's. "Tell them the truth, Murph. Tell them how you feel and speak from your heart. The truth is harder, but it's the best solution in the long run.

"Six years ago, when Jess and I decided to get married, one of the hardest things we had to face was coming out to our straight friends. We didn't want to make a big deal out of our wedding, but we didn't want to hide our relationship from them either." Stuart flashed Murphy a grin. "And, like you, we were 'nervous as hell' about it.

"Because we were honest about our intention, we found that, given the opportunity, most of the people who already knew us accepted our relationship.

"Jess was particularly concerned about Jakob Spencer. He'd known the man most of his life, and Jakob was one of his highly- regarded clients."

Stuart slanted Murphy an apologetic glance. "Jess suspected Jakob's position on openly gay couples was a lot like yours, and he wasn't sure Jakob would continue to retain him."

Murphy nodded. He hadn't seen Jakob since Dad's funeral, but they were of the same generation and had been raised with similar beliefs.

"Cora was our lifeline. She and Jakob weren't close at the time, but she enlisted the support of her friend Willa Samuels. It turned out that Willa and Jakob had been in love for years. Willa persuaded Jakob to reexamine his beliefs. As a matter of fact, the two of them have recently gotten married.

"It took Jakob a while, but like you, he cared enough to consider a different perspective and finally came around."

As Davey's brother, Jakob would be Shannan's uncle and entitled to know that he had a niece and a great-niece. Murphy realized that Shannan had numerous blood relatives in Spencer whom she deserved to be informed about. He would urge her to contact Jakob, but allow his daughter to decide on what she wanted to do with the information.

"Murph, I know Cora. She's got a pretty forgiving heart and honesty goes a long way with her." Stuart shrugged. "I don't know your daughter, but if she's anything like her mother," he beamed at Murphy, "I think you're going to be okay."

He hoped Stuart's optimistic outlook was accurate. Leaning forward, Murphy folded his arms on the desk. "What about Jesse's letter? Do you have any questions?"

Stuart steepled his fingers in front of his mouth, his gaze turned inward. "I don't have any questions." He glanced at Murphy. "I have a few choice comments I'd like to make, but I'll keep my opinions to myself." He blew out a breath and stared up at the ceiling. "Jess was right. Life is too short to hold grudges. Damn, Murph. I miss him."

Murphy pictured Jesse's youthful face, his blonde crew cut, and the fond, tolerant look in his blue eyes when Murphy had asked him dumb questions. He stood and squeezed Stuart's shoulder. "I miss him too, buddy."

Wiping his nose on a rough paper towel, Murphy chuckled. He dug in his pocket for the key Trinity had given him earlier. "Here, Stuart, unlock that drawer in front of you. Jesse left us some great pictures to remember him by."

❧

Cora trailed her granddaughter down the stairs. Trinity's insatiable curiosity about David had kept Cora occupied all afternoon. She'd enjoyed the time spent with her lovable granddaughter, but her thoughts had continually drifted to Shannan and Murphy.

Minutes ago, Shannan had knocked and peeked inside the doorway of Trinity's room. She'd had a nap and wondered if anyone else was as hungry as she was.

Relieved that Shannan was feeling better, Cora craved a few quiet minutes alone with Murphy to comfort him and be comforted in return.

The office door swung open, and Stuart appeared, followed by Murphy. Cora's pulse quickened.

"Stu. When did you get here?" Trinity tripped down the remaining steps and hugged the older man. "Has Gramps caught you up on all the news? We've been upstairs looking at retro photos of Grandma and my grandfather David in her cool scrapbook." She grinned up at Cora. "Grandma, can I show your book to Stu?"

"Hi Stuart," Cora said, embracing the dear man. "You and Trinity are welcome to look at my scrapbook, but first I think we all need to eat."

She glanced behind Stuart and smiled into Murphy's brilliant gray eyes. He replied with his endearing crooked grin. "Shannan will be down as soon as she gets off the phone with her manager."

"I'll warm up the pizzas. I brought plenty." Stuart turned to Trinity with a doting expression. "I'd love to look at the album later. Why don't you fill me in on all the excitement that happened this morning while we set up in the dining room?"

Her granddaughter followed Stuart into the kitchen. "Sure. Oh, and before I forget, Mom is buying the shop, and she's bringing Binx back from San Francisco with her."

"Cora Rose?" Murphy opened his arms.

As she stepped in his direction, he strode toward her and gripped her in a fierce embrace against his warm chest. She wrapped her arms around his neck and laid her head on his shoulder. "I've missed you, Murphy Webster."

He rested his cheek against hers. "I've missed you too, sweetheart."

Cora closed her eyes and inhaled his familiar lime and spice scent. "What a day this has been. I feel so much better now."

Murphy's soft lips brushed her temple. "Let's step into the office." Curling his arm around her waist, he guided her into the room and shut the door. He stared into her face and tucked a lock of hair behind her ear. "Cora, I'm so sorry for the pain I've caused you and Shannan. I should have told her about her adoption after Nan died. She would have searched for you and you would have found each other years ago."

Murphy's apology and the sincerity in his voice kindled an aching tenderness in her heart. Before she could speak, he placed a finger against her lips. "Let me finish, please. I love you Cora Rose, and I love Shannan and Trinity. You three girls are more important to me than the *Stargazer*, and my voyage around the world. I know you agreed to come to San Francisco with me, but that was before we knew about Shannan. If you want to stay here in Spencer, here is where we'll live."

He sighed and rubbed the back of his head. "Please bear with me. I have one last stupid question that I have to ask and then I'll shut up." He flashed a quick, hopeful smile. "What about Davey? I know you've stopped wearing his ring. You've told me you love me, but now that you know Davey was Shannan's biological father, does that change how you feel about us?"

Cora cradled his face between her hands and kissed him. "Murphy, my darling, the past cannot be changed. A part of me will always love David, but I'd created a fantasy in my mind. I wore his ring and clung to his memory far too long. I don't believe love is meant to be calculated. My love for

David doesn't diminish my love for you. Does your love for Nancy diminish your love for me?"

❧

Murphy studied Cora's cherished features. Her question had caught him off guard. "Of course not," he stated. He realized what she was trying to drive home and he softened his tone. "You're right, Cora Rose. A part of me will always love Nan, but my love for her doesn't diminish my love for you."

Cora soundly kissed him and Murphy told himself to stop doubting the damn evidence.

A knock sounded on the office door. Cora startled in his arms and Murphy reluctantly released her. Shannan poked her head inside the doorway and her face pinked up. "Excuse me. We're ready to eat."

Cora's expression of pure motherly love directed at Shannan reminded him of the occasions he'd glimpsed a similar look on Nan's face. Observing Cora and Shannan standing together, Murphy was astonished at their resemblance to one another. Mother and daughter shared the same doe-like brown eyes and willowy build.

Shannan caught Cora at the door. His daughter smiled shyly and hugged her. "Thank you for spending the afternoon with Trinity. I'm relieved that she's so readily come to terms with the adoption. She still loves her nana and treasures her memory. Trinity also confided that she'd already asked you to be her adopted grandmother, and finding out you were her biological grandma was absolutely perfect." Shannan beamed. "I'm looking forward to getting to know you better."

Cora's brilliant smile mirrored Shannan's. "I am too, honey. I'm so glad you feel that way." Cora glanced briefly at him, her eyes shining with happiness. She addressed Shannan in a confident tone. "I know our relationship has experienced a rough beginning, but together, with love and understanding, we will work the kinks out." Cora hastily pecked Murphy on the cheek. "I'll see you two in the dining room."

After the door closed, Shannan's brow furrowed, and her large brown eyes brimmed with distress. She bit her lower lip, reminding Murphy of the occasions she had come to him because her feelings had been hurt.

He gathered his grown daughter in his arms and stroked her silky hair, remembering all those times he'd comforted her when she'd been small. "I'm sorry, honey-bunny. Your mom and I should have told you. Can you forgive me?"

Shannan lightly rubbed noses with him like she had always done when he'd called her by her pet name. She gave him a sad little smile. "I did a lot of thinking this afternoon. I wish you and Mom had told me I'd been adopted, but I'm sorry I screamed at you and Trinity like I did. I realized that I've always felt that I was loved, thanks to you and Mom."

She stepped back, grasping both his hands tightly in hers. "Cora helped me understand your reasons a bit better. She told me about you and Mom losing the baby. Dad, after trying so hard to carry a baby myself and finally giving birth to Trinity, I can imagine how horrible the stillbirth was on you, and especially Mom."

Murphy nodded, squeezing her hands in reply. "Your mother was in a bad place. I don't want to think about what might have happened if we hadn't found you.

"Shannan, I read Jesse's letter. Shortly before he passed, he discovered some documents that shed more light on the circumstances surrounding your adoption. Some of the news may be more disturbing to Cora than to you, but I'd like to meet together with you and Cora to read the letter here in the office after we eat. I think Trinity should be present too, but that's your decision to make."

His daughter sighed. Rubbing her arm, she walked over to

stand at the window, apparently thinking over his suggestion.

Murphy slipped his hands into the pockets of his trousers and clenched his fingers. This day had been one of the longest in his life and it wasn't over. Although it was still raining, the sky outside looked to be lightening up. The pain in his stomach had eased, but he'd have another soda, even though a scotch sounded so much better. He smiled fondly, recalling Trinity's earlier concern regarding him and Stuart.

Shannan glanced back at him with a wry chuckle. "I don't know why I'm even considering the idea. Trinity has already notified me that as my daughter she should be informed if any new information is revealed pertaining to my adoption."

Murphy grinned. He joined Shannan at the window and slipped his arm around her shoulders. "Are you surprised? I'm glad you insisted I bring Trinity with me to Spencer. She's been a joy and a comfort, not only to me, but to Cora and Stuart as well. You've done a fine job of raising her."

Shannan briefly rested her head on his shoulder. She straightened and pointed across the street, her voice filled with delight. "I see a rainbow! Look Dad, there's a rainbow above The Attic."

❦

Cora limited herself to water, instead of soda, and two slices of pizza. Stuart, possessed with an everlasting sweet tooth, had brought dessert, a white bakery box filled with delectable cupcakes from Cookie's Coffee and Cakes. Cora had peeled off Cookie's unique sticker and shamelessly claimed her favorite, a rich, dense chocolate cupcake with creamy mocha frosting.

Murphy had followed suit, selecting a beautifully crafted red velvet cupcake, which he promptly began to devour.

Stuart offered to clean up after the meal. He and Murphy

carted chairs into the office and set them in front of the desk. Cora cast an apprehensive glance at her daughter, but Shannan appeared more interested than unsettled. Her brief conversation with her father before the meal had apparently eased her distress.

Trinity sat between her and Shannan. By mutual consent, Murphy read the letter out loud.

Cora clasped her hands tightly in her lap. As she listened to the letter's contents, the resentment she'd harbored toward her mother resurfaced. Mother and Henry Webster had played God with not only her life and her child's life, but with Nan and Murphy's lives as well.

Murphy glanced up at her over his reading glasses, his compassionate gray eyes holding hers in mutual under-standing.

After reading the passage where Jesse had urged him to tell Shannan that she was adopted, Murphy paused again and directed a repentant look at his daughter and granddaughter.

Shannan slipped her arm around Trinity and gave Cora a supportive glance that was balm to Cora's mangled emotions.

"*Know that I love you, little brother, and I hope to hear from you soon.*" Murphy rubbed his mouth and swallowed. He stared at Cora, his grief transparent.

Before she could respond, Shannan rose from her chair. She leaned over Murphy to hug him and kiss his cheek. "I'm sorry about Uncle Jesse, Dad."

Trinity reached over and grasped Cora's hand. She gifted Cora with an adorable smile that filled her with a divine sense of gratitude. Her granddaughter's simple gesture of love, and Jesse's hopeful wish that she, Murphy and Shannan would forgive each other, overrode her bitterness.

The past was behind her. Cora looked at the three people she loved most in the world and celebrated the present.

Murphy held the adoption papers out to her, but she shook her head with a serene smile. "No, thank you."

He handed the papers to Shannan. Her daughter perched on a corner of the desk and examined them. After looking the documents over, Shannan stared up at Cora, her dark eyes brimming with compassion. "How devastating the whole ordeal must have been for you."

Passing the papers to Trinity, Shannan approached Cora, her arms outstretched.

Cora rose to embrace her daughter. Shannan's first piercing cry echoed in her memory.

"Thank you for giving birth to me, for thinking about me, for searching for me and never giving up."

Her lovely daughter rested her hands on Cora's shoulders and shook her head. "We sure have our share of kinks to work out in this family."

Trinity wrapped her arms around Shannan and Cora. "Grandma, I'm glad you looked for Mom, but if Mom had to be adopted, I'm happy that she was adopted by Gramps and Nana. Nana, Mom and I enjoyed so many good times together, but now Mom and I will share good times with you."

Her granddaughter turned and wrapped her arms around Murphy's waist and hugged him. "David Spencer might be my biological grandfather, but you're the only grandpa I've ever known. I love you Gramps."

Murphy gazed at Cora above their granddaughter's tousled curls. His gray eyes shone with emotion. He kissed the top of Trinity's head. "I love you too, pookie."

He released Trinity and stood beside Cora, holding his splayed hand against the small of her back. She anchored her arm around his waist and nestled at an angle against his hip.

Shannan grinned and stifled a yawn. "I'm going to have to excuse myself. I have an early flight tomorrow."

Cora frowned at her daughter. "How are you getting to the airport?"

"I'm taking the shuttle. Three in the morning is too early for Dad to get up and drive me, and you have to work in the shop."

Murphy shrugged and kissed Cora's cheek. "I'll ask Stuart if he'll come along. We'll keep each other company on the trip back."

Cora smiled and tightened her arm around him. "How long will you be gone, Shannan?"

Parked in the desk chair, Trinity looked up from her phone with interest.

"I should be back in a week, maybe a little longer. I told Stuart I'll be here for Jesse's Celebration of Life." Shannan arched her brows with an enigmatic smile. "I've had a couple of casual conversations with Astrid regarding my business. I have nothing concrete to tell you yet. I know you don't want us to have any more secrets between us Cora, but what I'm working on isn't really a secret. If my plan succeeds, it will be more like a surprise."

Trinity's hazel eyes widened and she grinned from Shannan to Cora to Murphy. "I don't know how many more surprises our family can take!"

EPILOGUE

*T*he wind off the Bay whipped Cora's hair into her face. She smiled and tied it back with the elastic band from around her wrist. Murphy had talked her into growing her hair longer, and she'd been happy to oblige. She'd kept the lowlights because they were flattering.

"The champagne is ready for our toast." Murphy came up behind her and wrapped his arms around her waist. He pulled the band out of her hair.

"Murphy, I just tied it back because of the wind. It's going to get tangled."

"I'll untangle it," he said, lifting her locks to press his lips to her nape.

Cora shivered and closed her eyes. He knew how to make her crazy. "How much longer until we're out to sea?"

He rested his chin on the top of her head. "Factoring in the wind and the tide, our captain estimates another thirty to forty-five minutes."

She tipped her head back for a kiss. "Are you getting excited? I promised Shannan and Trinity I'd send pictures."

"Oh, boy, a selfie in every port." Murphy laughed. "It sounds like Trinity enjoyed her first day at Spencer High."

Cora's heart warmed, remembering her granddaughter's enthusiastic account of her class schedule. Trinity was taking art and she planned to apply for the yearbook staff.

"Shannan sounds like she's got a full plate, remodeling the house while keeping the shop open. I'm glad she sold her decorating business. Shannan told me Astrid was ecstatic about buying the company."

"That was a nice surprise, but that girl thrives on busy. As if expanding the shop weren't enough, the house she purchased from me and Stuart is already on her list of upcoming projects." Murphy cupped Cora's shoulders with his hands. "Shannan has been that way all her life. She reminds me of someone else I know and love."

Cora smiled and leaned against him, catching a faint whiff of lime and spice. "We're a lot alike though I'm glad she's not as bull-headed as I am."

"Nobody is as bull-headed as you are, Cora Rose Fleming," Murphy teased tenderly, sliding his arms around her. "You know what Shannan told me over the phone last night? It was late when she'd called. You'd already gone to bed." Murphy's voice in her ear softened with emotion. "She said Trinity had pointed out to her that I was the only father Shannan had ever known.

"Shannan told me she'd thought about what Trinity had said and realized I was always there for her, to bandage her skinned knees, give her my handkerchief to dry her tears, to walk her up the aisle on her wedding day. I thought that was nice," Murphy added.

Cora turned and gazed into the softened expression in his gray eyes and caressed the hard plane of his cheek. "I think so, too. I love you, Murphy Webster, because of the man you are."

❧

One of his two-person crew walked up on deck. "Mr. Webster. Captain says we're about ten minutes out before we hit open sea."

Murphy reluctantly released Cora and went below to open the champagne. He paused, a flute in each hand, and thought of Jesse. His quiet, kind, older brother, who'd left behind a partner Murphy had come to know and regard as a second brother. He raised his glass to Jesse and Stuart in a silent toast before climbing back on deck.

Cora had her phone in hand. "Hurry, Murphy."

The famous landmark spanning the strait loomed directly ahead.

Murphy swore good-naturedly and positioned himself beside Cora, their smiling faces framed within the phone's screen. She snapped two photos in rapid succession.

The Stargazer cruised beneath the bridge, the wind off the Pacific whipping her sails. Smiling broadly, his heart bursting with the joy of dreams realized, Murphy tapped his glass to Cora's and gazed lovingly into her beautiful brown eyes. "May we love as long as we live, and live as long as we love."

❦

Turn the page for the recipe for Aunt Cora's Incredible Iced Lemon Cookies.

AUNT CORA'S INCREDIBLE ICED
LEMON COOKIES

Makes 4-5 dozen cookies

2 ½ cups flour
    1 ½ cups sugar
    1 cup butter, softened
    2 large eggs
    1 tablespoon lemon zest
    1 tablespoon lemon juice
    1 ½ teaspoons cream of tartar
    1 teaspoon baking soda
    ¼ teaspoon salt

Icing
    2 ½ cups powdered sugar
    ¼ cup lemon juice
    1 teaspoon lemon zest

Preheat oven 400 degrees. Mix first nine ingredients in a large bowl. Beat at low speed, until well mixed, scraping bowl often. On ungreased cookie sheet, drop rounded teaspoonfuls of dough 2 inches apart. Bake 6-8 minutes until edges are slightly browned.

Mix icing ingredients in bowl. Stir until smooth. Frost warm cookies with icing.

THE ASPEN GOLD SERIES

Dear Reader,

Once upon a time a group of writer friends—helping a member with a particularly difficult thread in a continuity series contrived by her editors—got the grandiose idea to create a continuity series of their own.

Yes, this was us, and we threw ourselves wholeheartedly into developing characters, fashioning families, family dynamics, and a setting, which evolved from one member's love of all things Colorado. We created family trees, character profiles, detailed maps, brainstormed titles and themes. We collected photos and researched and even started the stories. We proposed our idea to a few publishers and got no traction. So, after a time the contracted books came first, two members dropped out of the group, a couple new ones came and went. But the core group remained.

In a tragic turn of events we lost a beloved friend and co-writer. Grief took the remaining wind from our sails. We recovered slowly, welcomed a new friend to our critique group. Then came a day when we got together and said, "We're going to get serious and do this!" Energy built, and the series took on new life. A previous co-creator joined us again. Now, here we are, years after the initial idea, sharing the finished stories with you and hoping you will feel the same intensity and appreciation for this project as we do. We have many more stories to share, and the ideas keep coming. Look for more books to follow in Aspen Gold: The Series.

So, come along. We welcome you to Spencer, Colorado, to have a look inside the families, to laugh in their good times and cry in their sad times, to follow them as they solve mysteries, expose secrets, recover from their pasts, reach for their goals, and most importantly—as they fall in love.

❦

These Aspen Gold books are independently published by the authors. We thank you for your support, and we take pride in giving you quality books and excellent stories. We're thankful you've chosen to follow us and be part of the AG community.

Reviews help readers discover and connect with new authors. Every review is important to us and is greatly appreciated. Please consider leaving an honest review of this book at your favorite bookseller and Goodreads.

❦

Be sure to follow all the Aspen Gold Series updates at:

Aspen Gold: The Series Website. https://www.aspengoldseries.com/

Aspen Gold twitter. Https://twitter.com/@gold_aspen

Aspen Gold: The Series on Facebook

https://www.facebook.com/AspenGoldSeries/

Rocky Mountain Rumors, the newsletter

https://www.subscribepage.com/n9n7p3

We love to hear from our readers. Contact the Aspen Gold authors at mailto:rumors@aspengoldseries.com

❦

The Aspen Gold Books

Dancing In The Dark Cheryl St.John
He had everything a man could want--except her forgiveness...
Call Me Mandy Debra Hines
The last man Miranda loved took everything from her...
Ryder's Heart *lizzie starr
She can't allow secrets to steal love from her...
For Keeps Barbara Gwen & *lizzie starr
Hiding the truth is like denying the sun...
Second Chances Donna Kaye
She tried the fairy tale and the fairy tale didn't work...
Sleepin' Alone Bernadette Jones
Hunter Lawe...riding the line between enforcing the law and breaking it...
Stay A Little Longer Bernadette Jones
Death didn't frighten Gage Ewing. Living scared the hell out of him,,,
Speechless *lizzie starr
How many peonies does it take for Vianna and Ryder to get married?

❦

COMING IN 2020

•*Finding Hope* Donna Kaye
•*Fortunate Cookie* *lizzie starr
•*Lonely Eyes* Bernadette Jones
•*Whisper My Name* Cheryl St.John
•*Gorgeous Scars* M.A. Jewell

ABOUT THE AUTHOR

Colorado native, Debra Hines and her husband have lived everywhere from California to Oregon and now call Iowa/Nebraska home. She's a world traveler, with stickers from England, Ireland, Scotland, New Zealand, Australia, Italy and Sicily on her passport. Somehow on her whirlwind planes, ships and automobiles tour, she still manages to spend most Friday evenings with her critique group and is invested in writing tales about the fictional residents of Spencer, Colorado. Debra is a long-time member of Romance Writers of America and its local chapter Romance Authors of the Heartland, of which she has been vice-president, program director and is currently treasurer. She's a devoted mom to three, grandmother to four, and will follow Hugh Jackman anywhere.

Find Deb on Facebook: https://www.facebook.com/debahines19/
Email Deb at debraia94@gmail.com

Made in the USA
Monee, IL
11 September 2020

41929526R00154